MY HEART STILL BEATS

A NOVEL

#1 *NEW YORK TIMES* BESTSELLING AUTHOR

HELEN HARDT

Entangled Publishing, LLC
644 Shrewsbury Commons Ave., STE 181
Shrewsbury, PA 17361
rights@entangledpublishing.com

Amara is an imprint of Entangled Publishing, LLC.

Visit our website at www.entangledpublishing.com.

Cover design by Bree Archer
Stock art by Tunatura/Gettyimages
Interior design by Britt Marczak

ISBN 978-1-64937-682-4
Ebook ISBN 978-1-64937-683-1

Manufactured in the United States of America

First Edition May 2024

10 9 8 7 6 5 4 3 2 1

AMARA
an imprint of Entangled Publishing LLC

MY HEART STILL BEATS

A NOVEL

ALSO BY HELEN HARDT

For everyone who suffers or has suffered the darkness of depression—I understand. I've been there. Please don't ever give up. You are worth it.

My Heart Still Beats is a dark, emotional romance with a happy ending. However, the story includes elements that might not be suitable for all readers. Sexual assault, physical assault, rape, child molestation, suicidal thoughts, suicidal ideation, depression, anxiety, PTSD, panic attacks, murder, and blood are shown in the novel. Readers who may be sensitive to these elements, please take note.

PROLOGUE

Ben

"Did you really think you could hide from me forever?"

I turn as the voice I hoped to never hear again crawls up the back of my neck.

Inconceivably, he looks much like he did when he was seventeen. He's now thirty-two—the same age as I am.

Dirk Conrad.

My senior year in high school, I was lost. My brother, Braden, had graduated three years earlier and was working with our father in his fledgling construction business. Our mother had died several years before, and after school I was expected to not only get my homework done and bring back decent grades, but also to work the business at least twenty hours per week.

We needed the extra money to make ends meet.

This was my senior year, and it was supposed to be fun. Football games, parties, and girls. But not for Benjamin Black. I had to work my ass off at school and then work my ass off at some construction site until my fingers bled and my muscles ached. I'd much rather have been playing sports, but the one good thing the work did was give me a physique that any athlete would envy.

One day, though, I was sick and tired of it.

So I didn't go to work that day.

I didn't do my homework, either.

Instead, I went out looking for some fun.

And that's where I found Dirk Conrad.

The same Dirk Conrad who insisted on meeting me at my office today.

So here he is, same brownish hair—though the hairline's a little higher—same crooked smile, same attitude. Same well-worn jeans that hang low on his waist. A gray hoodie and brown work boots complete his outfit.

"What the fuck do you want?" I ask.

"Did you really think I wouldn't come after my share eventually?" He presses his thin lips together.

I hold back a scoff. "Your share of *what*?"

He takes a step toward my desk. "You owe me, Black. Me, Jerry, and Carlos. All of us."

Carlos hightailed it to Mexico right after high school, and Jerry's serving time for second-degree murder. He's eligible for parole in five more years. I'll worry about him then. Dirk? Last report from my PI said he was living in Bumfuck, Alabama, and had a few baby mamas. I'm guessing that's what this is about.

He needs cash, and he thinks I'm his meal ticket.

He can think again.

"I don't owe you shit."

"You *do*." He smirks, keeping his tone even. "You do, or we're going to go to the newspapers. We're going to tell everyone exactly what went down that night."

The skin on the back of my neck contracts, making it feel like it's choking me.

But I'm a businessman now. I help my brother and father negotiate multimillion-dollar deals, so I know how to bluff.

"You mean the *royal* we? Because Jerry's in prison, and Carlos is nowhere to be found. This is all you, and you have no proof. Plus, you don't have the balls."

He runs his fingers over the smooth mahogany of my desk. "You think I don't have proof?"

"If you did, you'd have squirmed out from underground before now. Maybe when Braden and I *started* to make it big."

"Everybody knows Braden is the brains behind your success," Dirk says. "And I'm sure your big brother—your goody-two-shoes big brother—would *love* to know what you were up to that day."

This time I let the scoff come out. "You don't know my brother at all."

Indeed, he doesn't. Atilla the Hun is a bigger goody-two-shoes than Braden Black.

Still, though, I can't let this dark secret come to light. There is no statute of limitations for what happened all those years ago, and quite frankly, I don't want to spend the rest of my life behind bars.

I shrug, maintaining a casual demeanor. "There's a flaw in your plan, Dirk. If you have any evidence at all, it will implicate you and the other two just as much as it may implicate me."

He grins, only it's not a grin so much as the look a snake gets before he sinks his fangs into your flesh. "You'd think so, wouldn't you?"

My heartbeat increases, but I stay composed. "You're bluffing."

"Am I?"

"Absolutely. Why now? Why not before, when we first started

raking it in?"

"I don't have to tell you nothing, Black. Just know I need three million. A million each for me, Carlos, and Jerry. And that's the last you'll ever hear from us."

I walk from behind my desk to face Dirk straight on. "Money won't do Jerry any good from inside the slammer."

"It'll take care of his mother."

I shake my head, chuckling. Jerry's mother passed away two years ago. I keep tabs. "Why don't you tell the fucking truth, Dirk? It's all for you. You and your gaggle of illegitimate kids down south."

He says nothing, but I can read the redness creeping up his neck. I hit the nail on the head.

And I'm not giving this fucker a damned dime.

Paying off a blackmailer only makes him stronger.

He'll consider me a cash cow after the first payment, and once it's gone, he'll be back for more.

And then I'll never be rid of him.

Once you have money, you want more. Braden and I are constantly adding to our wealth, and it's not because we need it.

It's because we want it.

"You're not getting anything from me."

Dirk scratches the light brown stubble on his chin. "I see you're going to have to take some convincing."

"The answer is no. Whether you convince me or not."

"Have it your way, Black." He turns, heads toward the door, and then looks over his shoulder. "Expect something in the mail tomorrow."

"Your so-called evidence?"

He turns and then looks over his shoulder. "You wait and see."

CHAPTER ONE

Tessa

THREE MONTHS LATER...

Sometimes I'd rather die than go through one more day of feeling like this.

But I'm not suicidal. I don't have a stash of sleeping pills or razor blades hidden at my place. The thought of anything like that sickens me. I've spoken to my therapist ad nauseam about these feelings, and she agrees I'm not at risk of ending my life.

She originally called it "passive suicide ideation," but then she explained that term means actively thinking about one's own death without having any plan for bringing it about.

Then after several sessions, she agreed *that's* not me, either. I don't actively think about ending my life or even about dying. Sometimes, though, I just feel like I'd rather be dead than go through one more day of this agony.

On my computer screen are photos of a private Jamaican resort. The featured image on the website is, of course, the gorgeous beach. The blue of the ocean contrasts with the dazzling white sand. Palm trees frame the outer edges, adding a lush green to the scene.

The photo must be enhanced. Nothing can be that beautiful.

My mood changes daily.

Today's a bad day.

But I also have good days, and I remind myself of that when I'm having a bad day. I remind myself that I love the beach, the blue sky, the feeling of sand squishing between my toes. The sound of seagulls flying overhead. Stepping around jellyfish. Finding a starfish and throwing it back into the water, to its life.

Right now, I'm busy—or at least trying to be—planning my best friend's bachelorette party in Jamaica. Skye Manning is marrying the blue-collar billionaire Braden Black, so no expense will be spared. Funny, the old Tessa—before Garrett Ramirez changed her—would love planning the most amazing bachelorette bash on the planet for her best friend in the world.

I'm glad to have a reprieve when my phone buzzes. It's my father. Comfort settles over me. My father is such a strong and kind man, and I know he'd bear this burden for me if he could.

"Hey, Da," I say into the phone.

"Hey, angel," he says in his low voice. "Just wanted to hear your voice. Let you know your mom and I are thinking of you. How are you getting along?"

"I'm okay." It's not a lie, exactly. I'm not having a great day, but I don't want him to worry. "I'm working on the bachelorette stuff for Skye."

"Tessa, what have I told you your whole life? About lying to me?"

Good old Da. He always knows. Knows me better than I know myself sometimes. "I'm sorry. Today's a bad day."

"You want me to come get you? You know you can always come home if you need to."

"I know, Da. Thanks. But I'm fine. Some days are harder than others, but I'm muddling through."

"You're a strong woman, Tessa. Just like your mother and your grandmother before her. You've got that Esparza spunk. Don't forget that."

"Sometimes I don't feel very strong."

"I know. We all feel that way occasionally."

"Even you?" My father is so strong and robust. Sometimes I think he could face a Sherman tank and come out on top.

"Even me, sweetie. But you already know that."

A lump forms in my throat. My father and I have always been close, and he's been a rock for me these last few months. "I don't know what I'd do without you, Da."

"You never have to worry about that. Call me tomorrow, okay?"

"I will. Love you."

"I love you too, angel."

I end the call, and my adorable terrier-mix rescue dog, Margarita—Rita for short, named after my favorite cocktail, even though I no longer drink—climbs up into my lap.

The fact that Saint Rita is the patron saint of impossible and desperate causes isn't lost on me. Nana used to tell me about the saints when I sat in her lap as a little girl.

She was my safe place.

How I wish she were here now.

• • •

EIGHTEEN YEARS EARLIER…

Nana has an altar in her room. I love Nana's room because it has pretty gold wallpaper, and it always smells good. Kind of like smoke and perfume. Mommy and Da are Catholic, and so is Nana, but she's a different kind of Catholic. She goes to Mass with us, but she also prays to the Virgin Mary at home, at her altar. She calls her "Our Lady of Guadaloop."

The smoky and perfumy smell is from the incense she burns. Mommy and Da don't do things like that.

I stand at her door and wait until she opens her eyes and puts down her rosary.

"Come in, little one," she says without turning toward me.

I rush in and scramble into her lap.

She kisses my forehead. "I always know when you're there," she says. "You and I have a special bond because you're named after me."

"I am? But your name is Nana."

Nana smiles and strokes my hair. "But my given name is Teresa Maria, just like yours."

A warm feeling, kind of like a hug, spreads over me. I love sitting with her at her little altar.

So many candles and incense. It smells kind of like cinnamon but also like something else. "It's called frankincense," she once told me when I asked about the woodsy aroma.

"Like what the wise men gave to baby Jesus?" I asked.

"Yes. The smoke helps carry my prayers up to Mary in Heaven."

I love hearing Nana tell me about Mary and the other saints she prays to.

"Tell me about one of the saints, Nana," I say to her now.

"All right." She smiles. "I'll tell you about one of my favorite saints."

"Santa Maria?" I ask. "The Blessed Virgin? Our Lady of Guadaloop?"

"It's Guadalup*ay*," she corrects me, "and you know all about her, little one."

"Saint Michael, then. The Archangel."

"You know all about him as well."

I squint as I try to remember some of the other saints. "Saint Peter, Saint Paul."

"No, little one. I want to tell you about Saint Rita."

My eyes pop into circles. "I didn't know there was a Saint Rita."

"Oh, yes." Nana stares at her altar. "Saint Rita holds a special place in my heart. She is the saint of impossible or desperate causes."

"What does that mean, Nana?"

"It's when people lose all hope."

"Why would people lose all hope?"

Nana sighs and smooths out my dark hair. "Sometimes, little one, life takes a turn. A bad turn. But that's not going to happen to you. Not while I'm alive."

I snuggle into her, inhale her scent that's like roses and oranges put together.

She kisses the top of my head. "Saint Rita was born in 1381 in a small town in Italy. She wanted to become a nun when she was little, but her parents didn't like that idea, so they arranged for her to be married to a man named Paolo. They had two sons together, but the marriage was not a happy one, not like your mommy and da."

"Mommy and Da sometimes fight."

Nana smiles. "All married couples fight. Your papa and I used to fight before he died, but we were always happy, and we loved each other very much."

"That's good. I don't want to think that my mommy and da are unhappy."

"Your mommy and da are very happy. I'm blessed that they let me live here with them. I love being here with you and your sister, little one."

I smile, looking up into Nana's dark brown eyes. Her skin is darker than mine. "Are you from Italy, Nana, like Saint Rita?"

"No. I'm from Mexico. But I came here when I was just a little girl."

"But Saint Rita was from a place called Italy."

"Yes, and her marriage was unhappy. Her husband was not a nice man."

"Did he hurt her?"

Nana frowns and doesn't say anything for a minute. "No one really knows, little one. But what we do know is that Rita prayed for her husband, and eventually he repented, and she forgave him."

"So then they were happy?"

"For a little while, but eventually Paolo died."

I drop my mouth open. "How did he die?"

"He was killed, but Rita was a very religious woman. She was able to forgive his killers."

Sometimes Nana says things that I don't understand. "What's forgive?"

"It means she wasn't angry with his killers anymore."

"What did she do then?"

"She decided to do what her parents had forbidden her to do. She became a nun. She was very devoted to Jesus and often prayed about his suffering. Her greatest wish was to offer her own physical and spiritual pain for the salvation of souls."

"I don't know what that means, Nana."

"It means she was willing to go through pain so that others would be saved. That's why she's known as the saint of impossible or desperate causes." Nana touches her forehead, her chest, and then each of her shoulders before touching her chest again. She calls it "making the sign of the cross."

"What's an impossible cause?" I ask.

"It's when things are hard, little one. Or when someone hurts you."

"Why would anyone hurt me?"

She squeezes me in a hug. "No one will hurt you as long as your nana is alive. And even the day that I'm no longer with you, your mommy and da will protect you."

"But why would someone hurt someone else?"

Nana sighs. "Oh, my innocent little one, I don't know. But some people do. Some people hurt others."

"Do those people go to Hell?"

Nana doesn't answer me.

"Do they, Nana?"

"I don't know. Sometimes I hope that they do, and other times I hope that they don't."

"Why do you change your mind?"

"Because human beings aren't perfect, Tessa. Sometimes I feel more forgiving than other times."

"But Saint Rita forgave her husband. And she forgave others."

"And that's why she's a saint and I'm not." Nana lifts me up off her lap and sets me down on the floor. "Run along, little one. I hear your mother calling for lunch."

• • •

PRESENT DAY...

Seriously, I named Rita after the cocktail, but now, as I stroke her soft head, I feel like she's my own little guardian angel. My own saint helping me with my own desperate situation. She's my safe space, since Nana is no longer here.

Why would anyone hurt me?

No one will, as long as your nana's alive. And even the day that I'm no longer with you, your mommy and da will protect you.

I believed Nana that day. I continued to believe her, even as I grew up and left Catholicism behind me. I believed her even after she passed away.

But now, I no longer believe her.

My therapist helped me get Rita designated as my emotional support animal, and I swear the little pup is somehow able to get inside my head. She's there whenever I need her. And right now? I need her badly.

I stroke her soft head. "Such a good puppy. What would I do without you, Rita?"

I continue perusing the website for the private resort Braden Black booked for his and Skye's bachelor and bachelorette parties when my phone buzzes next to my laptop. I pick it up. Unknown number. Though I'm tempted to let it go to voicemail, Skye told me to expect a call from Braden's brother and best man, Benjamin Black. He's coordinating the bachelor party, and apparently, he and I need to chat.

A couple months ago, I would have been thrilled about this. Ben Black is one of the most eligible bachelors in Boston. Hell, in the country. He has dark hair, dark eyes, and he's model-level handsome. He's moved up a notch since his brother is now off the market. Any other time, any other place, I'd want to be first in line.

Funny how things can change in the blink of an eye.

"Hello?" I say into the phone.

"Tessa?"

"Yes, this is she."

"This is Ben Black." His voice is rich and low. "I'm sorry we haven't met yet. In fact, I can't really believe we haven't, considering my brother is marrying your best friend."

I could tell him why. Because I've closed myself up like a hermit for the past several months. I only leave my apartment when I have to. I've been working at home as much as I can since I got out of the hospital. I'm an accountant, so most of my work can be done remotely. The few times I've met with Skye to talk about the wedding and the bachelor and bachelorette parties, it's either been by phone or just the two of us alone here at my place.

"Yeah. I've been pretty busy," I say instead, keeping it simple.

"Would you be able to meet me for a drink tonight?" he asks. "I feel like we should meet in person to go over everything. We should at the very least be able to pick each other out of a lineup."

That's a laugh. Every woman in the free world can pick Ben Black out of a lineup. His face is splashed all over the gossip rags and social media feeds.

"Like I said," I emphasize, "I've been busy at work, and I still am. Maybe we could just chat over the phone?"

"I'm more of an in-person kind of guy. Can you meet me at The Stargazer tonight? Around seven thirty?"

I hold back a sigh. I really don't want to go out, but this is Skye Manning—my best friend in the whole world since we met freshman year of college. In fact, I'm the one who encouraged Skye to let her hair down when Braden Black first began to pursue her. To say Skye is a control freak is the ultimate understatement. She is a classic type A. But she and Braden seem to fit together like two puzzle pieces, and I've never seen Skye happier.

I was horribly jealous at first. I felt like I was losing my best friend. But I didn't lose Skye. In fact, I gained a friend in Betsy

Davis, who I met through Skye. Of course, I haven't seen much of Betsy lately, either. I've blown her off when she's tried to make plans because I didn't want to go out *anywhere* with *anyone*, but I can't keep doing that. She's one of Skye's bridesmaids, so I need to get in touch with her and the others and sort things out for the wedding.

That's all Ben is trying to do, so I have no excuse to tell him no.

"All right," I say into the phone. "Fine. We can meet."

"I can swing by your place and pick you up if you like," Ben says.

My skin turns to ice and my heart thumps hard against my sternum, the tremor visible in my shirt.

Panic sets in.

Ben Black is probably a nice man, but the thought of being alone in a car with any man sends me into a tailspin.

"That's kind of you, but no." I try to keep my voice steady. "I'll get there on my own."

"Sure. See you then, okay?"

"Yeah. See you then."

He must know what happened to me. Braden and Skye have certainly told him everything.

I may as well have a tattoo written in red letters across my forehead.

Tessa Logan was drugged and raped by Garrett Ramirez.
Tessa Logan almost died.

That's how I know I'm not actually suicidal.

I don't *want* to die. There are just days—like today—when I have a hard time with the simplest of tasks. When my torment is so great that I'm not sure I can get through one more day.

Honestly? Figuring out how to end my life would be too

much effort.

I stroke Rita behind her ears. "Guess I've got to go out tonight, Rita."

When did I last shower?

Working remotely has had a detrimental effect on my personal hygiene. On those days when I have to do a teleconference, I simply put on the bare minimum of makeup, brush my hair until it looks decent, and put on a clean blouse. I'm usually wearing my sweats, or sometimes only underwear—always a color, I hate white panties—as I sit in the meeting, forcing myself to engage. So far, I've been able to get my work done, and I have enough PTO for Skye's bachelorette party and the wedding.

No problem, right?

I go through the motions, day by day. Force myself to get out of bed, get to my computer, do my work.

Despite the fact that I've been subsisting on bacon and Ben & Jerry's, I've lost ten pounds. Yes, those stubborn ten pounds that I've always wanted to take off are finally gone, yet I can't be happy about it. When I look at my naked reflection in the mirror, I see the body I've always wanted.

Except it's someone else's body, and I can't bring myself to care.

I log off the website, set Rita down, rise, and head to my bathroom.

Maybe a shower will help.

I turn on the shower, listen to the soothing sound of the water pelting onto the tile floor. Again, I take a look in the mirror. How many days has it been? Three, I think. My hair is starting to look oily at the roots. I walk into the shower and—

"Shit," I say out loud.

My shampoo bottle is empty. I squeezed the last of it out

during my previous shower.

I have to meet Benjamin Black at The Stargazer in a couple of hours, and I have no shampoo. At least I have conditioner.

"For God's sake," I grumble.

Time to do something the old Tessa never would have done—never would have been caught dead doing.

I squeeze shower gel into my palm and lather it through my hair.

Once my hair is shampooed and conditioned—or rather, shower-gelled and conditioned—I lather up my shower pouf and notice my legs.

From my Mexican-American mother, I inherited a gorgeous head of nearly black hair. But from my Irish-American father, I inherited the wonderful European trait of body hair everywhere.

Yeah, I'm basically the link between man and the ape.

But I can't bring myself to shave. I just don't have the energy.

I'll wear jeans or leggings or something, even though it's summer and I'll be sweltering. The bar will be air-conditioned. I gather the energy to at least shave my armpits, and then I turn the water off and step out of the shower, grabbing a towel. Once I wrap myself in it, I grab another to wrap over my long, thick hair.

My face appears in the mirror once more, but this time I can't see it because it's steamed up from the shower.

What a metaphor for my life right now.

I'm just existing.

Existing in a fog.

I go to therapy twice a week, and my mother checks on me once a week.

I've been keeping up with work, but here's the thing.

Next week, my boss expects me to go back to the office full-time. No more remote work unless I'm physically sick. I used to love going to the office. Talking to people, looking good, having in-person meetings.

I've known for a while that this was coming.

Just like I've known Skye and Braden's wedding is coming, and still I've put off planning anything until the last minute.

I'm going to have to pick up the shattered pieces of my life and put them together into something that will hopefully resemble the Tessa Logan I used to be.

CHAPTER TWO

Ben

"What'll it be, Ben?" one of my favorite bartenders, Leanna, asks.

"Like you have to ask."

She shoves a lowball glass filled with two fingers of Wild Turkey at me with a smile. "You never know when it might be something else."

I give her a wink.

The Stargazer is a little hole in the wall in downtown Boston. It's my own little secret. There's always a seat at the bar for me.

"You meeting someone?"

I nod. "Braden's fiancée's maid of honor. She and I need to put together bachelor and bachelorette parties for the happy couple."

"You're doing it on your own? No party planner?"

"Braden rented out this private resort near Ocho Rios, Jamaica. It's big enough that we can have both parties there, and yeah, they have a planner, but I feel like I should be involved. Best-man duties and all."

"Will you be able to get a stripper?"

I let out a chuckle. "Braden doesn't want a stripper."

She laughs heartily. "That's what they all say."

I nod, grinning.

I've already looked into getting a stripper. If my big brother thinks he's getting out of bachelorhood that easily, he can think again. It's going to be a proper party. Not just one stripper, but several.

I glance at my watch. Tessa's late. I would've been okay with planning over the phone, but Skye asked me to try to get Tessa to meet with me in person. She's had a hard time of it, and Skye thinks she needs to get out more.

I don't know that I agree with pressuring Tessa to leave her place if she doesn't want to, but Skye knows her better than I do and—

I jerk to attention when a woman sits down next to me.

It's Tessa.

And it may sound cliché, but the woman takes my breath away.

I've seen photos of her. She's a knockout for sure. But in person?

Man, photography doesn't do her justice. Even the photos taken by Skye herself—and she's an amazing photographer. Skye's become a major influencer, largely due to the fact that she started dating my brother, but in short order, people recognized her for the talent that she is. Spectacular images.

But not when it comes to her best friend. Skye's camera didn't capture the subtle freckle on Tessa's lower lip, the way her hair catches the light with plum more than mahogany highlights, the lovely warmth of her light tan complexion.

Tessa is wearing black leggings and a blousy black tunic.

Black sandals on her feet, and her toes are unpolished.

Not that I would normally notice such a thing, but most of the women that I come across—except for Apple Ames, my ex-friend-with-benefits—have freshly manicured toes.

But what's more noticeable than the lack of polish on her toes is the sheer beauty of them. I'm no fetishist when it comes to feet, but Tessa Logan has the most beautiful pair I've seen.

Once I've noticed her bottom half, I look up, into her eyes.

I've never been serious about a woman in my life, and I've always gone for a hot body over a pretty face.

But Tessa's eyes...

They're large, dark, and long-lashed... And my God...

They look so fucking sad.

A wave of empathy surges through me, and it almost makes me shiver. It's an odd feeling—a foreign feeling. I know what Tessa's been through, and in this moment, I would move heaven and earth to get that look of pure remorse and resignation off her beautiful face forever.

Those beautiful eyes were meant to show happiness, excitement, love.

"Thanks for coming, Tessa." I hold out my hand. "I'm Ben Black."

"I know you are."

Leanna places a cocktail napkin in front of Tessa. "What can I get for you?"

"Just some sparkling water, please."

According to Skye, Tessa's favorite drink is a margarita. But also according to Skye, her assailant, Garrett Ramirez, laced alcohol with ketamine, which nearly cost Tessa her life.

I imagine she's purposely staying away from booze.

"So..." I begin. "I thought we should, you know, talk about

our plans for the respective parties. Make sure they can both happen on the same premises without any issues."

"Yeah. Of course."

Even her voice sounds sad. She taps her fingers on the wooden bar. Her nails are also not polished, but her hands are shapely and beautiful, with long fingers and oval nails cut short, filed smooth. She doesn't wear a watch or bracelet or any other jewelry. Her hair falls in gentle waves around her shoulders and midway down her back.

"Why don't you tell me what you're planning?" I ask.

She shrugs. "Just the usual stuff. We'll shower her with gifts."

"No strippers?"

She turns and meets my gaze for the first time. "No. I don't want any men there."

"Is that what Skye wants?"

Her gaze narrows. "Yeah. She specifically told me that she and Braden don't want strippers."

I chuckle under my breath.

"What's so funny?"

"Nothing, nothing."

She raises her eyebrows. "You're going to have a stripper at the bachelor party, aren't you?"

"I didn't say that."

She shakes her head. "Fine. Do what you want. I'm not having male strippers at Skye's bachelorette party."

The way she phrased that makes me think it's more about Tessa's preferences than Skye's, but given what she's been through, I can't blame her for being cautious when it comes to nearly naked men. I'm not sure how to respond, so I take a long drink of my bourbon and then change the subject. "Okay. So if we have the parties that Friday night, how do we get everybody together at the end?"

Tessa looks down at the bar. "Why would we do that?"

"Isn't that what Skye and Braden asked for?"

"Oh." She wrinkles her forehead. "Yeah, you're right. At midnight, we're supposed to bring the two parties together into one big party."

"Yeah. So...any ideas?"

She draws in a breath, holds it for a few seconds, and then exhales slowly. "We really could've discussed this over the phone."

She's not wrong. And now I feel like a dick for setting this up.

A man clad in jeans and a T-shirt walks into the bar. He takes a seat next to Tessa.

In a flash, she hops up off her stool and moves closer to me.

"You okay?" I ask quietly.

She swallows. "Yeah. Fine." She slides into the empty seat on my other side.

My God, she's skittish. And of course I understand why.

I turn to her. "You want to get out of here?"

She frowns. "And go where? This was your idea."

"We could go back to my place, or yours."

Her eyes widen into circles.

That was the wrong thing to say.

"Or to...someplace where we can have our own table." I glance around the bar. "I see an empty table in the back."

She nods and hops off her stool again.

"Leanna, could you bring her sparkling water to that table in the corner?" I gesture toward it.

"I've got it right here." She slides it across the bar to Tessa. "Sorry for the wait."

Tessa thanks her, picks up her water, and I follow her to the table. She sits down, and then she glances over her shoulder and all around the bar, becoming aware of her surroundings.

I clench my jaw. That asshole did a real number on her.

I'd like to pound him into next week, and I don't even know the shithead. He's out on bail right now, I've heard, but he was let go from his architecture firm. Out on bail, out of work, facing trial for rape… He'd better stay the hell away from her.

I'm not one to talk to women about serious stuff. Hell, I'm not one to talk to anybody about anything serious. I'm usually the one who's the life of the party, telling the jokes, getting the crowd excited.

But for some reason, I want Tessa to talk to me.

"You doing okay?" I ask.

"I'm fine." She takes a sip of her sparkling water and wipes her lips with her cocktail napkin.

"Are you hungry? They make a good burger here."

She doesn't reply, simply shakes her head. Her lips tremble a bit. They're full and dark pink.

So sexy.

I recently took a break from my alternative sexual lifestyle and ended my long-term friends-with-benefits relationship with Apple. Some things from my past have resurfaced, and the last thing I need is to be focused on a woman.

But Tessa Logan—Tessa Logan, with her sad eyes—has my groin reacting.

Easy, I say to myself. *I am the* last *thing she needs right now.*

It's been a long time since I've had this intense of a reaction to a woman. Have I ever?

I don't know much about her except that she's an accountant. And, of course, what she went through with that asshole architect.

"You want to tell me anything about yourself?" I ask.

She blinks. "Why would I want to do that?"

"I don't know. Maybe make yourself a little more comfortable."

She draws in a breath again, holds it for a few moments. "You know all about me. You're Braden's brother. You know from him, and he knows from Skye. So you know what happened to me."

I absently reach forward to lay my hand over hers, but she pulls her hand back quickly.

"I'm sorry," I say. I'm fucking this all up.

"I don't like to be touched."

"I get that. I respect that. I was just trying to offer you some comfort."

"I don't want any comfort."

"I won't do it again."

"Let's just do what we came here to do, okay?" Then she sighs. "Look. I'm not trying to be rude. I'm not a rude person. I just… Just tell me what you have planned. I'll work around it."

"I need to know what you have planned as well."

She gnaws on that gorgeous, full lower lip.

And I realize…

She doesn't *have* anything planned.

"Nothing's final yet," she says. "I'm flexible."

"Okay. I can work with that. The men and I will have a golf game in the afternoon. The private resort has an amazing golf course. We're going to play nine holes. Then we'll have dinner, catered by the resort. We'll roast him. And boy, do I have a lot of stories." I smile.

Disappointment creeps through me when she doesn't return my smile.

"Then," I continue, "we'll pop open the champagne, toast the groom, and…"

"The stripper…"

"Strip*pers*," I say.

"More than one?"

"I'm sending my brother off in style."

She rolls her eyes. "Okay. And then we'll be getting close to midnight at that point?"

"Yeah. That'll take us up to midnight."

She nods. "I don't have anything planned for the afternoon." She purses her lips. "I don't have anything planned at all, actually. You've probably figured that out. But I thought we would spend the afternoon on the beach. Relaxing."

"You could book massages and facials for everyone."

Her eyes light up. "Yeah, that's a good idea. Why didn't I think of it?"

I could answer for her, but she doesn't really want me to. She didn't think of it because she hasn't put any thought into this. She's been focusing inward lately, and there's nothing wrong with that.

She takes her phone out of her pocket and makes some notes. "Beach day. Massages and facials. Then dinner. If you guys are having dinner at the resort, where should *we* have dinner?"

"It's a large resort. They have two separate dining rooms plus two outdoor dining areas."

"All right. Just tell me where you're having yours, and I'll arrange to have mine somewhere else."

I nod. "Good enough."

"Then after dinner, we'll give Skye her gifts. And then I don't know what the hell we'll do until midnight."

"You could go dancing," I suggest. "There's a DJ, and you could arrange for him to work one of the ballrooms. You guys can dance, have a drink. Toast the bride."

She makes more notes on her phone. "Great. Sounds good."

I can't believe this. *I'm* planning the bachelorette party.

Who would've thought?

"Hey, Ben!"

I turn toward the voice I recognize.

Apple Ames strides back toward our table. Naturally blond, Apple colors her hair black and wears long flowing dresses in dark colors. She's heavily tatted and pierced and doesn't look at all like the hotel heiress that she is. That's what I like about her.

"Oh, sorry," she says. "I didn't realize you were with somebody."

"No problem." I rise and give her a hug. "This is Tessa Logan. Skye's maid of honor."

"Oh, hi. I'm Apple." She reaches out with her right hand.

"Nice to meet you," Tessa says, but she doesn't return Apple's handshake.

Apple pulls back, the brightness in her face dimming a bit. I could explain Tessa's preference to not be touched, but it isn't my place. If Tessa wants to tell her, she will.

But she doesn't.

"You want to join us?" I ask Apple.

"No, that's okay. I'm meeting some friends. Good to see you both." She smiles and walks away.

"That's Addison Ames's sister," Tessa says.

I return to my seat. "It is."

Addison Ames is the woman who gave Skye her big break as an influencer. Long story there, but the relationship didn't end well.

Tessa grabs a wallet out of her small purse and takes out a few five-dollar bills.

I scoot the money back toward her. "Please. It's on me. Leanna's got my tab up at the bar."

"All right. Thank you." She stands. "If we're done here…"

I suppose we're done. But something inside me doesn't want her to leave.

Not yet.

"Tessa…"

She raises her eyebrows at me.

"Skye asked me to have you meet me. In person."

"I figured as much."

"I'm sorry. I should've told you when I called. We'll do the rest of the stuff over the phone if you want. The last thing I want to do is make you uncomfortable."

"I'm perfectly comfortable," she says. "But if we're done, I'd like to go."

"All right." Though I desperately want her to stay.

I would never hurt a woman. In fact, I got out of the BDSM lifestyle because I no longer wanted to hurt women, even if we both got pleasure out of it.

But Tessa doesn't know that. Right now, to her, *every* man is a threat.

And while I understand it's justified, I wish there were something I could do to ease that fear in her.

I stand. "Would you like to…go on a walk sometime? Tomorrow is Saturday. And for once, I'm not working this weekend. Braden and Skye are in New York. We could—"

She gestures for me to stop. "Thank you, but no."

Then she turns, and within seconds she's disappeared into the ladies' room.

I've never had a woman practically running to get away from me before. *What a brilliant fuck-up, Ben.* If we weren't going to be forced to see each other again because of Braden and Skye's wedding, I doubt I'd ever see Tessa Logan again after tonight.

CHAPTER THREE

Tessa

I grip the edges of the counter, looking at my reflection in the bathroom mirror.

The tingling begins in my fingers, travels through my hands up to my elbows, and then branches into my arms and over my chest. My heart beats quickly, slamming against my sternum and then pulsing throughout my body. I hear it like a drum in my ears, drowning out everything else. My body trembles, and perspiration erupts on my hairline.

And in the mirror...

In the mirror is a woman I don't recognize.

She looks like me, but she's not me.

She's someone who has detached herself from her body. And she's looking at me, judging me, telling me I'm nothing.

You're nothing, Tessa. You're nothing.

• • •

THREE MONTHS EARLIER...

"**Y**ou're nothing, you cock tease."

Garrett shoves his cock inside me.

How did I think I was falling in love with this monster?

How did I...

I'm not me anymore.

I'm simply a vessel. A vessel that he's masturbating into.

I turn my head.

"No, you *look* at me. You look at me while I fuck you."

But I no longer feel him.

My body feels it, but not my mind. I go inward, to that safe place.

My grandmother's embrace.

"Why would anyone hurt me?"

"No one will hurt you as long as your nana is alive."

• • •

I swallow hard when a woman exits the stall.

Quickly I turn on the water. Put on my game face. Pump some soap out of the dispenser and wash my hands while I feign a smile.

She smiles back at me as she washes her own hands and then slides them under one of the automatic dryers.

Leave. Leave. Leave.

When she finally opens the bathroom door and exits, I let out a deep breath.

I look in the mirror, and this time I see myself. I see Tessa.

My body has recovered.

Still, just to be sure, I grip the counter once more. Breathe in, breathe out, breathe in again.

Exhaustion weighs on me. I haven't been eating right, and I haven't been sleeping well.

When I do manage to fall asleep, nightmares plague me.

But I have to get a grip.

And not just on this counter.

My best friend is getting married—married to the man of her dreams. Married to the man of anyone's dreams, really. I can't let her down.

I draw in a breath again. Check my reflection in the mirror to make sure I'm still me.

I nod to myself.

Then I leave the bathroom and—

Thud.

I look up, get my bearings. I ran right into Benjamin Black.

He grabs my shoulders. "I'm so sorry. Are you okay?"

"Yes." I pull out of his grasp. "Were you waiting for me?"

"No... I was heading to the bathroom."

Oh. Of course he was. The men's room is right next to the ladies' room.

"Right. Sorry."

He gazes up and down my body. "You sure you're okay?"

Is he serious?

Of course I'm not okay. I just had a fucking panic attack in the bathroom. I haven't eaten, haven't slept, and he's the one who made me come out tonight.

No. My best friend, Skye, made me come out tonight.

Never again.

"I'm fine," I grit out.

He stands in my way.

"If you'll excuse me," I say.

He cocks his head, looks me over. "Tessa, wait right here for me while I go to the bathroom. I want to see that you get home safely."

"That's not necessary."

He reaches out, but he doesn't touch me. "Please."

Something in his voice makes me think about it.

Please.

I have no reason to fear Ben Black. He's the brother of my best friend's fiancé. I'm certainly safer with him than I am with a strange cabdriver or Uber driver, aren't I?

"How?" I ask. "Do you have a car here?"

"I just need to call my driver. He'll pick us up here, and I can see you home."

"A driver?"

"He's paid very well by my company. He has top security clearance. I assure you that you'll be safe."

I look down, nibbling on my lower lip. He knows what's bothering me, all right. I *hate* that everyone knows.

I may as well be wearing a scarlet letter like Hester Prynne. Except I haven't committed adultery. No. And it would be a string of letters, not just one.

Tessa Logan was drugged and date raped. Tessa Logan almost died.

"Please," he says again. "Let me do this for you. Let me do this for Skye and Braden."

I swallow. Nod. "All right."

He smiles at me then, and I see kindness in his brown eyes. The old Tessa would've found him extremely good-looking. The old Tessa *did* find him extremely good-looking. I've seen him on television, all over the internet, in magazines.

The old Tessa would be doing a lot more than just noticing his looks. She'd be flirting up a storm.

But that Tessa doesn't exist anymore. In her place is a shell. The shadow inhabiting my body.

Ben takes out his phone and taps on it. "Sherlock will be here in just a minute."

"Your driver's name is Sherlock?"

"Sherlock Gatsby," he says.

I can't keep my jaw from dropping. "Someone really named their kid Sherlock Gatsby?"

He cracks a grin. "Stranger things have happened."

Can't argue with that. "Thank you," I say. "For, you know. Your kindness."

"No thanks needed. I will always help a lady who needs it."

His words and his strong-yet-gentle voice—not to mention his rich, low timbre—almost send a shudder through me.

Almost.

The old Tessa would be making the most of this evening. She would've had a margarita—maybe two. She would've talked to Ben about his likes and dislikes, and she would've found a way to innocently slide her fingers over his arm, lean in, and whisper something suggestive into his ear.

Now?

The thought of doing those things threatens to send me reeling.

Already I feel the tingling in my fingers once more.

I draw in a deep breath and stave off the impending panic.

All I need to do is get into a car. Get in a car with a driver who has passed the best security clearance there is with this man who, though I don't know him, can be trusted because his brother is marrying my best friend.

Ben returns from the bathroom, checking his phone. "He's here."

He takes care not to touch me as he leads me out of the bar. His car—a black BMW—is parked outside on the street. Sherlock, a tall man with brown hair mostly hidden under his chauffeur's hat, gets out, comes over to the sidewalk, opens the back door, and offers his hand to me.

I don't take it.

"I'd offer to help you in the car but..." Ben says.

"I'm fine, thank you." I slide into the back seat, edging over so that I'm behind the driver's seat. Ben gets in after me, keeping to his own side.

"Where do you live?" he asks me.

I rattle off my address, and Sherlock begins to drive.

I don't know what to say, so I say nothing.

But I'm very aware that I'm sitting next to a man. A man who doesn't frighten me nearly as much as I expected him to.

Still...I feel frozen. My skin feels numb, and I'm antsy. I just want to get home. Get out of the car. Get up to my apartment and cuddle with Rita.

We don't speak the whole way there, and when we finally arrive at my place, I immediately try to open the car door.

It's locked, of course.

Locked.

I'm locked in.

The tingles start again—

Ben's low voice eases the panic. "Sherlock will get that for you, and I'll see you up."

"That's not necessary."

A man hasn't been to my apartment since...

"I'm not asking to come in, Tessa. I just want to see you to your door. Make sure you get in safely."

What I'm feeling is such a contradiction. Part of me wants the security of his presence. After all, what if someone is waiting for me? What if Garrett is waiting for me?

But on the other hand...

His nearness makes my skin prickle, and not in a good way.

I desperately want to be free from him. Yet I also want him to walk me to my apartment.

Sherlock opens the car door for me and extends his hand, which I don't take. He doesn't seem offended, though. He just closes the door behind me and gets back into the driver's seat.

Ben follows me to the building entrance. "Which floor are you on?" he asks.

"Fourth."

My place doesn't have an elevator, which sucks, but it's part of the reason why the rent is so cheap.

Ben follows me up the stairs, staying close but careful not to touch me.

We get to the fourth floor, and I walk the two doors over to my apartment. Rita's barks pierce through from the other side.

"You have a dog?" Ben asks.

"I do. I need to take her down to do her business."

"It's dark outside, Tessa."

"I know that, but the dog has to go out."

"I'll take her for you."

"She won't go with you," I say. "You're a stranger."

"Then we'll go together."

The man has an answer for everything.

Nausea makes its way from my stomach up my throat. I swallow it back. "This is a safe neighborhood, Ben. I'll be fine."

But he stays outside my apartment as I unlock my door, calm Rita down, and get her leash attached to her collar. I'm equal parts annoyed and relieved.

Ben doesn't say a word—neither do I—as we walk down the stairs together.

I usually take Rita on a short walk every morning before

work to give her some exercise. But the rest of the time, we only stay out until she goes to the bathroom. Lately, I've been lazy about the walks, though.

Normally it's just a pee in the evening, but tonight it's number two as well. And of course, I forgot the bag. Ben has me flustered, off my usual routine.

"I've got to go back upstairs and get a bag," I say.

"You think she'll stay with me? That way you don't have to drag her up with you." He kneels and scratches her behind her ears. "You're a sweet girl, aren't you?"

Surprisingly, Rita takes to Ben, and it *will* be easier for me to trudge back upstairs to get the bag without her tagging along. But that isn't entirely the point. I pin Ben with a look. "You mean you're going let me go alone, when a few minutes ago you wouldn't?"

He simply smiles. "If you're not back in five minutes, Rita and I are coming up."

Something in me wants to return his smile.

But I don't. I just turn and leave to get the bag.

CHAPTER FOUR

Ben

I love dogs. Always have. But I don't have one of my own. I travel so much between here and my place in New York and abroad that I never thought it would be fair to the dog.

Rita's a cute and scruffy little thing, white with gray markings—an obvious rescue. I'd say she's mostly some kind of terrier, and I can't guess her age, exactly. She doesn't seem old, but she's definitely not a puppy anymore. She doesn't seem bothered by me as she continues to sniff the ground.

"Hey, pup," I say.

She wags her tail at me. She's small enough that I can easily pick her up, so I kneel and take her in my arms. She licks my face. And I can't help myself. I laugh.

Yeah, I've got to get a dog.

"She doesn't usually let people pick her up."

I turn at Tessa's voice. She opens a bag and scoops up the poop, knotting it closed. Then she walks over to the trash can close to the entrance and drops it in.

Rita is wriggling in my arms. I let her down and hand the

leash to Tessa. "I'll see you back up."

"Ben, I was just up there."

"I know. But I'm going to see you to your door. It's what I do. Besides"—I bend down and give Rita a pet—"Rita and I are good friends now."

She sighs but doesn't argue.

We walk back in, up the four flights of stairs, and Tessa unlocks the door to her unit.

I make a point to stay in the hallway. "It was great meeting you."

"You too." She looks at the floor as Rita runs into the small apartment.

Resignation exudes from her. She's depleted. So depleted, and I yearn to help her. To at least do something within my power.

"Tell you what," I say. "I'll make the arrangements for your bachelorette party if you'd like. I've got all the details about the resort, and Braden gave me carte blanche. He's planning on paying for everything."

"I know," Tessa says. "Skye told me. He's very generous."

"He is, especially where Skye is concerned. He'd buy her the moon if he could."

"I believe he would." She looks over at Rita, who has settled herself on a chair. "Skye fell in love with a puppy when I rescued Rita. Her place didn't allow pets, but I..." A small smile curves her lips.

She's so beautiful.

"I called Braden," she continues. "I told him about the pup, about how much Skye loved it, and Braden adopted the pup for Skye."

I nod. "I'm familiar with the tale."

"It's so..."

"So...what?" I ask.

She sighs. "It seems like years have gone by since then, but in reality it's only been a few months. I remember telling her to go for it when Braden asked her out. To let her hair down. Skye was never like that. She thought everything out. *Over*thought everything. Tried to control every minor facet of her life."

"And now?"

"She's still like that, but not to the same extent. Braden has been good for her."

"She's been good for him too," I say. "I've never seen them happier."

That gets another small smile out of Tessa.

"Goodnight," I say.

"Goodnight. Thank you for the drink."

"Anytime. I'll be in touch about the arrangements. That way you can..."

She meets my gaze. "I can what?"

"Nothing. I'll be in touch. I'll take care of all of it."

"Thank you." She nods and closes the door. I wait until I hear the deadbolt click into place, and then I leave.

I hope I haven't done Tessa a disservice by offering to take care of the arrangements for both parties. It's clear she's not in the mood, not in the headspace, but this is her best friend. I know how much she loves Skye. I can see it in the way she talks about her and how happy she is for her and Braden. I don't doubt Tessa wants the bachelorette party to be perfect and she's just struggling to focus.

The signs are loud and clear to me. I've been where Tessa is. Not for the same reasons, of course, but I've been to that dark place where you're not sure you'll ever be able to climb back out of the hole. The best thing you can do is to have something to focus on, and I just took that away from Tessa.

I wanted to help her, yearned to help her, but I may have only made things worse.

Sherlock is waiting for me, and I scramble into the back seat as he holds the door.

"Where to this time, Mr. B?" he asks.

It's early yet on Friday evening. I could go to a club, but I'm not really in the mood for crowds and dancing and loud music.

Watching Braden and Skye find each other and follow their love has made me wonder if maybe it's time for me to look for the same thing. Indiscriminate sex no longer has the thrill it once did. I'm looking for more. An emotional connection that matches the physical.

"I think just home," I say.

I see Sherlock's eyebrows rise in the rearview mirror. He's surprised, and I can't blame him. Since when do I go home before ten o'clock on a Friday evening?

But it's been a rough week at work. Braden and Skye are in New York, and frankly? I'm exhausted. Home, a glass of Wild Turkey, and a little Netflix marathon sounds great.

"Just home," I say to Sherlock again.

This time he nods.

· · ·

The next night is Saturday, and I usually spend it at a local downtown dance club called Ballroom Blitz. The owners have been known to look the other way if people get a bit physical on the dance floor.

I dreamed about Tessa last night. The funny thing is, it wasn't even a sexual dream, but when I woke? I felt a pulsing need that was new to me.

I'm feeling horny, but I don't have any desire to do anything about it. That's new.

My phone dings. I glance at it.

Apple: *I know you ended our mutual fun, but...I'm kind of horny.*

She sends me the devil emoji, with horns and all.

I send back a laughing emoji. She texts back.

Apple: *Your place or mine?*

Apple and I have been friends with benefits—on-again, off-again—since she was barely eighteen. She and her twin sister, Addison Ames, had a huge party at their daddy's mansion while the parents were out of town, and somehow Braden and I ended up there. We were both working construction at the time for our father, Bobby Black. Addison chased after Braden big time, but Apple and I? We just clicked. Nothing romantic at all. We love each other as friends, but nothing more. And we have a good time in the sack.

I consider it, given my raging hard-on over Tessa, but then I text her back.

Ben: *Sorry. I'm busy.*

Apple: *Are you?*

Ben: *No.*

Apple: *It's okay. You don't have to lie to me. You okay?*

Ben: *Yeah. I guess.*

Apple: *How was your date with Tessa?*

Ben: *Are you kidding me? That was hardly a date.*

Apple: *Yeah. I could see it wasn't from her end, but I saw the way you were looking at her.*

Ben: *Why shouldn't I look at her? She's a gorgeous woman.*

Apple: *She is. And she's Skye's maid of honor. The two of you will be thrown together a lot during the next couple months.*

Ben: *I suppose so.*

Apple: *Are you hoping something will happen there?*

Am I? Tessa Logan has baggage. Baggage I'm not equipped to handle. So no matter how attracted I am to her—and I'm *damned* attracted to her—I need to leave well enough alone.

Apple texts back before I think of how to reply.

Apple: *Have a good evening. I'll slake my horniness elsewhere. Ciao!*

Ben: *Take care.*

I shove my phone in my pocket and walk around my rec room. I have a house in a luxury community. I only recently moved there from my downtown Boston penthouse. It's the quintessential bachelor pad with a sleek contemporary design, lots of glass, steel, and stone accents. My large lawn is home to elegant shrubs and a fountain and koi pond.

The inside is spacious with high ceilings and floor-to-ceiling windows that flood the space with natural light. The colors are a masculine mixture of blacks, grays, and whites, accented with bold artwork and high-end furnishings. The place boasts a home theater, a game room, and a fully-equipped gym.

And of course a spacious master bedroom complete with king-size bed, walk-in closet, lounge area, and en-suite bathroom with shower, jetted tub, and infrared sauna.

I love it all.

Apple's been there many times, and I could have easily accepted her invitation. She'd have come over, and together we could have taken care of business. No different than any other time we screwed.

Except everything has changed.

I met Tessa Logan. Tessa Logan, who I know damned well I should stay far away from.

Only problem?

I can't get her out of my mind.

CHAPTER FIVE

Tessa

It's Monday morning, and I have a meeting with my boss. I'm back at the office, which freaks me out a little, but I suck it up, put on work clothes, and enter my building by eight o'clock.

All eyes are on me—at least it feels like they are—when I walk into the office suite, as if I'm flashing that neon tattoo on my forehead.

They all know I've been gone for a few weeks. That's no secret.

Most likely they all know why.

I don't make eye contact with anyone, and I wave hastily to the receptionist after her, "Welcome back, Tessa."

After grabbing a cup of coffee, I head into my office and fire up my computer.

I go through emails until my meeting at nine.

Then I rise, walk the hallway to my boss's office, and knock.

"Come in," Charlotte Peterson says, her gaze never straying from her computer monitor.

Charlotte's new, and I haven't worked with her for long. Since

I've been working mostly remotely, this is the first time we've talked in a while.

"Tessa, please have a seat."

I do my best to paste on a smile and take a seat across from her desk.

"How have you been?"

I nod. "I'm fine. Thank you for asking."

Charlotte looks up from her computer screen and frowns. "I won't beat around the bush, Tessa, and trust me when I say this has nothing to do with your quality of work. But we're making cutbacks, and unfortunately we're going to have to terminate your employment."

The news should shock me. Worry me.

But all I feel is numbness.

"Tessa? Did you hear me?"

I blink. "Yes. I've been here for a couple of years, though."

"I know. Unfortunately, shit runs downhill. I've had to make some decisions I didn't want to make. You'll of course receive three months' severance pay and benefits. Then if you need to retain your benefits under COBRA, you can do that for another year and a half."

Benefits, yeah. I definitely need benefits. Health insurance covers my therapy.

"I…" Words don't form in my head. What am I supposed to say? Thank you? I should hardly thank her for firing me.

"Since you're not being terminated for cause, if you don't find another position once your severance package is up, you can always apply for unemployment."

Right. Unemployment. That'll make me feel good.

I'm upset yet not upset. A little nonplussed, actually. "All right. Is that all, Charlotte?"

"Yeah. That's all." She begins tapping on her computer. "You can clear out your office today if you feel like it. Your current salary will continue to be paid for the next three months. I can get all of that to you in writing for your signature."

"Yeah. Sure. Whatever."

I leave, walk back to my office, not talking to anyone along the way. Is this truly not for cause? I've done my job to the best of my ability since the incident, but everyone knows I haven't been myself. I've hardly been to the office.

Perhaps they *did* need to cut costs, and I was the obvious choice, since I haven't had my head in the game lately. Maybe this is why I felt all the eyes on me when I walked in. Maybe everyone knew I was getting canned.

Whatever the reason, I don't feel concern. In all honesty? I just feel relief.

Now I don't have to go to work.

I have three months of salary coming. A decent amount of savings in the bank. I'll be fine.

And if I'm not?

I can't go there. Absolutely can't go there. I have to stay focused so I can get through Skye's bachelorette party and wedding.

I laugh out loud—wow, when was the last time I did that?—as I leave the building with my box of items.

Well, now I have all the time in the world to focus on Skye. I'll even have money.

You're going to have to search for a new job, Tessa.

Yeah, I know that.

Skye's back from New York now, and I should call her and let her know what's going on with the bachelorette party. Which I would totally do, if I had a clue. Ben said he'd handle everything.

But now I have the time, and I need something to prod me

along. Because frankly? I'm so tired of feeling like I'm trudging through mud, each step a challenge. My work was getting me up each morning. That's gone, so I need something else.

Once I'm back at my apartment, I decide to call Skye.

"Ben Black," the voice on the other end of the line says.

The phone slips from my hand and clatters to my floor, scaring Rita.

"I'm sorry, baby." I pet her quickly and pick up the phone.

Ben Black?

Did I tap his name instead of Skye's?

I look at my recent phone calls. Sure enough, Ben called me right after Skye did. I had my phone on silent during the meeting with Charlotte.

I put the phone back to my ear. "Hey, it's Tessa. I'm really sorry. I thought I was calling Skye."

"That's not a problem. Always glad to talk to you."

"Well, since I've got you on the phone, I have some more time to deal with this bachelorette party fiasco."

"Do you?"

"Yeah. I just got laid off from my job."

He pauses a moment. Then, "I'm sorry to hear that. You doing okay?"

Such a loaded question. I hardly know this man, and he doesn't give a damn if I'm doing okay. How could he?

"As a matter of fact, no, I'm not doing okay. You know my past. I'm having a fucking hard time, Ben. And I've got this bachelorette party and wedding looming over me. The last thing I need is for strangers to ask me if I'm okay."

Silence on the other end of the line.

This is not who I am. I don't go around looking for pity by spouting out my problems or snapping at people for expressing sympathy. But I can't bring myself to apologize.

For a moment, he says nothing, and just as I'm about to open my mouth to tell him I'm ending the call—

"Sorry, I didn't mean anything by that. Tell you what. I don't have a lot on my calendar today. Why don't I come get you, we'll go have some lunch, and I'll let you know what's going on with the parties? I have to get the final details to the resort by tomorrow. I'd say we could handle it via a phone call, but I want to show you some photos."

The parties are this weekend. Invitations have already gone out. Skye handled them for the bachelorette party because she knew who she wanted to invite. Braden is footing the bill for everything. Still, it will be small. Skye, Betsy, me, a woman named Kathy Harmon who used to date Ben's father and remained friends with Skye, and her other bridesmaid, Daniela Cruise.

So far as I know, they've all RSVPed yes.

Why wouldn't they? An all-expense-paid trip to Jamaica? No-brainer. Old Tessa would be loving this. She'd be listening to reggae and shopping for bikinis.

I sigh into the phone. "Yeah, sure. Let's have lunch." Why not? He seems like a nice guy, and I'm unemployed. I may as well take the free meal.

"I'll be by around noon to pick you up," Ben says. "Just watch for Sherlock."

"Fine."

This time, my skin doesn't prickle at the thought of seeing Ben. I have no reason to fear him. Sherlock drove me home Friday night and nothing happened. Ben saw me to my door, even helped me take Rita out, and nothing happened.

Funny. A year ago, if I'd lost my job, I'd be devastated.

Today I don't even feel it.

. . .

I sit across from Ben in a booth at a local diner.

I try not to look at him, but my gaze keeps getting drawn to his face. To his warm brown eyes.

The whole world knows his reputation as a ladies' man, but his eyes… They seem so kind and comforting. As if you could tumble into them and land safely.

Part of me wants to lose myself in them.

And that feeling? It scares me.

It scares me how attractive I find him.

And it scares me that I'm not *more* scared.

"The Reuben is great here," Ben says, perusing his menu.

"I'm not a fan of sauerkraut."

He peeks over the top of his menu. "What kind of food do you like?"

"Normally I eat most anything. But lately I've been living on bacon and ice cream."

He laughs then, and it's a joyful sound. It's not forced, and it's perfect. I made him laugh. Granted, I didn't mean to, but I'm glad I did.

And I'm glad that I'm glad. Which is strange, but why fight it? It's okay to feel glad. It's a good thing.

"It's time you had a decent meal, then," he says.

"You're probably right." I glance at the offerings.

"They make a solid burger here. My favorite is the black-and-blue burger."

"I don't like blue cheese."

He laughs again. "Tessa, you just told me you eat pretty much anything, but we've already eliminated sauerkraut and blue cheese."

"Yeah. But not bacon or ice cream."

"If you tell me you don't eat oysters, you may break my heart."

"Are you kidding me? I'm a Bostonian. I love oysters."

I listen to the sound of my voice. Those words were more animated than I've sounded in months. Maybe losing my job and going out to lunch with Ben Black wasn't such a bad thing.

Ben smiles. "I should've taken you to the Union Oyster House. Braden and I have a standing date there each week. Did you know it's the oldest restaurant in Boston and even claims to be the oldest restaurant in continuous service in the United States?"

"Uh…yeah. I grew up here too, remember? I also know Daniel Webster and JFK were big fans."

"Make fun of me if you want, but Braden and I love the place. It epitomizes the American dream. We usually sit at the bar and listen to Charlie, Tony, and the other shuckers tell stories. Once Mickey—he's retired now—invited us behind the bar and taught us how to shuck. It's a lot harder than they make it look."

"Fascinating."

I'm not trying to be rude, but I thought we were here to talk about the parties.

And now I feel bad that I was belittling his interest in oysters—which is better than feeling numb, but still, I should say something more. "I've never sat at the oyster bar."

"That settles it," Ben says. "You and I. Tonight. Union Oyster House. We have a date to sit at the oyster bar."

You and I.

Date.

My skin tingles.

Not in a good way.

But also not in a *bad* way.

I find myself wanting to smile, and I do. With my eyes, even though I'm not sure it reaches my lips.

CHAPTER SIX

Ben

I want to make this woman happy.

I don't have a clue why, but I do. I know she's been through some shit. Who hasn't? I've been through shit of my own, but this is a woman who—according to Skye—used to love life. Used to live in the moment, smell the roses, and live life to the fullest every day. Let her hair down.

It's literally down now, and it falls like a sleek curtain around her shoulders. So dark brown it's almost black, but there's a warmth to it. Her skin is a light tan, and her eyes big, dark, and beautiful. Her lashes are longer than I've ever seen on a woman.

Maybe she's wearing mascara, maybe extensions, but as I look at her, I don't think she is. Everything about her looks purely natural. Even the dark pink of her full lips.

Did I just ask her on a date?

I don't date. Not really. When I do, I tend to pick the wrong women, so my friends-with-benefits relationship with Apple was a good thing for both of us. Until I ended it because… Because I watched my brother fall in love, watched how it changed him for the better.

I want that.

And when Tessa's eyes lit up at the idea of the Oyster House and sitting at the bar, I couldn't help myself.

Her eyes sparkled, and they were so beautiful.

They should always sparkle.

I want to make them sparkle.

"Where did you get Rita?" I ask.

"A shelter over by Betsy's place," she says.

"Who's Betsy?"

I know very well where Tessa got her dog, and I know who Betsy is, but she doesn't know that I know. I may as well move the conversation along.

"She's a friend of Skye's and mine. She's in the wedding party, so you'll get to meet her soon. She owns a pet treat shop called Betsy's Bark Boutique. I helped her put together an online business. She's doing great."

"Good, glad to hear that."

"I thought we were going to talk about the details of the bachelor and bachelorette parties."

"Yeah, sure." I set down my menu. "I have great news for you. Both the—"

"Hi, I'm Olivia." Our server—a bubbly redhead—interrupts us. "I'll be taking care of you today. Would you like a drink besides water?"

"Water is fine for me," Tessa says.

"I'm good with water as well."

"Awesome. I'll give you a few minutes to look over—"

"I'm ready," Tessa says. "I'll have a burger with fries. Burger medium. No cheese, but I do want lettuce, tomato, and onion."

"Absolutely." She turns to Ben. "And you, sir?"

"I'll have the Reuben, also with fries."

"Very good. I'll get this right in." She smiles and flounces off.

"So you were saying?" Tessa asks.

"Right. Good news. Everything's taken care of."

She cocks her head. "Then why are we here to talk about the details?"

I shrug. "When we had a drink last Friday, I said I'd take care of it, and you said okay. So I took care of it. Everything you asked for. The lunch, the spa day, the beach day, the dinner, the gifts, the dancing."

"You took care of *all* of that?"

"Braden gave me carte blanche," I remind her. "All I had to do was call the coordinator at the resort. She set it all up for me."

Tessa sighs. "Must be nice…"

"To have Braden Black's wallet at your disposal? It is."

"You have your own wallet at your disposal."

She's not wrong. I may not have the net worth of my brother, but I'm a close second.

She sighs again. "I'm sorry."

"What for? I'm not. It's great having money."

"That's not what I mean." She takes a drink of her water. "I had a shitty day."

Right. She got laid off. And I'm talking about parties and having an obscene amount of money.

Good going, Ben.

"You're an accountant right?" I ask, even though I already know.

"Yeah. I know it sounds boring as hell, but I've always had a thing for numbers."

"We can use good accountants at Black Inc. Do you want me

to put out some feelers for you?"

She raises her eyebrows. "Feelers? Really?"

I chuckle.

"I'm sure you could find a place for me with one phone call," she says, "but I don't need a pity job."

"It wouldn't be a pity job. It would be a *job*."

That actually gets a smile out of her.

It's a tentative smile, but it's a smile nonetheless, and it makes her face brighten just a bit.

My God, how radiant she must be when she's actually happy, when she's smiling because she's ecstatic.

And I make it my goal, right here and now, to find a way to put that kind of smile on Tessa Logan's face.

"Seriously, I can probably get you a job." I raise my hand to stop her from interjecting. "And no, it would not be a pity job. We crunch so many numbers at Black Inc. that we can never have too many accountants."

She pauses a moment, appears to mull it over. "It's kind of you to offer. I'll think about it."

"Good enough. That's all I ask. You can let me know tonight at dinner."

She chuckles again, shaking her head. "You're something."

"Better than being nothing." I wink at her.

Her cheeks redden then, and she looks away.

So she *is* attracted to me.

I like that. Like it a lot.

"Are you excited?"

"About what?" she asks.

"This weekend. The trip to Jamaica. The bachelor and bachelorette parties."

"Oh yeah. Sure," she replies. Her tone sounds more bothered

than excited.

"All right, Tessa. I'm going to get you excited about this." I pull up all the details on my phone. "Did you know we're flying out on the company private jet?"

"Yeah."

"You ever been on a private jet before?"

She scoffs. "Are you kidding? Only about a hundred times." Her lips curve upward once more.

Yeah! I'm getting there. Sarcasm is a good thing. "You have such an amazing smile," I say.

The redness hits her cheeks again, this time spreading to the top of her chest.

"You're a beautiful woman, Tessa, but I think you probably already know that."

Her smile fades. "Don't tell me I'm beautiful," she says.

"Why not?"

She looks down. "Because I don't *feel* beautiful. Sometimes I look in the mirror, and I see…"

"You see what?"

"I see…a shadow. No features. Just a blank face."

My heart cracks a little. "I know you don't want to talk to me about this. And you don't have to. I'm not going to insult you and say I understand, because I know I don't. But I do know what it's like to be fighting something, Tessa. It's not pretty. But there *is* help."

"I'm getting help."

"I'm glad to hear that. And if there's anything I can—"

She holds up a hand. "Stop. I don't want to go there. I was actually having a semi-good time, and this will just ruin it."

I nod. "I hear that."

Olivia returns with our lunches and sets the Reuben in front of Tessa by mistake.

"That's mine," I say. "The lady doesn't like sauerkraut."

"Oh my goodness. I'm so sorry."

"It's okay." Tessa frowns at me. "You don't need to make a big deal out of it, Ben."

I wasn't trying to do that. To the contrary, I wanted to make Tessa smile. She shouldn't have to be in such close proximity to sauerkraut.

Olivia reddens, flustered. She probably thinks I'm angry with her.

"Olivia, it's okay," I assure her with a smile. "Honest mistake."

She attempts a smile in return, but it's wary. I really don't want her thinking I was upset. I'll give her a huge-ass tip.

She sets the hamburger in front of Tessa. "I hope you like this. We're famous for our burgers."

"I'm sure it will be delicious," Tessa says.

"You all let me know if you need anything else." Olivia whisks away, pulling out a pad to take an order for another table.

I'm a gentleman, so I wait for Tessa to take the first bite of her burger.

I wait and I wait, and finally my stomach lets out a growl.

"Sorry," I say. "The enticing scent of sauerkraut and all."

"Oh, please. Go ahead. I'm just"—she looks at her burger, her eyes widening slightly—"gearing up for it."

"After the pork fat and dairy diet you've been on, this will probably taste pretty good."

"It does smell good," she says. "My appetite has just been…"

"Hey. I get it. I do."

"Please don't insult me like that."

I shake my head quickly. "You're misunderstanding me. I'm

not saying I get what you've personally been through. It's like what I said before. I understand how it feels to fight demons."

"Please." She scoffs. "I honestly don't mean to be disrespectful, but you're a billionaire, and you can't deny that money does make a lot of things easier. What the hell kind of demons have you ever had to fight?"

Her comment is one I've heard many times before. People seem to think money can take care of everything.

It can take care of a lot. That's true. But it can't erase demons. It can't bring light into darkness.

The funny thing about darkness is that it's actually not dark. You can still see. You can still hear. You can still smell.

You can smell rotted flesh, that sweet—sickeningly sweet—aroma that gets inside your nostrils and never really leaves.

It's the smell of death.

My mother's death.

Something I always blamed my father for—my father and his drinking. But recently I found out there was another culprit.

My brother.

He confessed it all to me.

I told him not to worry about it. It was in the past.

But doing the whole best-man thing with his confession still in my mind has been more difficult than I imagined.

I tell myself nothing has changed. This all happened decades ago, and we have the world at our fingertips now. We're billionaires. A couple of construction guys from South Boston are fucking billionaires.

But that's not the only demon I've had to fight.

Not by a long shot.

• • •

FIFTEEN YEARS EARLIER...

The day comes when I finally decide not to go to work after school. I had a shit day. I had to break up a fight in the boys' room. Three football jocks were shoving a freshman's head into the toilet.

Poor kid. He was a nerdy-looking thing—skinny with freckles and bucked teeth. Voice hadn't dropped yet. So I helped him up, got him dried off, and then chased the motherfuckers down the hallway. And who got sent to see the principal?

Me. Not the jocks, of course. They're the big men on campus.

I did. The blue-collar brainiac who was trying to save a kid from three bullies who think they own the freaking school.

I didn't end up getting in trouble, but only because the principal believed my story. When I asked what would happen to the jocks, I got no answer.

Wrong. I *did* get an answer. Just not in words.

Nothing.

Big fat nothing would happen to those Neanderthals who tormented that poor geek.

I'm sick and tired of what my life has become.

So I don't go.

I don't go to work.

I'm sick of it.

Braden, the good son, always went straight to work when he was in high school.

But I'm *not* the good son.

I never wanted to be the good son.

I miss my mother, but I don't have a lot of memories from before the fire. I was only three.

Now? This is the life I lead. Working my ass off while I'm still expected to go to school and maintain perfect grades and attendance.

Today I'm not going.

Instead, I walk to the convenience store to get some beef jerky. I've got a few bucks in my pocket, and beef jerky is what I'm craving.

Dirk Conrad and his two minions, Jerry Thompson and Carlos Ortiz, stand on the side of the store, smoking cigarettes.

"Hey, Black," Dirk says to me.

"Hey." I walk past them.

"Come here," he says.

These three are no good, and I know that. Still, I turn. I turn because I'm curious. What the hell do they want with me?

"What is it?" I ask.

He offers me a cigarette. "Want a smoke?"

"Sure." I grab one.

I haven't smoked a cigarette in years. Last time was in middle school with my friend Junior, who later moved away. We coughed and hacked the first time, but then that nicotine high drifted over us and we lit up again.

By the third cigarette, we had stopped coughing, and by the fifth, we no longer felt the high, so I stopped.

Just to be on the safe side, I hold the smoke in my mouth before I exhale. I don't want to hack in front of Dirk and his cronies.

"What are you guys up to?" I ask.

"Hanging. Looking for some fun." He blows a puff of smoke toward me. "What are you doing? We never see you around here."

"Playing hooky from work."

"Seriously?"

"Yeah. I'm supposed to work with my brother and father

at their construction site after school every day. Didn't feel like going today."

"Good on you, Black," Carlos says. "This is senior year. You should be having fun."

"You know what, Carlos? I couldn't fucking agree more." I take a drag on the cigarette, this time inhaling.

I don't choke or hack.

And since it's been so long since I've had a cigarette, I feel the nicotine high.

I take another drag.

"You're just the kind of guy we need, Black," Dirk says.

"You think, huh?"

"You've got brains *and* brawn. We need some brains."

"What the fuck for?"

"We're going to rob the convenience store," he says, "and you're going to help us."

· · ·

Darkness. One childhood caper can go wrong.
So very wrong.

"You don't know anything about me," I say to Tessa.

"I know *enough* about you," she replies hotly. "You're in the news all the time."

I cock my head, ready to scowl, but I hold it back. "You think what you hear about me in the news and the internet and the brag rags is all there is to me? That's what you think I am? A fucking caricature?"

She widens her beautiful eyes, and my God, I could get lost in them so easily. Even though I'm kind of irritated with her at the moment.

"I...I'm sorry," she says. "I guess I just thought—"

"No. You didn't think, Tessa. You didn't think at all. I never have to worry about money another day in my life. But don't think for one minute that I don't spend every day being grateful for that. Don't think I haven't seen or felt pain in my life."

She looks down at her plate. "I didn't think that."

"You asked me what kind of demons I've ever had to fight." I shake my head. "Maybe one day I'll tell you, but not now. Not today."

All I wanted to do was make her happy, and instead I've taken a mental detour onto the dark road of my past.

Fuck.

Good going, Black.

CHAPTER SEVEN

Tessa

I look up at Ben Black. His face is twisted. He's still the most handsome man I've ever seen, but I've dislodged something in his brain.

I can't believe I said something so cruel. I know about the fire that destroyed his home when he was only a kid. A really young kid. I know his mother was burned badly and scarred in the fire and died years later. I know about his father's drinking.

Is that what he's talking about? Because that's common knowledge, and I should have remembered it.

That's all bad enough, but is there something more?

The old Tessa would ask him. The old Tessa would want to help him.

This Tessa?

This Tessa can't handle anything more in her head right now. No more torment. Even if it's someone else's. I just can't take it.

And I hate how selfish that sounds in my own head because part of me wants to help him. Part of me is drawn to him in a way that's new to me.

"So I suppose our dinner at the Union Oyster House is canceled now," I finally say.

He wipes his lips with his napkin. "Why would it be canceled?"

"You're obviously upset with me."

"Why would I be upset with you?"

"Because I…" I shake my head. "Never mind, I guess."

"Tessa," he says, his tone serious, "I know you feel like you've been marked with what happened to you. I get that. You probably hate the fact that I know about it. But I'm glad I do because it helps me understand you. I'm not one to use kid gloves. You don't become a billionaire doing things that way. I can't just turn off my personality." He pauses a moment and looks me right in my eyes. "What I *can* do is be as understanding as possible about your situation. I can keep a safe distance from you. I can help you feel safe and secure. Why do you think I asked to see you home last night?"

I twirl a lock of my hair. "I understand. I get it."

"I want you to learn to trust me." He places a hand on his chest, as if pledging allegiance. "You have nothing to fear from me, Tessa. But I understand why you feel that way. I'm a man, and a man did you harm."

I simply nod.

"Now that I've seen you home, you've driven in my car with my driver, I've taken you up to your apartment, helped you with your dog… Now that you know that I'm not a threat, please trust me." He reaches across the table. "Depend on me. I can help you get through this."

I don't take his outstretched hand. "What? You some kind of psychoanalyst now?"

He wants to roll his eyes. I can tell by the look on his face, but he resists. Good for him.

"No," he says. "I didn't mean I can help you get through what happened to you. What I meant was I can help you get through the bachelor and bachelorette parties and the wedding."

Okay. Now I feel like the scum on my shoe. He's trying to be nice, and I'm throwing it back in his face.

"I apologize," I say, and I'm surprised at how much I truly mean it.

"No apologies necessary."

"Damn it. Don't say that. I was being a bitch. Let me own it."

He chuckles a bit. "All right. You own it."

"And honestly, I appreciate the help with the weekend." My fingers twitch. I actually want to grab his hand that's still reaching toward me. But I don't. "Skye's an only child, and she always told me I'd be her maid of honor. I was so psyched when she asked me back in college. I always wanted to help give her the wedding of her dreams. But now... It seems like such a heavy burden on my back."

"I know it does. But we have to be thinking about Braden and Skye now."

"You think I'm not?"

"That's not what I said." He sighs, takes a drink of his water. "Clearly I'm really bad at this."

"Well, you're *not* a psychoanalyst." I give him a smile, and to my surprise, it's not forced.

"No, I'm far from that. But Skye is your best friend, and I know you'd never forgive yourself if you didn't do everything within your power to give her the bachelorette party and wedding of her dreams."

He's right on point about that. The fact that it's been so difficult for me has added guilt to the already ridiculous load of crap in my head.

"Now eat," he says.

I look down at my untouched burger. His Reuben is already half gone.

I pick it up, take a bite, and grease runs down my chin.

Normally on a date, I'd be completely embarrassed to have grease running down my chin.

But I don't embarrass so easily anymore. I put the burger down, pick up my napkin, and wipe my chin as I chew and swallow.

Surprisingly good.

"So?" Ben asks.

"Good," I say.

"Just good?"

I sigh. "Just good is about all I can handle these days. It's actually an improvement."

He smiles, his eyes crinkling at the corners. Demons? If he has demons haunting him, I certainly can't tell from looking at him.

I take another bite of my burger. The meat is juicy and full-bodied without the smokiness and fattiness of bacon that I'm used to. The tomato, lettuce, and onion add freshness and crispness, something else I've missed. Maybe it's time to eat real food again. I wash it down with a sip of water and wipe my chin once more. Then I grab the ketchup bottle from the side of the table, remove the top bun, and squirt some onto the burger.

I take another bite.

This time it's even better. Ketchup is a miracle condiment. I almost smile, thinking about what Nana would say to that. She hated ketchup. Said it was a poor man's salsa.

Ben smiles at me from across the table.

Warm quivers shoot through me.

Ben is gorgeous, and I haven't felt a tingle like this in a long time.

And it feels...*good*.

It feels good to know I'm with a man who won't hurt me.

Because Ben won't hurt me.

I know that already.

But knowing I can trust him and actually trusting him are two completely different things.

Still, a blanket of appreciation covers me, keeping me warm.

"Thank you," I say.

He lifts his eyebrows. "For the burger? You're welcome."

"Well, yeah. For the burger, for getting me out, but also for making me feel safe."

"You'll always be safe with me, Tessa." His face is serene. "Always. Take that to the bank."

CHAPTER EIGHT

Ben

I'm exhausted after a slew of afternoon meetings, but I don't want to break the date with Tessa at the Oyster House. She wants to get out more. She nearly said as much after lunch. And she seems to feel safe with me, so I'm the perfect person to escort her. Doesn't hurt that I enjoy spending time with her, either.

Braden is back from New York, so before I leave work for the day, I knock on his cracked open door, peeking in.

"Yeah, come in, Ben."

I enter, closing the door behind me, and take a seat opposite his desk.

"What's up?" he asks.

"Tessa Logan got laid off from her job."

He widens his eyes. "She did?"

"Yeah. After everything she's been through. Can you believe it? I told her we could always use a good accountant here at the company."

"Yeah, of course. Whatever she needs. We'll find room for her."

"Thanks. She needs to be keeping busy right now. If she's out of work, she'll just—"

"Sit around and ruminate. Yeah. Believe me, I get it."

"I know you do. And so do I." My brother doesn't know the half of it.

Braden grabs a pad of sticky notes and writes some things down. "I'll take care of it. From what I know, Tessa's more than competent, but I'll give her previous employer a quick call to verify. She can start right away. With all these new business deals we've got brewing, we can always use more help."

"That's what I told her, but she thought it was a pity job."

Braden chuckles. "She ought to know better than that. You and I don't give out pity jobs."

"That's what I tried to tell her."

"Cut her some slack," Braden says. "She's having a rough time."

"I know. I want to cut her all the slack she needs, but that doesn't include sitting around unemployed. She'll feel useless, and that's the last thing she needs."

"I agree with you there."

"I'm meeting her for dinner tonight at the Oyster House to wrap up the final details for the weekend. Text me once you talk to her previous employer. Then I'll tell her she's got a job if she wants it. My concern is that she won't take it."

"You're going to have to insist."

"That may make her want to take it less."

"All right…" Braden rubs his chin. "Tell her you talked to me, and there's a job available starting tomorrow if she wants it. But if she doesn't, that's okay. We totally understand. If she does want it, she can report to HR tomorrow at ten a.m."

"Okay. We'll make it *her* choice." I scratch at an itch that pops up on my forehead. "Although I guess it's her choice anyway. But she may decide to take the week off since we're leaving Thursday night for Jamaica." I shake my head. "I hope not. I shudder to think about what she will do for two days sitting alone in her apartment with nothing to do."

"I know. It's not a good thing to be alone with your thoughts sometimes. Especially when you're getting over trauma."

"Exactly," I say. My brother gets it. And not for the first time, I'm both grateful to have him and consumed with guilt to be keeping secrets from him.

. . .

"Ben," one of my favorite shuckers, Charlie, says, "who's the pretty lady?"

Tessa looks gorgeous in dark blue jeans and a pale pink blouse. She's glancing around, no doubt feeling like she's stepped back in time. At least that's how I always feel when I come here. I can't believe she's never sat at the oyster bar. The bar is made of dark wood, and the stools have brass footrests. It's iconic, and I love it here.

"This is Tessa," I say. "Tessa, this is Charlie, one of the shuckers."

"Nice to meet you." Tessa moves her gaze to the star of the show at the oyster bar—the impressive display of fresh oysters. The counter showcases the day's selection of oysters on ice, their shells glistening with seawater.

I inhale the briny and slightly sweet scent of the raw oysters— one of my favorite aromas. Nothing quite like slurping a fresh oyster between your lips.

I look around at the exposed wooden beams, low ceilings, warm lighting, and maritime decor. Seriously, I *love* this place.

Charlie wears a traditional white apron, and his graying hair is pulled back into a net. He wears an oyster glove and holds the oyster securely in his other hand with a white towel. With his oyster knife, he expertly breaks the seal of the oyster shell, cuts the muscle, and then pries the two halves apart. He inspects the oyster for any debris or shell remnants and then hands it to Tessa.

"For you, pretty lady."

She blushes slightly and looks down, but then she takes the oyster and slurps it expertly into her mouth. "Delicious," she says once she swallows. "You make that look so easy."

"It's not easy," I say. "Braden and I once—"

"You told me," Tessa says.

Right. I did. Today at lunch. So much I'd like to talk to her about, but I'm afraid something I say may inadvertently upset her.

"That's a Wellfleet," Charlie says to Tessa.

"From Wellfleet in Cape Cod," Tessa says.

"Give the pretty lady a star." Charlie smiles. "You know your oysters."

"I've lived in Boston my whole life," she says. "Do you have any Chincoteague today?"

"Not today."

Tessa frowns. "That's too bad. They're my favorite."

"I like them, too," I tell her. "They're so briny and minerally."

"They are, plus they're from Chincoteague Island, where the wild ponies live."

"You like horses?" I ask.

"Love them." Her dark eyes light up. "They're such gorgeous creatures. *Misty of Chincoteague* was one of my favorite books when I was a kid. My nana used to read it to me."

Her dark eyes soften when she mentions her nana.

"Your nana?"

"Yeah. My mother's mother. I was named after her. Teresa Maria. Teresa after Saint Teresa of Avila, a Spanish mystic and writer, and Maria after…well, after the Virgin Mary."

"You're Catholic?" I ask.

"Was," she says, her mouth tightening a little. "I left the church after college."

"Teresa Maria," I say, letting the syllables flow off my tongue as if they're poetry. "That's beautiful."

"My grandmother was a beautiful woman. And a beautiful person."

"As are you." I smile.

Tessa looks away from me, a rosy blush on her cheeks.

"Give us a dozen of the Wellfleet," I say to Charlie. Then I turn back to Tessa, urging her to meet my gaze. "Tell me more about your grandmother."

Tessa smiles slightly. "She was my favorite person in the world. I suppose she felt close to me because I was her namesake. Eva—she's my younger sister by two years—wasn't nearly as close to her as I was. Nana was very devout. My parents were—*are*—too, but Nana was different. Her faith was more to her than Mass or a set of rules to follow. It was part of her."

"How so?"

Tessa sighs. "It's not easy to explain. You'd have to have known her. I can tell you about the altar in her bedroom, about the incense and candles she burned when she prayed to the saints, about her favorite rosary made of rose quartz. About her deep brown eyes that held so much wisdom… About how snuggling in her lap when I was small was the most comforting place in the world. But none of it would truly describe her."

"Can you tell me why you left Catholicism?" I ask.

She turns away. "That's personal."

"I'm sorry."

A glance back at me. "Are *you* Catholic?"

"No. We were raised Christian, but we didn't really go to church. Only on Christmas and Easter, and that ended when my mother died."

"I'll never go back," she says. "Never."

Interesting. Her grandmother was her favorite person and was also a devout Catholic, but Tessa will never go back? There's a story there—and I sense it's not a good one—but I won't pry. Instead, I grab another oyster from the bar.

Briny and delicious, the oyster slides over my tongue and down my throat.

I order a Wild Turkey, and Tessa orders sparkling water. Charlie serves our dozen oysters, and I take one, add a twist of fresh lemon, and slurp it.

Tessa takes another one and downs it like a champ. "Mmm. So good."

"Great. You had a hamburger earlier. Now you're eating oysters. Tell me this isn't better than bacon and ice cream for dinner again."

"I'm not really that hungry," she says, her tone noncommittal.

"Then this is the perfect place for you. I don't think anyone could actually fill up on oysters on the half shell. I've been known to eat them until I burst, but that's a heck of a lot of oysters. Way more than we'll be eating tonight."

Charlie shucks another oyster, and his eyes widen. "Here's a special one for your lady, Ben." He hands the oyster to Tessa.

She gasps. "This can't be."

"It's unusual, for sure," Charlie says, "with the stuff that we get. That, my dear lady, is a pearl."

I look inside Tessa's oyster. Sure enough, nestled against the oyster meat is a tiny black pearl.

"I can't accept this." She hands the oyster back to Charlie. "You found it. This should be yours. Or your wife's or girlfriend's or whatever."

He smiles with a shrug. "Don't have a wife or girlfriend, and my mother is no longer with us. I don't have any sisters. I was shucking it for you, young lady, so it's yours."

"Do you know how many times I've come to this place?" Ben says. "Never once has a shucker found a pearl."

Charlie nods. "It's rare."

"How?" Tessa asks. "Pearls come from oysters, don't they?"

"They're mostly cultured now," Charlie says. "It's uncommon to find them in oysters raised for consumption."

"Must be a good-luck charm," I say.

"I don't know about that." Tessa fishes the pearl out of the shell and wipes it off on her napkin. "It's such a unique shape. Kind of like a teardrop." She wrinkles her forehead. "Not round like cultured pearls."

Charlie laughs. "That's how you know it's real."

"I guess I can assume it's real, since I watched it come out of an oyster."

"Absolutely, young lady." Charlie shucks another oyster and hands it to me.

"Definitely a good-luck charm," I say to Tessa again. "And I've got another piece of good luck for you."

"Oh? What's that?"

"I talked to Braden. He got rave reviews from your previous employer, and you can start work tomorrow in our accounting department."

She frowns. "I told you I didn't want a pity job."

"I told you earlier and I'll tell you again, this isn't a pity job. Braden texted me after he talked to your old boss. She hated to let you go. We've got so many new deals in the works that we always need more number crunchers. We can hire you or we can hire someone else. It's up to you."

"Honestly, I was looking forward to some time off."

"You're going to get some time off this weekend. A four-day weekend in Jamaica, starting Thursday and ending Sunday."

"I know that."

"But before then, come into HR tomorrow morning at ten and they'll get you set up."

She laughs, but the tone is disbelief rather than humor. "I didn't say I was taking the job."

"I suppose you didn't. It's your choice. Show up or don't show up. But if we don't hire you, we'll just hire someone else." I slip another oyster into my mouth, enjoying the brackish saltiness.

Then I watch Tessa eat another.

For a moment, I wish I were that oyster touching her lips. She is the most beautiful woman I've ever met.

And I've met my share of beautiful women.

Stop thinking of her that way.

She's likely not ready for sex, if just being around a man makes her anxious. Or a relationship, for that matter. I'm not sure I am, either, despite the fact that I'm leaving my old ways behind, hoping for something more. I love what I see between Braden and Skye, and I want it, but—

"Well…" Tessa says, interrupting my thoughts. "What kind of pay are you offering?"

Good, she's thinking about it. "HR can tell you all the details, but I'm sure we'll be able to meet or exceed what you were making. We make it a point to keep our salaries competitive."

"All right. I'll go tomorrow. And…"

"And what?"

She looks at the pearl, rolling it around in the palm of her hand. "Thank you. Again. Thank you for everything, Ben."

CHAPTER NINE

Tessa

I shower and shave my legs the next day—that alone has me feeling better—and then I dress in simple black slacks, patent leather pumps, and a white blouse. I tuck the black pearl from last night in my pocket for good luck.

"May I help you?" the receptionist asks when I get to the front desk of the well-secured Black Inc. building. I've been here before to meet Skye, and I'm always mesmerized by the ornate marble lobby and the clack of my heels on the tiles. This is the first time I'll see another part of the building.

"Yes, I'm Tessa Logan. I'm supposed to report to HR this morning at ten for an accountant position."

A sharp nod. "I'll let them know you're here." She pauses. "Hi, Leona," she says into her headset, "it's Margaret at reception. I have a Tessa Logan here." Another pause. "Very good." She looks back to me. "I just need to see your ID. I'll make you a temporary ID badge to get you up to HR. Once you finish your paperwork, we'll get a permanent one for you."

I give her my driver's license. She scans it and then hands me a sticker.

I remove the backing and place it on my blouse, and then I take the elevator up to the designated floor. Again, I have to check in with reception.

"You must be Ms. Logan," a young brunette says with a smile. "I'm Leona, the receptionist here in human resources."

I paste on a smile. "Nice to meet you. Please call me Tessa."

"Absolutely. One of our HR managers will be out to collect you in a— Oh, here she is now." She gestures. "Barb, this is Tessa Logan."

"Good morning, Tessa." Barb, an older woman with dark hair graying at her temples, holds out her hand. "The misters Black told me a lot about you. They speak very highly of you, as does your previous employer."

I shake Barb's hand, attempting a smile once more. "That's kind of them."

"Come back to my office. We'll get your paperwork filled out, and then I'll take you to the accounting department where you'll meet your manager."

With a smile still pasted on my face, I follow Barb down the hallway to another office.

"Have a seat," Barb says before firing up her computer and peppering me with questions.

I answer her questions robotically and sign all the papers she gives me.

I widen my eyes when I see my salary. Quite a hefty raise from what I was making before.

"Does everything look in order?" Barb asks.

"Yes, thank you so much. I truly appreciate this opportunity."

"We're happy to have you here at Black Inc." Barb rises. "I'll take you up to accounting now."

Accounting turns out to be one floor up, and a few moments later I meet my manager, Luke Barr. Once Barb leaves, Luke asks me to his office.

"Let's get down to business, Ms. Logan." He holds out his hand.

I shake his hand firmly. "Tessa, please."

"Tessa. Please call me Luke. I'll be your immediate supervisor, but we all report to the vice president of accounting, Marietta Wilson. She's not a micromanager, which we all appreciate." He smiles.

"I'll do my best to do an excellent job for you," I say.

"I have no doubt." He sits down behind his desk. "You come highly recommended."

Something is a little off in his tone. He knows why I'm here. Nepotism at its finest.

But I need the job, so I'll do my best to show Luke and the others that I'm a good addition to their staff.

"I'm going to ask you a few quick questions," Luke continues, "just to make sure we're all on the same page."

"Of course. I can tell you about what I did at my last job, if you'd like."

"No need. Mr. Black already talked to them and got a detailed summary of your duties. I'm interested in other things. For example, how do you keep up with current accounting laws and regulations?"

"I regularly read accounting journals and attend workshops, when I can. I personally subscribe to *CPA Practical Advisor*."

He raises his eyebrows as if he's surprised. He really does think this is a pity hire.

"Good." He looks down at his iPad. "How do you manage tight deadlines?"

"By meeting them. I prioritize tasks and keep a detailed calendar. I work extra hours when necessary. I've never missed a deadline, Luke. I pride myself on that."

He seems to warm up to me a bit. "Excellent." He looks back down at his tablet. "I don't think I need to bother you with any more questions for now. Welcome aboard."

"Thank you, and I can't tell you how much I appreciate your faith in me." I pause a moment. "I hate to be the person who gets a job and then asks for time off, but I'm scheduled to go to Jamaica on Thursday. I'll be back Monday for work."

"Oh, yes. We've already been told."

The tone is back.

"If this is a problem, I—"

"Can cancel going to your best friend's bachelorette party? Is that where you're going with this?" He raises his eyebrows.

"No."

I'm not sure what else to say, so I leave it at no.

He rises. "Let me show you to your desk."

"Thank you."

Luke leads me to a small interior office. It's windowless, but at least it's better than a cubicle. "We use all the standard accounting software, but if you're not familiar with it, there are user manuals in your file cabinet or you can access them online."

"I'm familiar with all the standard software," I say. "I won't have any problem, Luke."

"I'm sure you won't. Check your inbox, and you'll see your assignments. Everything should be self-explanatory, but if you need me, I'm just down the hallway."

In his office with windows.

But he's a manager, and I'm not.

Management is no longer my thing. I used to aspire to

management, but it means dealing with people.

I used to be good at that.

Now? Not so much.

I like numbers. Numbers represent order and structure in a chaotic world. Numbers don't mess with your head or play with your emotions. With numbers, you can usually find a right answer. An answer that makes sense. An answer that follows the rules. Numbers don't talk back, and numbers don't manipulate you.

I get through the day and even stay past quitting time so I'm not leaving any projects unfinished. Luke leaves at six thirty, and I leave at seven.

It's a decent job, and nothing I can't handle.

Am I thrilled about it?

No.

But nothing much thrills me anymore.

Once I get back to my place and take Rita out, I see that I have a voicemail from Ben.

Funny, I didn't hear my phone ring.

I check it and realize I turned the ringer off during my meeting with HR and forgot to turn it back on.

"Hey, Tessa, Ben Black here. Just wanted to let you know that everything is finalized for the two parties this weekend in Ocho Rios. I've emailed you the information to distribute to the other bridal attendants for the shower. Everyone will go on our private jet. All the details are in the email."

I read through the email that tells me where to go in the airport, which terminal, how to get through security for private jets, and whatnot.

He really did take care of everything.

I owe him one.

Hell, I owe him a lot more than one. I'm not sure I could have done this myself in my current mental state. I have a great new job because of his recommendation, too. I should be happier about this than I am, but I can't help but wonder if he wants anything in return for it. Then I feel bad for assuming he'd manipulate me like that. Then I feel *worse* because I remember why I tend to jump to those conclusions lately, especially with men. It's a nauseating mental spiral, and only one thing will pull me out of it now.

I grab Rita and pull her into my lap, cuddling her.

"Rita, Rita," I say to her. "The little dog who saved me."

After I was drugged and date raped by Garrett Ramirez, I was in such a depression that the only thing that got me out of bed in the morning was Rita. She had to go out, and I certainly didn't want a dogshit-infested apartment.

My mother stayed with me for the first week after it happened and then came by once a week. She would've moved in with me, but it wouldn't have worked. I only have one bedroom, and my couch doesn't roll out. Besides, I love her dearly, but she's a devout Catholic and would've been praying over me every second.

Not that I can't use the prayers. I need all the help I can get these days. My mother means well. She truly does.

But I need more than prayers, that's for certain.

As for what it is I need?

I wish I knew.

My stomach lets out a growl. Rita scrambles off my lap as I rise and go to the freezer. No ice cream. No bacon in the fridge.

Neither sounds good to me, anyway. I'm ready for real food again. I loved the burger and oysters I had with Ben, and now...

Now I want some of my mom's Mexican fare. Some gooey cheese enchiladas and refried beans with rice and pico de gallo.

Man, it actually sounds good! Am I getting excited about *food*? Yes, I am, and realizing that excites me even more. I'm actually *excited* about something.

My mother gave me all her recipes years ago, but I never bothered trying to make any of them. Whenever I needed a fix, I just went home and got the real thing. It's nearly nine p.m., way too late to expect Mom to whip up a batch of enchiladas for me, and also too late to go out shopping for what I need.

But maybe…

Actually wanting to eat something decent and wanting to learn how to make it for myself?

Maybe it's a start.

CHAPTER TEN

Ben

I still get a thrill when I travel on the company private jet.

Braden and I had a very modest beginning to our lives. After the fire that scarred our mother, things were so tight that we had to get food from a food bank.

We're truly living the American dream now, and it's all thanks to my brother's genius. He brought my father and me along for the ride, and I'll be forever grateful.

Not that I don't pull my weight.

I'm the chief operating officer of the company, so I'm responsible for the business end. I keep the trains running on time.

I do a damned good job if I do say so myself.

Braden's the creative genius behind our signature product, plexiglass goggles for construction workers. But our business has gone so far beyond construction equipment. We have investments in real estate, precious metals, foreign currency—and just about everything else.

We've had this jet for several years now. It's a Boeing 737

with reclined seating and a bedroom in the back.

No one will be using the bedroom for this trip, though, because along with Braden, Skye, Tessa, and myself, we also have Skye's three bridesmaids, Braden's three groomsmen, and our father, Bobby Black.

Once we take off, our flight attendants, Glory and Marissa, distribute champagne—Dom Perignon, of course—and it's up to me to make a toast.

"Welcome to Black Inc. Airlines," I say jovially, holding up my glass. "Let me be the first to toast my big brother and the love of his life, Skye. We're here to celebrate the two of you this weekend, and I know that you're going to love what Tessa and I have planned. The big bachelor and bachelorette gigs will be tomorrow night, and then we'll all be together Saturday night for a large dinner and the prelude to the impending wedding. So here's to Skye and Braden!"

Everyone raises their glass and cheers.

I glance at Tessa, who's sitting in a row by herself.

She lifts her glass and smiles—though it seems forced—but she doesn't take a drink.

She didn't drink with me at the bar the other night, either.

Not a huge deal. My father doesn't drink, either. He's a recovering alcoholic. The flight attendant poured him sparkling white grape juice instead of champagne.

We could've done that for Tessa if I'd known she wanted it, but she didn't say anything.

That's on me. I should have known. Or at least asked. I'll be more in tune with her needs for the rest of this trip.

When Glory comes by to ask Tessa if she's finished, she nods. Glory grabs her full glass of champagne and steps down the aisle.

Braden and I could afford to drink Dom Perignon every day

for the rest of our lives and we would never run out of money, but the blue-collar boy in me hates waste.

"I'll take that, Glory."

She hands it to me, and I take a sip of Tessa's champagne.

I walk down the aisle and sit in the empty seat next to Tessa. She's staring out the window of the plane.

"You don't like champagne?" I ask.

She doesn't bother moving her gaze from the window. "Just didn't feel like it tonight."

"Not a problem. Just tell me what you want. I'll make sure that you get everything you need."

"It's not a big deal." She frowns and looks down at her lap. "I'm sorry to waste it."

"It's not getting wasted." I take another sip.

She turns to me then. "That's *my* glass?"

"Yep. It's delicious, too. You want a taste?"

"No, thank you. I just haven't felt like drinking since…"

I hold up my other hand. "No explanation needed. I'll make sure you get sparkling water for the rest of the weekend."

"Thank you." Then she truly does meet my gaze. "I don't know how I'll be able to thank you. You know, for making all the plans for this weekend." She sighs. "This is something I used to love to do. I'm really letting Skye down."

I lean toward her and lower my voice, even though no one can hear us on the plane. "It's our little secret. As far as Skye knows, you and I planned this entire shindig together."

Her shoulders slump a little. "You're a lifesaver. I don't know what I'd do without you."

"You don't have to worry about that. If you need anything at all this weekend, you've got my number. You call or text me and I will be there. Got it?"

She twists her lips. "You don't have to do that."

"Yes, I do. I know you're going through a rough time, Tessa. I'm so sorry about that, and I wish I could make it easier."

She gives me a weak smile. "You are, Ben. You're making it quite a bit easier."

"I appreciate you saying that, but that's not what I meant."

"I know what you meant." She looks out the window. "I miss Rita."

"Braden's staff will take great care of her."

"I know. I still miss her. I thought about bringing her, but she's never flown before, and…" She sighs. "I just miss her."

"She's having a great time with Sasha and Penny. She'll hardly miss you."

Tessa frowns.

Uh-oh. The wrong thing to say.

"I mean…of course she—"

"It's okay. I know you didn't mean anything by it. She's a dog. She's having fun with other dogs. I miss her a lot more than she misses me."

I decide not to talk about the dog anymore. Instead, "The flight attendants are going to serve a light supper. It's seared ahi tuna on a bed of greens with sticky rice and edamame. Does that sound good to you?"

"Yeah. Sure."

"Good. I'll make sure you're served first."

"Don't be silly. Skye and Braden should be served first."

"Do you think they really care about that?" I chuckle and gesture toward my brother and his fiancée. "The two of them are making googly eyes at each other. They won't even notice. I'm in charge this weekend, and I'm going to make sure you're served first."

She lets out a laugh. Or maybe it's more of a choke. I'm not sure, but it's something.

"So…you good? Do you need anything?"

"I'm fine," she says. "Thank you for checking on me. Thanks again…for everything."

"Absolutely. Don't you worry about a thing, Tessa." I give her a quick wink before rising from my seat. "I've got you covered."

CHAPTER ELEVEN

Tessa

When I was a little girl, I used to dream I could fly. I told my therapist about that once, and she said it's a very common dream for children. Children like to believe they can do anything, to the point that some fall down the stairs in an attempt to *actually* fly.

I never did that, but my parents had an old barstool out on the back porch. Every once in a while, I would take it out to the yard, climb on top of it, and jump as high as I could, flapping my arms.

I always ended up on the grass, and fortunately I never hurt myself because I couldn't jump that high.

But each time I always thought... Maybe this was the time... Maybe this was the time that I would actually fly.

The dream I had about flying was similar. I would jump and then become airborne, and I would move my arms and legs as if I were swimming underwater, only I was flying through the air instead.

It was my favorite dream as a kid, flying.

A year ago, flying on a private jet would have me excited, joyous.

Right now, the best I can do is stare out the window and feel…okay. We're at thirty-five thousand feet, and it's a clear day. We're immersed in the blue sky, and cottony clouds are scattered below us.

Such beauty.

I've always wanted to go to Jamaica. I've heard the people are so friendly and the food is excellent. We're staying at a private resort, so I won't get to see much of the sites. Not that I'll have the energy to go sightseeing anyway.

But there is a part of me—albeit a tiny part—that feels…not excited, really, but slightly eager.

Objectively, I have no worries in this moment.

I have a brand-new job thanks to Ben. The bachelor and bachelorette parties are all planned and should be executed perfectly, again thanks to Ben.

I'll have to repay him somehow, even if he isn't expecting anything in return. It just seems like the right thing to do.

Then I let out a sarcastic laugh. How can I repay Benjamin Black for anything? He literally has *everything*. Including a private jet.

There's no way I can pay him back.

Good thing he doesn't expect me to. If he did, he surely would have given some hint by now.

He's doing all of this for Braden and Skye. He doesn't want their big weekend ruined, and I was well on my way to doing just that.

He's not doing this for me at all. Why should he? He doesn't know me. To him, I'm just some pathetic young woman who's trying to heal from a rough ordeal.

He feels sorry for me—and God, I hate that.

My therapist says I shouldn't hate being pitied when I'm pitying myself.

But I don't feel like I'm pitying myself. I don't really feel like anything. It's like Garrett Ramirez took my emotions away from me. On the days when I'm not feeling completely depressed, I simply feel…nothing.

I'm doing everything I can. I was working until I got laid off. I just spent two days working at Black Inc. The work is simple, not overly challenging. But simple is fine for me right now. The old Tessa would have wanted a challenge. She would have wanted to do something besides simple accounting.

But this Tessa? The new job is working out just fine for now. Maybe sometime in the future I'll want more. Now, I'm content to do simple tasks and collect a paycheck.

"Hey, Tess."

I turn as Skye sits down in the seat next to me. She looks radiant, her brown eyes glowing.

"Hey." I give her my best smile.

"Nice try," she says.

Skye knows me better than anyone. She knows when I'm faking it.

"Sorry," I say.

"You don't have to be sorry, Tess." She squeezes my shoulder. "What can I do? What can I do for you?"

"Oh, Skye. If only it were that simple." I give her the weak smile again. "You're doing everything for me. You're giving me this weekend. This amazing weekend. Not just for me but for all of us."

"That's Braden, not me. Last time I checked, *I'm* not a billionaire."

"Yet," I remind her. "You will be after the wedding."

"Yeah." Her eyes dance. "It's crazy to even think it."

"I'm so happy for you."

The words aren't a lie. I *am* happy for her. Except I kind of forget what happy feels like. But she's my best friend, and I remember being happy for her, and of course I'm thrilled that she's found the man of her dreams—with all the fringe benefits he comes with.

It's like my feelings have gone on hiatus, and I don't know how to get them back. I get twinges of feeling now and then, like when I found the pearl in the oyster, or when I was thinking about making my mother's Mexican recipes.

Or when I got a warm tingle when Ben smiled at me at the diner.

Skye leans into me and gives me a side hug. "I really appreciate this, Tess. I know this isn't easy for you."

"I'm okay. Truly. I want you to have an amazing long weekend that you'll never forget."

Skye smiles broadly. "I'm so excited! I've always wanted to go to Jamaica."

"Well…" I look down at my watch. "Looks like we'll be there in a couple hours."

"We will. And I'm going to do everything in my power to make sure you have an amazing time."

I reach toward her then, grab her hand. "No. You don't worry about me at all. This weekend is for *you*, Skye. For you and Braden. *You* have a wonderful time. Please. Don't worry about me."

She squeezes my hand. "I'll always worry about you, Tess. You're part of me. You know that."

Her words move me. "That takes me back."

"I know. Spring of senior year, when I was trying to decide whether to go back to Kansas or to stay in Boston. You sat me down, looked me straight in the eye, and told me you wanted me to stay but you'd be okay with whatever I decided."

I smile, and this time, it's not forced. "Except I was really trying to get you to stay."

"I know." She chuckles. "You said, 'Wherever you end up, you'll always be a part of me.' I never forgot those words, Tess. Even when you thought I had."

Skye is referring to a rough patch we had recently, but I don't want to go there, so I draw in a breath. "Just promise me you'll have a great time. That's all I ask."

"I will. We both will." She beams. "Dinner will be served in a minute. If you need anything, you let me know."

"Of course."

But I won't. She doesn't need to be worrying about me. I should be the least of her concerns.

Skye rises then and returns to her seat next to Braden.

The two of them put their heads together and talk, presumably about me.

And damn it.

I do *not* want to be the subject of Skye's unhappiness. I don't want her focusing on me. I want her beaming like she did a moment ago.

Ben himself brings my dinner to me and then sits down beside me as Marissa, one of the flight attendants, serves him as well.

"I hope you don't mind a dinner companion," he says.

"No, I don't, because I need to talk to you."

He raises his eyebrows. "Of course, what is it?"

"I need you to make sure that Braden and Skye aren't worried about me. This long weekend has to be about them."

He nods. "I couldn't agree more, Tessa."

"So what do we do? How do we get them to quit focusing on me?"

He shrugs. "You need to have a good time. If they see you enjoying yourself, they won't worry."

I roll my eyes. "I know you won't believe me, but I'm trying."

"I do believe you," he says. "And you're right. I *don't* know how you're feeling. But like I said before, I've wrestled with my own demons, Tessa. It's not always easy. But there's one thing that keeps me going."

Right. His demons. Those demons he mentioned the other day. The demons I questioned him about, that he said he might tell me about someday. "What's that?" I ask, genuinely curious now. "What keeps you going?"

He takes my hand, and for once I don't think about pulling away. He places it on his chest. "It's knowing that my heart still beats."

My lips part. I want to say something, but I have no idea what.

"Life, Tessa. Life is a gift."

"I'm not going to disagree with you, but your life is pretty easy, Ben. You have everything in the world. Literally."

"I didn't always." He squeezes my hand that's still touching his chest. "Not a day goes by that I'm not grateful for my fortune. For everything good that has happened to me. But that doesn't mean I haven't fought demons."

I don't want to fight forever, though. I'm tired of fighting. "Have you won against them?"

He pauses a moment, his forehead wrinkling. "It's not winning that's important. It's moving forward. The journey. It's not letting them eat at you, suffocate you."

"Good to know that's possible."

He smiles. "It's not only possible, Tessa. It's necessary. It's necessary because you're a beautiful and vibrant woman, and you deserve to have a life that you love. So make a deal with me, okay?"

A deal... "And what would that be?"

"This weekend, you have a good time. I'm not saying to forget what happened to you. That's not possible. Believe me, I know. But have a good time in *spite* of that."

"Depression isn't something that you can turn on and off."

He nods. "That's correct. You can't turn it on and off. But what you *can* do is choose how to deal with it when it happens. Instead of sitting in your room eating a pint of Ben & Jerry's, you can be active. Go on a run. Walk by the beach. We're going to be on one of the most beautiful beaches in the world."

I bite my lip and let my gaze fall to my lap. "What if I can't?"

"What are you talking about can't? Do your legs work?"

"Of course." There was a time when they felt like they didn't, because the depression was so bad. Some days I couldn't move if I tried. But that isn't where I am anymore, thank goodness.

"Then you *can*, Tessa," he says gently but firmly.

He's not wrong. When I'm having a bad day, I always feel a little better when I do something productive. Even if it's just taking Rita on a short walk. Sometimes it's as simple as taking the trash down to the dumpster.

"Do it for Skye," Ben says. "Like you said, she needs you to be happy."

"I don't believe in faking it, Ben."

"I don't, either. Faking it can lead to bad things. It can lead to people not knowing you're in pain, and then... Well, let's not go there. I'm not asking you to fake it. I'm asking you to, when you're feeling bad, get up and do *something*. It doesn't matter what it is. Get your ass out of bed and do it. You said you didn't want Skye and Braden to worry about you this weekend. This is how you accomplish that."

He lets my hand go then, and I absently place it against my own heart.

My heart still beats.

And that, alone, is a reason to be grateful.

Is it a reason to be happy? Ecstatic?

Yeah, it is.

So why am I not feeling that way?

"I'm just saying, Tessa, at least for these four days, if you're having a particularly bad time, get up. Walk across the room. Take a shower. Get dressed. Go outside."

I swallow.

"You can do this," Ben assures me with a smile. "And if you find that you're having trouble? Call me. I will be at your side. I will drag you out of your room, if you ask me to. I will do whatever it takes to help you make this long weekend perfect for Skye and Braden."

"All right," I tell him.

So I'll suck it up.

I'll feign emotion.

And I will make sure that my best friend has the best long weekend of her life.

CHAPTER TWELVE

Ben

One smooth landing in Montego Bay and a two-hour limo ride to Ocho Rios later, we arrive at the beachside resort. The three luxury suites have been divided among Braden and Skye, Tessa, and me, as best man and maid of honor.

My suite has a masculine vibe. The living area is decorated in black lacquer and burgundy leather furniture. The kitchenette includes a small dining table, and the bedroom sports a king-size bed covered in royal-blue silk. Even the bathroom is decadent, with a tub and separate walk-in shower and a double vanity in blue-and-white marble.

For a moment I think about how wonderful it would be to share this with someone. Apple Ames would hate this place. It's too done up for her hipster tastes. Most of the women I've dated recently would love it, of course. But none of them were born for this.

Tessa Logan, though?

She was born for a place like this.

My baggage has already been delivered, and the housekeeper

has unpacked for me. No formalwear this time. That's for the wedding itself. Mostly nice jeans with button-down shirts and flip-flops for dinner. All other activities? Trunks and—hopefully—bikinis.

I'll bet Tessa looks luscious in a bikini. A white string bikini would perfectly accent her tan skin.

And all that beautiful dark brown hair.

I should check on her.

Her suite is right across the hall from mine, so I leave, making sure I have my key card, and I knock on her door.

"Who is it?"

"It's me, Tessa. Ben."

"Just a moment, please."

She opens the door, her hair piled on top of her head.

"Getting ready to go down to the pool or the beach?"

"I was planning a quiet night inside," she says.

"How about a quiet walk on the beach instead?"

"Well…"

I gesture toward her window. "We're in Jamaica, Tessa. Let's make the most of it."

She crosses her arms. "You're certainly welcome to make the most of it without me."

"What did you promise me on the plane?"

"That I would make sure this is a wonderful weekend for Braden and Skye. But we don't have any plans with them tonight, and I'm sure they would prefer to be alone."

"Maybe… But whether they want to be alone or not, *I* don't want to be alone."

"There are many young women here who I'm sure would be happy to spend the evening with you."

She's no doubt right. But I want to spend the evening with

her. Something about her has gotten under my skin. I'm attracted to her, of course. Who wouldn't be? But there's something more.

In fact, I'm not sure I would've gone for the old Tessa. From what I understand from Skye, she was wild and flamboyant, always living in the moment.

Sounds a lot like me. The few times I've tried to date women who are exactly like me, it's never worked out.

I can't force her to walk on the beach with me.

So I decide to ask her nicely.

"Would you please accompany me to the beach?" I say with a smile.

She sighs and then holds the door open. "All right. Let me get my suit and my coverup on. Wait here."

"I'm right across the hall from you. Just knock on my door when you're ready. I need to get my trunks."

She nods.

I return to my suite and hurriedly put on a pair of navy board shorts. I throw a light-blue T-shirt over my head, grab a towel, and slide my feet into my flip-flops.

Then I wait outside my door.

A moment later, Tessa emerges—

And I nearly lose my breath.

Her hair is now in a sleek high ponytail that falls down her back, and she's not wearing a white bikini. No. It's royal blue, and she looks like a fucking model. Her coverup is simple black mesh, and she holds a white towel from her bathroom.

I can't gawk at her. That will make her uncomfortable.

"You look amazing." I hold out my arm. "Shall we?"

I don't expect her to take my arm, so I'm surprised when she does.

We say nothing as we walk to the elevator, descend, and then walk out the resort the few steps to the beach.

The sun is going down, and we pass Betsy and others. They're having a drink at the beachside bar.

"Tessa!" Betsy waves us over.

Tessa and I head to the bar.

"Hey, you guys," Betsy says. "Frankie makes a mean margarita, Tessa."

"I'm sure he does, but I think I'll stick to water."

Betsy frowns a bit but then says, "Of course."

"I'll try a margarita," I tell the bartender. "And I'd like an ice water for the lady, please."

"Coming up, Mr. Black."

Frankie pours a glass of water and mixes my drink quickly. I hand the water to Tessa and hold up my margarita. "To an amazing evening."

Betsy and the other girls join in, giggling.

I take a sip of the margarita. The combination of salt, lime, and tequila is a little too much for me.

Margaritas are okay, but I may as well be drinking limeade with some salt. I'd much prefer a Wild Turkey.

"Shall we?" I say to Tessa again.

I hold up my arm, but this time she doesn't take it. She does, however, follow me away from the others.

Tessa and I dump our towels and then walk along the shoreline, away from the commotion.

The sun is setting, and its tangerine-and-purple hues over the horizon are mesmerizing. The rays cascade over the rippling blue of the ocean.

I gaze outward, and then I gaze at Tessa.

And I think I may have found something more beautiful than this breathtaking Jamaican sunset.

CHAPTER THIRTEEN

Tessa

Something's happening in my hand. My fingers are tingling, but for once it's not from nerves.

Except it is, in a different way.

And I recognize it.

I recognize it from something the old Tessa used to feel when she was attracted to a man.

Tingles starting in my fingers. Tingles that made me smile, giggle, flirt.

This Tessa doesn't smile, giggle, or flirt.

Still, the tingles are there.

Part of me wants to step closer to Ben, maybe grab his pinky with mine, feel his warmth as he entwines it around my own.

Part of me is scared to death of that prospect.

I stop walking, turn, and look at the ocean.

It's so beautiful, a sparkling dark blue as the sun sets.

I take a drink of my water, and I look at Ben. The soft ocean breeze drifts over his hair, messing it up.

And if possible, he's even more handsome.

This is a man who is equally at home in a suit and tie as he is in trunks and a T-shirt, walking along the beach.

"You okay?" he asks.

"Yeah, why?"

"You stopped walking."

I turn and meet his gaze. His dark eyes are so beautiful and searching. "I wanted to look at the ocean. I've always loved it. It's so vast. Its beauty is unequaled, especially right at sunset. If we stay here and just watch, we'll be able to see the very last edge of the sun go beneath the horizon. Beneath the waterline."

"It is gorgeous," he says. "But it's not as beautiful as the woman watching it."

The tingles in my fingers again.

Ben stands beside me, gazing out at the ocean with me.

Again, my pinky itches to grab his.

Such a tiny tender touch, and I want it.

But I'm afraid to want it.

What if my body reacts in a bad way? What if the fear overpowers the desire?

It's too soon.

Way too soon.

Besides, Ben Black is a player. He's in the tabloids with a new woman on his arm every week.

I can't get involved with him.

Especially if he has demons.

Perhaps he truly does.

Part of me wants to learn about him—everything that makes him who he is.

But I haven't conquered my own demons. Adding his to the mix wouldn't be a good thing.

A tingle flashes through me as his flesh touches mine.

Just the pinky. The pinky that I've been thinking about.

I yank my hand away.

He turns to me. "I'm sorry. That was an accident. I got too close."

"No, it's… You didn't do anything wrong. I just…"

"I understand, Tessa." He pauses. "But I'm not going to deny I'm attracted to you. Very attracted to you."

His words put me on edge, but they don't elicit as much fear as I expect them to.

Because I find him very attractive as well. More than I've even admitted to myself.

I want to tell him that he's pretty much the best-looking man I've ever laid eyes on. That his broad shoulders make my heart flutter, his full lips make me wonder how they'd feel against mine, and his hypnotic dark eyes make me want to get lost in them and never be found.

The old Tessa would have made a move by now, or she would have coyly encouraged *him* to make a move.

"Maybe you weren't ready to hear that," Ben says. "I won't do anything to make you uncomfortable, though. I won't do anything you don't want me to. I'd love to help you if I could—"

"You've already helped me. You took over the planning of both of these parties. Your only responsibility was the bachelor party, but you took on the bachelorette party for me."

"That wasn't a big deal. I had Braden's wallet and an expert party planner at my disposal. It was nothing, really."

I reach toward him, but I don't touch him. Yet I feel him—his stubbly jawline, his warm skin. A phantom caress. "No, it *was* something, Ben. It was something I couldn't handle—or didn't think I could, anyway—and you took it off my plate."

"Like I said, it was easy for me. I had everything I needed

at my disposal." Then he cocks his head. "But I'm wondering if perhaps I did you a disfavor."

I lift my eyebrows. "What do you mean by that?"

"Nothing," he says. "Forget I said it."

"I can't forget." Because I know what he's thinking.

I can see it in the gorgeous contours of his face.

"You think I was sitting at home doing nothing when I could have been working on the bachelorette party."

"Well…" he hedges.

"Is that why you offered me a job? Because you didn't want me dwelling on things any more than I already am, and you'd already taken over the bachelorette party?"

He sighs. "I offered you a job because our company needs good accountants."

"Is that the only reason?"

"What if it isn't?" he asks, his gaze meeting mine. "Does it matter, as long as my heart was in the right place?"

His dark eyes are so warm and inviting.

When a warm breeze drifts over my skin, I feel something.

I feel something familiar yet foreign.

I like this man.

I like him a lot.

I like him more than I should.

I'm not sure I can ever even have sex again.

I'm certainly not there yet.

Certainly not when the idea of his pinky touching mine makes me flinch.

But Ben makes me *want* to heal. He makes me want to want those things again.

And while that should scare the hell out of me—and it does—part of me also relishes the thought.

Part of me…

I grab his pinky.

The feel of his finger on mine doesn't scare me, doesn't make me flinch.

Because *I* chose to do it. I *chose* to do it. The power is mine.

He cocks his head once more. "Is this okay?"

"It's okay."

Then we turn, neither of us saying a word, our pinkies still entwined, and we continue walking along the shoreline.

CHAPTER FOURTEEN

Ben

I meet Braden the next morning for breakfast and a cold plunge. The cold plunge first.

He and I started this ritual after we made our first million. It's forced meditation.

Because when you're submerged in icy-cold water—I prefer fifty-five degrees, which isn't exactly icy cold, but it sure feels that way—all you can think about is not freezing your ass off.

You focus on your breaths—in and out and in and out—keeping them slow and steady.

No other thought enters your mind, so yes, it's forced meditation.

When you live the life that Braden and I live—running a billionaire company that employs thousands of people who depend on you to be your best every day—your mind is always going.

I know mine is. The cold plunge has helped me through some difficult times. Those demons I've mentioned to Tessa, to name a few.

Braden and I like to challenge each other.

He and I are both up to ten minutes in the cold plunge, but today I'm going to make it to eleven.

Hell, I need it. I had a hard-on all last night thinking about Tessa Logan.

And damn, I don't even *want* to think about her that way. Not before she's ready.

I wish I could help her. I truly do. But I'm not a psychologist, not a counselor. She has to take the lead on this, let me know what she wants and when, step by step. She's the one in control. And for me, that's all-new territory.

Braden and I stand outside, the morning air sliding over our bodies.

"We're at fifty-five," the resort trainer says, holding the thermometer out of the water. "You sure you want to do ten minutes? That's a long time."

"That's what we do," Braden says.

"I'm doing eleven this time," I say.

Braden shoots his eyebrows up. "Ten is pushing it, Ben. You sure?"

"Fuck yeah." Chills are already running through my body at the thought. "I have to. I need it. Besides, it'll make our hike up Dunn River Falls seem like nothing."

"That'll be nothing anyway," Braden says. "We're in the best shape of our lives. You sure about eleven?"

"Absolutely."

"Great, then. I'll do eleven as well."

I roll my eyes. "Figured you would."

Braden gives me a good-natured punch to my upper arm. "You know I can't be bested by my little bro."

The trainer, a muscled Jamaican man named Spencer, sets

his timer. "All right, fifteen seconds to work yourselves up. Get in when you're ready. I'll tell you when the timer starts."

I breathe and move my feet in a high-kneed march for a few seconds. I close my eyes, ready myself for the icy water that's going to meet my body.

"You ready?" Spencer asks.

I close my eyes. "I am."

"Good here, too." From Braden.

I step into the cold tub and submerge myself within a second.

I want to keep my teeth from chattering, so I close my eyes and begin to breathe.

The first minute is the most difficult.

All I think about is the cold.

How my body is turning into a glacier.

Fifty-five degrees can't freeze my body, but it sure as hell feels like it is.

I keep my face out of the water, but I submerge my shoulders and the tip of my chin.

But my whole body—including my face—feels the cold.

I breathe in, breathe out, breathe in again.

Keeping my eyes closed, concentrating only on my breathing.

Breathe, breathe, breathe…

Eleven minutes seems like a fucking year, but I'm determined.

Breathe, breathe, breathe.

"One minute down," Spencer says.

He won't mention the time again. Our minds need to go blank, not worry about hearing the time. Once the first minute is over, the body starts to numb.

You feel the cold, but it's not quite as harsh.

Breathe, breathe, breathe…

In, out, in, out…

I move my fingers. Nope, that makes it worse.

Stay still. Breathe, breathe, breathe...

The hands and feet never get warm.

Not that any of the body gets warm, but the hands and the feet stay freezing, as if my fingers have turned into icicles.

The body, when exposed to these conditions, attempts to keep your internal organs warm and working. Extremities are the first to go.

In, out, in, out...

No images form in my mind. No thoughts form.

I focus solely on my breathing and dealing with coldness.

Breathe, breathe, breathe...

Blank.

Blank mind.

Nothingness.

Nothingness...

Nothingness...

• • •

"Eleven minutes."

I dart out of the water at Spencer's voice.

He hands me a warm towel, and I wrap it over my shoulders.

I'm surprised to see Braden already out of his tub.

"You didn't make it for eleven minutes?"

"I told him to touch my shoulder at ten." Braden towels off her hair. "I have to hand it to you, Ben. You fucking nailed it."

"So I bested you, bro?"

"You did. I'm not sure how."

In truth, I'm not sure, either. I only know that I needed it.

I needed eleven minutes of a blank mind.

Because as soon as that warm towel is wrapped around my

shoulders, the one image I've tried to block out is back in my head.

Tessa Logan.

Braden and I sit in our towels for fifteen more minutes until we're warm enough to change into shorts and T-shirts. Then we head to the dining area for breakfast.

"I guess we're the only early risers here," I say.

Indeed, the dining room is vacant except for us.

"This is a vacation for everyone," Braden says. "I imagine most of them will be sleeping in. We're the only two idiots who will get up at six in the morning when we don't have to."

"Since we usually get up at four thirty, yeah." I laugh.

We fill our plates with bacon, eggs, and potatoes, along with the local Jamaican breakfast, ackee and salt fish. The ackee comes from the inside of the ackee fruit and looks a lot like scrambled eggs.

Once we're seated, servers bring us coffee and juice.

"Skye really appreciates you looking out for Tessa," Braden says.

"There's just something about her," I say.

Braden looks at me sternly. "Don't be thinking..."

I put my hands up in front of me. "For Christ's sake, Bray, I'm not. Besides..."

"Besides what?"

"I ended things with Apple. No more friends-with-benefits. And no more gold diggers, either."

Braden raises his eyebrows. "Are you saying you're looking for an actual relationship?"

"I never thought I would. I mean, you know my track record with women. They all seem to be after one thing. But I've seen what you and Skye have."

"But Tessa…"

"I'm not thinking of her that way." I sigh. "At least I'm trying not to."

"She's off-limits," Braden says in his big brother voice.

The voice that makes me want to punch him.

"I'm glad you're no longer hanging with Apple, though. I'd prefer that we all stay as far away from the Ames family as possible."

"Then you won't want to know that I actually considered a relationship with Apple."

He scowls at me. "Please be kidding."

"I'm not kidding, but I don't feel that way about her. She's great, and she's wildfire in the sack, but we're just too different."

"She did have one good quality."

"Really?" I spear a piece of potato with my fork. "You're going to admit that?"

"She has her own damned money, Ben."

"Hey, like I said. No more gold diggers." I sigh. "I'm not in any huge hurry. I'm going to concentrate on work. I'm not going to go looking for love. I'll let it come to me."

"I certainly wasn't looking for love when I found Skye."

"That's my point. It will find me when it's ready."

The only problem is…I think it might have already. In the form of Tessa Logan.

"I can't help but think," I say, "that when I look back through Skye's Instagram, and I see the pictures of her and Tessa, Tessa was an entirely different person then."

"She was. If not for Tessa, Skye and I might not even be together."

Right. Tessa mentioned that to me. "What was it about Skye that drew you to her?"

"The first thing that attracted me to her was her mouth."

"She does have nice lips," I say.

He narrows his gaze. "Right, and that's the last time I will hear you say that. You're not allowed to think of my wife-to-be that way."

"I'm not, Bray. Jeez. Skye's not my type anyway."

"I know she's not. She's a little too girl-next-door for you, isn't she?"

"Is it my fault that I go for the supermodel type?"

"I know your type, Ben. And I know someone who exactly fits that mold."

"Tessa Logan," I say without thinking.

"Exactly. Tessa is tall, gorgeous, with a body to die for. *Precisely* your type."

"Don't I know it." I sigh. "But don't worry. I understand that she's not ready for anything like that. Besides, this weekend isn't about me. It's about you and Skye. I'm not going to go looking for action. I'm here for *you*, big brother. To make tonight a night you will never forget."

CHAPTER FIFTEEN

Tessa

"Hiking? Seriously?" I say to Ben after I finish off something called ackee and about five slices of bacon before the dining room closes for breakfast.

"Hey, you told me to plan the whole damned weekend, Tessa." He laughs. "And I planned for us all to hike up Dunn's River Falls."

I take a drink of orange juice. "But tonight is the bachelorette party. I don't want everyone tired out from some hike."

"This isn't just *some hike*, Tessa. It's Dunn's River Falls. We're hiking up a waterfall."

"And that's supposed to make me feel better about the whole thing?"

"Yes! It will be exhilarating. All that oxygen coming off the water. You're going to love it, I promise. Everyone will."

"So everyone is going?"

"Yup! I've got a guide all set up."

"What am I supposed to wear?"

"Whatever you want," he says, smiling, "but I'd suggest a

bathing suit. It's a waterfall, Tessa. You're going to get wet."

I shake my head.

"Hey," he says again, "you told me to plan the weekend."

"You could have told me about this on the plane ride, you know. Around the same time when you were telling me to get out and do something when I was feeling down."

"Little did you know...I'd already planned for you to get out and do something." His eyes crinkle.

My God, those eyes...

I almost think he could get me to do anything when he looks at me with those warm dark-brown eyes.

"I'm not going," I say hotly.

"Have it your way," he says. "But everyone else is going."

"Betsy's going? Kathy? Kathy Harmon would rather die than exercise." She's one of those naturally thin women who never lifts a finger and gorges on dessert but never gains an ounce.

"Everyone, even Kathy," he says. "Except you, apparently. And it's not really exercise. It's...exertion. It's more energizing than tiring."

"Oh, well." I sigh. "I guess I'll find something to do."

He stares at me then. Really stares at me, and—

I realize I must look and sound like a petulant child. One hike won't kill me, I guess.

"Fine," I say. "When are we leaving?"

"Limos are picking us up outside the resort in an hour. Be there or be square."

"You did *not* just say that."

Ben laughs. "Afraid I did."

He is in entirely too good a mood today. And it's contagious. I can feel myself catching it from him.

"Wear that hot blue bikini you had on last night," he says.

"Put on a pair of shorts over the bottoms. Do you have shoes with tread?"

"What if I don't?"

"Then I'll have some sent over."

I roll my eyes. "I have water sandals with tread, lucky for you."

"Definitely lucky for me." He smiles. "And don't forget sunscreen."

• • •

We're not at all inconspicuous driving up to Dunn's River Falls in limos. Tourists stare as we exit the large black vehicles, and a guide meets us right at the entrance.

Ben walks toward him. "You must be Marcus," he says. "I'm Benjamin Black."

"Good to meet you, Mr. Black," Marcus says in a Jamaican accent. "Is the whole party here?"

I look around. One person is missing—Ben's father. How did he get out of this? Everyone else—including Kathy Harmon, in a gorgeous fuchsia tankini that shows off everything perfect about her body—is here.

"Yup," Ben says, "and call me Ben, please."

"Good enough, Ben." Marcus grins and then raises his voice. "All right, folks, welcome to Dunn's River Falls! I'm Marcus, your guide for today. Remember, stay close, and we'll make it to the top safely."

"Safely?" I whisper to Ben.

"Tessa, this is perfectly safe."

I don't reply.

"Wow," Skye says on a breath, a waterproof camera around her neck. "The pictures online don't do this place justice."

"The photos you take will," Braden says, taking her hand.

They're so in love, it's disgusting.

Except it's not. It's sweet, actually. Their impending wedding is one of the most anticipated events on social media. Skye is keeping a lot of it private, but she makes her followers happy by posting once a day about something. Today I have a hunch it will be Dunn's River Falls. She won't post about the party tonight. If I know my best friend, she'll consider that too private.

We walk to the falls. The whoosh of the water is oddly soothing. Chains of climbers holding hands move upward on the limestone rock, but I try to imagine the falls without the people. Just the natural beauty. The water glistens in the sunlight as it rushes over the rocks. The falls are surrounded by vibrant greenery that contrasts strikingly with the white limestone and the turquoise pools of water.

For a moment, I wish only Ben and I were here to experience this together.

Marcus shouts to be heard over the thundering falls. "Okay, everyone. We're going to wade in now. Make sure anything that can be damaged by water is secure because, folks, we're going to get wet! Anyone who wants to take my hand and form a chain, please do. Otherwise, be careful."

Ben grabs my hand.

I jerk slightly, but I don't pull away. I'm pretty athletic from running and yoga, and I'm sure I can make this climb alone, but Ben's hand... It feels good in mine. We don't join the human chain. Neither do Skye and Braden, but Betsy, Kathy, and most of the others do.

The cool water laps around my ankles, and it's refreshing in the hot sun under the blue sky.

"The rocks beneath you are naturally formed by the water,"

Marcus yells. "This is a unique hiking experience that you'll never forget!"

Betsy laughs. "The water's chilly, but it feels great!"

"Totally," Kathy agrees.

She's holding Marcus's hand and engaging him. Such a flirt. Betsy's next to Kathy, holding her hand.

"Keep going," Marcus says. "We're just getting started. Remember to watch your step on the rocks."

The water level increases as we go, and soon I'm up to my knees. It's cold, but it feels good. Invigorating, even.

"I think I know why you wanted me to do this," I say to Ben, my hand still in his.

"Oh?" He lifts his eyebrows.

"The cold. The water. It's…exhilarating. I mean…you just can't feel bad when you're among such beauty…and coldness."

"It takes you over," he says.

"Yeah, it does. In a good way."

"Wait until you see what I've got planned for you tomorrow." His eyes twinkle.

"Climbing Mount Everest?"

He laughs. "Did Tessa Logan just make a joke?"

Did I? The old Tessa made jokes all the time. This Tessa? It may be her first time.

"This is incredible!" Skye says from in front of me. "Can you believe how the water carved these steps from rocks?" She stops and takes a few photos.

Some of the silver-gray rock steps are crescent-shaped and some semi-circular, with natural ridges and depressions, providing sufficient grip to prevent slipping.

Braden turns around. "You two are bringing up the rear."

I look upward. Marcus and the rest of our group are way

ahead of us. I pull on Ben's arm. "We should catch up."

"We're fine, Tessa," he says. "Look around you. This is Mother Nature's handiwork. Enjoy it. Breathe it all in."

At his urging, I draw in a deep breath, inhaling the natural mist coming off the falls.

And I feel...

I feel almost...invincible.

And I like the feeling. I like it a lot.

How did Ben Black know that this hike was exactly what I needed?

I tug on his arm once more, and he turns around to meet my gaze.

His brown eyes are kind and beautiful and full of joy. Demons? Did he say he has demons? Because I don't see them.

"Yeah?" he asks.

"Thank you for this," I say. "For making me do this."

He chuckles. "Tessa, I don't think I can *make* you do anything."

CHAPTER SIXTEEN

Ben

This is my first time hiking the falls, but when the resort planner told me about it, I knew we had to do it.

I knew it would be perfect for Tessa—and for the rest of us, for that matter.

This is nothing for Braden and me. The cold plunge is much chillier and requires a lot more mental fortitude.

But for Tessa? This is the beauty of nature, the power of water, and the life force of oxygen in the air.

Exactly what she needs.

"This place is like a hidden paradise," Tessa says. "Yet we're not very far from the resort. Which is also paradise, but in a different way."

"Manmade versus nature," I say. "Nature wins every time."

I already had my cold plunge this morning, but being here revitalizes me with a rush of adrenaline and awe. The cascading waters and joyfulness of the tourists provide an absorbing soundtrack. Ascending the steps isn't particularly difficult for someone in good shape, but there's still a thrilling sense of accomplishment as the frothy waters curl around my feet and the Caribbean sun hits my bare chest.

I tug on Tessa's arm, helping her onto a particularly high rock. She turns around and gazes downward, joy filling her dark eyes.

Yes, this was definitely a good idea.

"The view from the top must be amazing," she says.

"This is so much fun!" Betsy says from a few steps above us.

"They've reached the summit," I say, taking Tessa's hand again. "Come on. Let's go."

A few more rocks, and Tessa and I join Marcus and the others at the top. Skye and Braden have fallen behind, Skye snapping photo after photo.

"Congratulations, everyone!" Marcus grins. "You've made it to the top of Dunn's River Falls."

I didn't bring a camera, and neither did Tessa. Plus, we left our phones behind so they wouldn't get wet. No matter. Skye will have her own photographs, and they'll be better than anything I could capture.

Besides, I don't need a photo. I'll never forget this place—or the serene look on Tessa's beautiful face.

"Take in all the scenery," Marcus advises. "The lush jungle, the Caribbean Sea. The silver, white, and gray of the stones around you. Just think." He gestures. "These steps were formed over centuries by the waters themselves."

Tessa is gazing outward. "It's so tranquil here. Even with the crowds of people. I almost feel like it's only you and I."

"I should have rented out the Falls for the day," I say, "and then it could have been."

I expect her to say something snide about me throwing my money around, but she surprises me. "Could you imagine that?

Only the two of us? No voices, nothing splashing us except the water itself. It would be heaven, Ben. Absolute heaven."

The look on her face, the sound of her voice…

I'd give up my fortune and surrender to my demons if it meant I could keep Tessa in her current state of mind, that beautiful, unflustered smile on her face.

Skye and Braden eventually make it to the top, and Skye snaps about a hundred more photos. Marcus and the others begin to descend, and Skye and Braden follow.

But Tessa and I…

We stay. The limos won't leave without us, and if they do? I'll call another.

Because right now, in this moment, Tessa is feeling something wonderful. I won't take that away from her.

We'll go at her pace.

Her breathing is deep, and every once in a while she closes her eyes. Then she opens them quickly, as if she doesn't want to miss one second of this spectacular view.

Finally she turns to me. "We should go."

I gently touch her shoulder. "We'll go when you're ready to go and not one moment sooner."

She nods. "I'm ready. Thank you for talking me into this. It's been wonderful, truly."

I give her a smile. "I'm glad." I grab her hand. "We need to be more careful going down. It's easy to slip and fall."

"I'll be careful."

I take the lead, navigating each step with care, balancing the exhilaration of the waterfall's force with care to maintain my footing. I grip Tessa's hand, helping her down each rock.

The water laps our knees, and in some places nearly hits our waists, but I hear no complaints from Tessa. We move with the water, smoothly navigating it, until—

"Oh shit!" I slide off a rock and into a pool of water up to my chest.

Tessa tumbles down after me, and I catch her in my arms, water cascading over us.

I expect to see fear in her eyes, but instead I see only jubilation.

She's laughing. Tessa is laughing!

Our bodies are touching in an embrace, and her lips are mere inches from mine.

Kiss her, kiss her, kiss her.

That's my body talking. My other head.

But I can't, even though I want to more than I want my next breath.

"You okay?" I ask.

"Fine," she laughs. "Are you?"

"Not my most athletic moment, but I'm good." I let go of her except for her hand. "Ready?"

Is that disappointment in her eyes? Or relief?

Did she *want* me to kiss her?

Did I miss the right time?

She simply nods, and we make it the rest of the way down the falls. We're soaking wet, of course, and Marcus hands us each a towel.

"You were the last ones down, Ben," he says. "You must have enjoyed it."

"You have no idea, Marcus," I say. "No idea. Thank you for everything."

CHAPTER SEVENTEEN

Tessa

When we returned to the resort, Ben said a quick goodbye with a squeeze of my hand and left to meet with the resort coordinator about the festivities for this evening. I took a short nap and then reported to the spa where all the ladies were treated to a hot stone massage and a manicure and pedicure.

Afterward, I went back to my room to change for the bachelorette events. I brought a little red number that doesn't leave a lot to the imagination, and for a moment, I consider dressing in something a little less risqué—especially since this dress has not-so-great memories for me. I was wearing it when I first met Garrett Ramirez.

I threw it into my suitcase on a whim, along with two black options and a blue strapless. I never wear white, and black... Well, I love a little black dress, but the red... It flatters me better than the others.

I stare at it laid out on my bed.

I'm safe here on this island. I'm safe with Ben. He's made that clear.

But the men and women will be segregated this evening. Ben won't even see me in the dress.

I grab one of the black dresses instead. If I get my courage up, I'll wear the red one tomorrow evening, at the big party where all the guests—women *and* men—will be present.

It's still on the bed, and every second it's in my line of sight, I hear Garrett's voice more loudly in my head. Feel him on top of me. Smell him…

No. I won't wear this at all. Too many bad memories.

I toss the dress in the wastebasket. I'll buy another red dress when I get home.

After a quick shower, I dry off and slide the dress over my body, paint my lips to match my newly manicured fingers and toes, pull my hair back into a sleek ponytail so it won't hang on my neck and make me sweat, and head down to the bachelorette party, carrying my gift bag for Skye—a red satin nightie. She always says she can't pull off the color red, but I'm sure she'll look fantastic in it.

The women are on one side of the resort while the men are on the other, and I have to hand it to Ben—he did a fabulous job with the planning.

A table is set up beachside, and to our right is a full bar featuring two specialty cocktails—the Skye and the Braden.

Braden's signature cocktail is a simple Wild Turkey on the rocks. From what I've seen, Ben and Braden both drink theirs neat, but apparently the barkeep was told to add ice. Whatever. I won't be drinking anything anyway.

Skye is also a fan of Wild Turkey. She drank it at home in Kansas, so her cocktail also features the bourbon, and it's a lovely sky blue.

"What's in that?" I ask one of the bartenders, a muscular

Jamaican man named Terry.

"Wild Turkey, simple syrup, lemon juice, and a touch of blue curaçao." He gives me a wide grin. "Can I mix one up for you?"

"No, thank you. Sparkling water, please."

"Of course." He pours my drink and hands it to me.

"Thank you." I take a sip and walk over to Betsy, who's standing on the beach and looking out to the ocean.

She turns to me and smiles. She's wearing her signature flowing Bohemian-style dress in light blue, and her feet are bare. Good idea. I kick off my sandals.

She holds a Skye cocktail in her hand. "You want to taste this? It's really lovely. You can hardly taste the Wild Turkey."

I shake my head. "No thanks, Bets."

"Tess, come on. This is Skye's bachelorette party. I'm not saying you have to get drunk, but you should taste her cocktail. It's so very…Skye."

I sigh. "Fine." I take a sip of the light blue cocktail.

And shockingly…it's good.

Not overly sweet, and I do taste a tinge of the bourbon, but it works with the blue curaçao and the lemon juice.

"Delicious, right?" Betsy says.

"It is good."

"Let's get you one."

"I don't know…"

"I understand. Never mind." Betsy jingles the ice in her glass. "Maybe you'll feel more comfortable when we toast Skye."

She's right. We have to toast Skye soon, and as the maid of honor, I'll be leading it.

Old Tessa would've written everything out, had a lot to say, including a little bit of a roast, talking about all the trouble Skye used to get into in college—which was none because she was always a control freak. Old Tessa would have been jovial and jolly and would have had all the women laughing and crying and nearly peeing themselves.

"You know what, Bets? I'll try the Skye."

"If you're sure."

I nod, and a moment later, Betsy brings me a Skye cocktail.

It is a beautiful shade of light blue, much like the blue sky above me—which I guess is the point.

"What's everyone else drinking?" I ask.

"Kathy's drinking bourbon shots." Betsy looks over at Kathy, who's sitting next to Daniela, several empty shot glasses in front of her. "That girl can hold her alcohol. And Daniela is drinking Skyes."

"What about champagne?" I ask. "Shouldn't there be champagne for a toast?"

Betsy laughs. "I have no idea. *You* planned this, Tess. Did you plan for champagne?"

Warmth slides into my cheeks. I'm sure I'm growing red. I didn't plan *any* of this. Ben did. Surely he'd think of champagne.

Wouldn't he?

I take a sip of the drink and look over at the bar. Terry motions to me. "Excuse me," I say to Betsy.

I walk over to Terry. "Yeah?"

"Are you ready for me to pour the Dom Perignon for the toast?"

Okay. Ben *did* think of champagne. Or the resort event planner did. Whoever it was, I say a silent thank you to them.

That means I need to think of something to say.

"Or you could do the toast after dinner," he says.

Yes! Saved by dinner. "After dinner, I think. Thanks, Terry."

"Not a problem." He eyes my drink. "I see you decided to try the cocktail after all."

"Yeah." I force out a laugh. "I mean, it's a party, right?"

"It sure is." He turns to Daniela, who's ordering another drink and acting pretty giggly.

I sigh. I'm filing that under the heading of *not my problem*. What can I do? Daniela is over twenty-one, and it's an open bar. It's not like anyone has to drive anywhere.

I look toward the beach, and I'm surprised to see Skye there, holding a cocktail. She looks lovely in bright pink.

I approach her. "Doing okay?"

She smiles at me. "I should be asking you that."

"Skye, come on. We've had this discussion. This weekend isn't about me. It's about you and Braden. We're going to give you a great sendoff."

"This party is gorgeous," she says. "I can't thank you enough."

Guilt gnaws at me. I did nothing.

"How did you come up with this cocktail? It was a wonderful idea."

"TikTok," I lie.

I hate lying to her, but you can find anything on TikTok.

"I love the idea. I think maybe we'll do this at the wedding, too. Have a Braden cocktail and a Skye cocktail."

"It's all the rage these days," I say, hoping I'm right. I bring my cocktail to my lips without actually taking a drink. "I was thinking about saving the toast until after dinner. Is that okay with you?"

"Of course," she says. "I like that idea. We'll all be sitting down, and I don't want to miss one word of what you're going to say."

I give her a weak smile. "Whatever you want, Skye."

Ugh. Now I *really* need to think of something to say.

The truth of the matter is that Skye and I had a difficult time when she and Braden were getting serious. I was being a brat and feeling left out of her life. Betsy and I got close, but then Garrett happened... And at first, I was thrilled. Garrett and I seemed like a match made in heaven.

We met at a MADD gala that Skye attended for her employer at the time, mega-influencer Addison Ames. For some reason, I was drinking daiquiris that night. Banana daiquiris instead of my usual margaritas.

I'll never drink a banana daiquiri again.

• • •

SEVERAL MONTHS EARLIER...

The band is playing Latin music, which I love, and I'm aching to dance and make a spectacle of myself in this gorgeous red dress, so when the handsome, dark-haired man approaches me, I'm ecstatic.

"Care to dance?" he asks.

"Sure." I give him a dazzling smile. "Watch my drink, Skye."

Skye always says that's her job at clubs, to watch my drink. She hates clubbing, but we're not at a club tonight. We're at a charity gala, the music is awesome, and my legs want to move.

"What's your name?" he asks once we hit the floor.

"Tessa!" I say loudly. "What's yours?"

"Garrett."

"Nice to meet you." I take his outstretched hand.

He knows the basic moves and the side-to-side, and we move in synchrony to the Latin beat of the drums. Once we're warmed up, Garrett leads me in front of him, in the cross-body move. I slide into each step, following his lead like a pro. I love to dance, and Garrett knows his stuff. The red dress is formfitting, but with each move I execute, I wish I were wearing something with a flowing skirt that I could twirl around in. We dance through three numbers before Garrett wipes his brow.

"Break?" he asks.

"Yeah, sounds good."

I head back to the table where Skye is still sitting, nursing her Wild Turkey, while Garrett walks to a different table.

I grab a tissue out of my evening bag and wipe my forehead. "Garrett can really move!" I pick up my daiquiri and drain most of it.

"Ready to go?" Skye asks.

I laugh. A big, boisterous laugh. She can't be serious. "Good one, Skye. Finish your drink. We need to get out there. This music is great."

"But I—"

"No excuses, babe. Just down it."

Skye downs it. I stop myself from dropping my jaw. Skye never downs it, but there's a first time for everything. We head to the dance floor, and I'm busting some serious moves when Garrett and a friend join us. We dance as a foursome through the next four numbers.

"Sorry, I need a break," Skye says.

"Need a drink?" Garrett's friend asks.

The two of them exit the dance floor, leaving me with Garrett. He grabs my hand and has me twirling around in no time, and I'm exhilarated. Is it the banana daiquiri? The music? The man?

All three?

Whatever it is, I'm totally down for all of it.

• • •

PRESENT DAY...

*U*gh.

I quickly erase the thought from my mind. I was ready to hand him my heart that first night. He had that playboy charm and such gorgeous hair and eyes. He was dressed in a tuxedo but was only wearing the shirt and pants. The bow tie had long been discarded, and his white sleeves were rolled up, accenting his gorgeous dark forearms.

We became an item—a happy item, or so I thought. He actually dumped me at one point, and I was so upset.

But then...

We got back together...

I was on top of the world...until I found out what he'd been doing to me the whole time.

Now I feel violated and ugly and used.

I glance down at my Skye cocktail.

Funny, if I had planned this party myself—rather, if old Tessa had planned it—we'd probably be serving pitchers of margaritas and dancing to Latin pop later.

This is better.

Ben Black did a better job of planning a bachelorette party for my best friend than I would have. It's almost as if he knows Skye better than I do. Old Tessa would have made this about her own tastes. Ben made these festivities perfect for Skye's tastes.

I can't help a chuckle at the irony.

"Something funny?" Skye asks.

"No. Just thinking."

"Whatever you're thinking about, I'm glad you are," she says. "I miss your laugh, Tess."

"I miss it too."

That's no lie. Life is so much easier when you're happy.

That gets another chuckle out of me.

"What is it this time?" Skye asks.

"Nothing." I look down at my bare feet in the sand. "Maybe it's just time... Time to heal."

Skye grabs my free hand. "I'd love for you to heal, Tessa, but you need to do it on your own time."

"But I want to make this a wonderful evening for you, Skye. You deserve nothing less. I was a brat when—"

She gestures for me to stop. "No, Tess, that was all me. I got so involved in my relationship with Braden that I left you out. That was never my intention, and trust me, it will never happen again."

"I know that."

True to her word, Skye has tried to involve me every step of the way. We've kept our Saturday morning yoga dates, and she calls me several times a week, texts me daily. Forces me to go out to lunch once or twice a week.

I think I see her more now than I did before Braden.

Still, we were such besties, and I did feel left out.

Now?

All I want is to be left alone.

But this weekend isn't about me. And certainly not about my need to be alone.

I'll do well to remember that.

I take another sip of my drink.

"I can't believe you're drinking," Skye says.

"Betsy talked me into it, and I have to admit it's a delicious cocktail."

"It is." Skye takes another sip. I simply smile. "I think we should probably head toward the table. They'll be bringing our dinner out soon."

"Wonderful. I'm famished." Skye finishes her drink quickly,

and we walk toward the table that has been set up inside a large cabana.

"What's on the menu?" Skye asks.

That's a good question.

"Just wait and see," I say.

Dinner turns out to be a Jamaican feast, including a colorful array of jerk chicken, pigeon peas, and roasted vegetables.

I have to admit it's tempting.

The savory aroma alone makes my mouth water.

I consider that a good sign. My mouth hasn't watered for food—or anything else—in quite some time, except for the other night when I wanted my mom's enchiladas, but that may have just been for comfort.

We enjoy our dinner, and no one notices that I don't talk much, because Skye, Betsy, Kathy, and Daniela chat animatedly the entire time. No one notices that I eat slowly, because they're all talking so much that they eat slowly as well.

I take a bite of the chicken, and it's moist, succulent…and spicy.

I adore spicy food. My mother's Mexican cooking has made me immune to most heat, but this—scotch bonnet peppers, according to the printed menu sitting at each of our places—has me feeling like smoke is coming out of my ears.

I take a quick drink of my water.

"Can I get you another cocktail?" a server asks.

"No, thank you. But more water would be great."

"Coming right up."

I take another bite of the chicken and then a drink of water. The vegetables and pigeon peas are easier to get down. When I finally realize I can eat no more, half of my chicken is left on my plate.

But I did okay.

The server brings out our dessert—passionfruit gelato. It's a beautiful orange color, and ice cream is one thing I have no trouble with.

I take a bite and let the creaminess flow over my tongue. The passionfruit gives it a mango-like sweetness plus a citrusy tang.

And it's good. I find myself enjoying it.

I take another bite when something touches my shoulder.

I nearly jump out of my seat.

"Whoa," Terry the bartender says. "I didn't mean to startle you, sweetheart."

I'm not your sweetheart.

The words are on the tip of my tongue, but he's been calling all the ladies sweetheart. I breathe in and exhale slowly. "It's okay. Did you need something?"

"I just wanted to check to see if you wanted me to pop the champagne. Everyone seems to be finished with dessert."

Great. But I can't put this off forever. "Yeah, sure. That would be great."

Terry ceremoniously opens the champagne, and I stare at the cloud of condensation that drifts off the lip of the bottle. He pours Skye's flute first and then moves on to Betsy, Kathy, and Daniela, saving mine for last. Then he bows quickly and leaves.

I pick up my spoon to tap on my flute but then realize they're already all staring at me.

Okay, then.

Showtime.

I rise.

"I want to thank all of you guys for coming tonight," I say.

"Are you kidding? An all-expense-paid trip to Jamaica to celebrate Skye?" Kathy laughs. "You didn't have to exactly twist our arms, Tessa."

Daniela and Betsy join in the laughter, and Skye's cheeks blush.

I force a smile and continue. "I'm thrilled to be Skye's maid of honor. When we met our first year at BU, we had absolutely nothing in common. I was a math major, and Skye was an art major. Totally different. But somehow we seemed to click, and within months we were besties. Skye's an only child, so she asked me to be her maid of honor long ago—way before she met Braden—and now I guess she's stuck with me."

I get a few laughs at that, though it's not really what I was going for.

Stop being self-deprecating, I tell myself. *Speak from your damned heart.*

I draw in a breath. "When Braden first approached Skye, she wasn't sure whether she should respond to his advances. He pursued her hard. We even joked that he was a stalker. I remember telling her to ease up. He's a damned billionaire, so until he boils a rabbit in your kitchen, you should go for it."

More giggles. At least I was *going* for laughter that time.

"Skye has always been a little bit of a control freak."

This time I get guffaws.

"You're kidding, right?" From Betsy, rolling her eyes.

But they laugh again, and I join in, forcing out some chuckles.

"But of course Braden Black was the catch of the century, as we all know. The blue-collar billionaire himself, and he was interested in my Skye. So I told her to go for it. To let her hair down and take a chance."

My words are true. That's exactly what I told her. And now? I can't even let my own hair down.

"And maybe," I continue, without realizing what I'm saying,

"maybe it's time I take my own advice." I pick up my flute of champagne. "So Skye decided to let her hair down, and she found something way better than a quick fuck with a hot billionaire."

More snickers and giggles.

"She found the love of her life, and when you're in the presence of Skye and Braden together, you can't help but feel that love. It emanates from them. It's thick and almost visible in its intensity." I meet Skye's gaze, tears forming in my eyes. "Skye, I love you. You're the best friend a girl could ask for, and I'm so, so happy for you. So here's to you, to your husband-to-be, and to the rest of you ladies as well. Let's celebrate the beauty and wonder that is Skye Manning!"

I raise my glass, clink it to each of the others around me, and then take a sip.

I used to love champagne. Not so much because of its flavor or the bubbles or anything, but because of what it represents. Class and decadence.

That was the Tessa of old. She appreciated all of those things. She let her hair down and was always ready for a party.

I take another sip of the champagne and let the bubbles dance over my tongue. And the tears... They're there, ready to spill. Emotion. I'm feeling something.

It's been so long that it nearly guts me.

"Speech, speech, speech," the girls chant.

They drag Skye to her feet, and she stands next to me.

"Tess, I love you more than anything."

"Not more than Braden," Kathy shouts.

"In an entirely different way," Skye laughs. But then she gets serious. "Tessa, you've always been there for me, even when I wasn't there for you. Thank you for forgiving me when I didn't deserve it. Thank you for this amazing weekend." She looks around at the tropical decor, none of which I had anything to do with. "I'm in awe of what you put together. You've always been great with parties, Tess, but this is amazing even for you."

Again the guilt gnaws at me. "I'm really glad you like it," I say sincerely.

"Are you kidding me? I love it. So what else is going on tonight?"

I wish I knew. Ben said something about putting together a DJ and some dancing in one of the ballrooms. But now I'm wishing we had just done it all outside. It's a beautiful night, and I don't want to leave it just yet.

"First we have gifts for you," I say, "and after that you'll just have to wait and see."

But then—

The beat of a drum, steel drums, actually—and some reggae music.

I look around. Where is it coming from?

And then I see.

Oh my God…

The band. A steel drum player, a guitar player, and…

Some of the best-looking men I've ever seen.

Jamaican men—their skin dark and their muscles rippled.

Oh. My. God.

All wearing tight white trunks—and nothing else.

Damn you, Ben.

Fucking damn you.

CHAPTER EIGHTEEN

Ben

The ladies are here, and they're hot.

And they come in a spectrum of colors.

From the darkest brown to the fairest white.

Four women, all with bodies to die for and luscious racks too, of course.

We've moved from the beach into one of the ballrooms. The ladies gyrate around us, and one by one, they shed their bikini tops.

They crowd around Braden, dancing for him.

And of course he's got a scowl on his face. "Jesus Christ, Ben. What did I tell you?"

"I believe you said no strippers." I smirk. "These ladies aren't strippers. They're topless dancers."

He shakes his head.

"Good call, son," my father says.

He gets up and starts dancing with the half-naked women, taking each one in his arms and twirling her around in a makeshift waltz.

I'm not surprised. My father likes them young. Kathy, one of Skye's friends here in Jamaica, used to date my father. I have no idea how or why that ended, and I'm not asking.

Braden finally lets his lips curve into a smile.

"You seriously thought I was going to let my big brother leave bachelorhood without a true party?" I chuckle.

"They're not hookers, are they?"

"No," I assure him. "Like I said, they're not even strippers. They're not taking the thongs off. Just topless dancers. No lap dances or anything. They're only here to party and have some fun with us."

He narrows his gaze. "Dad seems to be having fun."

Braden and I get along well with our father now, but we didn't always. During most of the formative years of our childhood, he was an alcoholic. Things I don't like to think about much.

But even those aren't the darkest secrets I harbor.

I have demons not even my brother knows about.

But tonight is not the night to think about those.

Tonight is the night to celebrate the end of my brother's life as a bachelor. I've never seen him happier than he is with Skye. My brother isn't the happy sort. He's carried a load on his shoulders for far too long, and Skye has helped him bear the burden.

He's finally forgiven himself—I hope—for his part in our mother's burn scarring and eventual death.

I've forgiven him, too.

Because God knows I've done way worse when I knew way better.

Braden was just a child.

I was not.

But again…

I erase the thought from my mind. I can't have those memories tainting this party for Braden. My father and I both owe him a lot. It was his genius that created the product that made us millions. We gained our billions through outside investments, and Dad and I both had a huge part to do with that. But we wouldn't have been able to do that without Braden first creating the company that put us on the map.

I take another sip of my Wild Turkey. "Get up and dance, brother. This is your sendoff."

He chuckles. "I'll leave that to Dad. And you. Why aren't you dancing?"

Yeah, I should be, actually. I haven't been able to get Tessa Logan out of my mind, but I also need to remember that tonight is about Braden and not me. I should participate in the fun.

I rise, head toward Dad, who's twirling one of the dancers around. I grab the first one I see. She has tanned skin and light brown hair.

"What's your name?" I ask.

"Teresa," she says with a Jamaican accent.

Teresa.

Tessa's given name.

So much for getting her off my mind.

I twirl Teresa, let her go, and turn to another—this one with fair skin and blond hair—and grab her. "What's your name?"

She smiles. "Amy."

Amy.

Good enough.

I take her into my arms.

Normally, holding a nearly naked woman like this would get me hard.

But not tonight.

Not a problem. These women aren't going to sleep with any

of us anyway, no matter how much my father would enjoy having all four of them in his bed. The resort planner made that very clear when I booked them to perform.

"I'm Ben," I say to Amy. "I'm the best man."

"The best man for what?" she whispers in my ear, her voice seductive.

I pull back a bit, gaze into her dark brown eyes. "I thought…"

"You thought what?"

"Nothing."

Then she whispers in my ear again. "You're better-looking than your brother. You have a…sexy darkness about you."

Interesting.

Braden's eyes are blue while mine are dark brown, but most people say he's the one with the darker edge.

Of course, since he met Skye, he smiles more than he has his whole life.

And I…

Demons I thought were dead and buried have since risen.

Nothing I want to bother Braden about.

Not when he's the happiest he's ever been, not to mention his impending nuptials.

"A darkness?" I ask, my voice low.

"Oh yeah. I can always tell." She pouts her lips. "What are you hiding, Ben?"

Nothing I'm going to tell her about.

I crush her to me, move in a slow dance. "I'm not hiding anything. What are *you* hiding, Amy?"

"I don't think I'm hiding it." She gyrates her hips into me. "I'm very attracted to you."

"I see."

"Are you not attracted to me? Not even a little?"

I blink. "Of course. You're a beautiful woman. All four of you are beautiful."

"Your father seems to like Stephanie." She glances toward the taller woman with dark brown skin still dancing with my dad.

"My father likes anything with tits." I smirk. "Correction. Anything *young* with tits."

"And you don't?"

"Sweetheart, I love all women."

She trails her fingers up my arm. "Do you have a girlfriend, Ben?"

"Nope. Not looking for one, either."

She frowns, an adorable little pout on her coral lips. "That's a shame."

"Why? You looking for a boyfriend?"

"No." She cocks her head and smiles. "Just a night of fun."

I grab her then, hold her to me, and hiss in her ear. "I don't think you know what you're asking for."

"Don't I?"

My tastes in the bedroom run dark. Though I recently left the BDSM lifestyle, I'm not the kind of lover who is soft and gentle.

I like to fuck, and I like to fuck hard.

"No, you don't." I remove her arms from around me and step back. "And I'm not looking for a bedwarmer tonight. If you are, maybe you'd better find another dancing partner."

"What if I've found the dancing partner I want?"

"If you can be content to just dance, maybe you have."

"I think I can convince you otherwise," she says.

I smile. "Don't let my friendly personality fool you."

"Oh, I don't." She wiggles her boobs. "I like things dark."

I dance with her for a few more moments, but then I let her

go. "Thank you for being here, Amy. Thank you for helping to make my brother's bachelor party something to remember. But I think I'm done dancing."

I head back to the table where Braden still sits. He's not dancing with any of the women, but he *is* watching them intently.

"Fuck," he says. "They're all so gorgeous. Where did you find them?"

I laugh lightly. "I'll never reveal my secrets, brother."

"Do you like that one you were dancing with?"

"She liked me more."

"You're not attached. You left the club, and you left the lifestyle. What the hell are you looking for, Ben?"

My brother doesn't realize it, but he just asked me a loaded question.

I want what he and Skye have. I long for it. But I'm not looking for anyone because I already know who I want. I need to go slowly for her. And for me, because there are things I have to take care of first.

If Braden knew what I've been hiding all these years, he'd disown me. It's so much worse than him asking our mother to go back into a burning house to get his comic books. Indeed, that was our mother's fault more than Braden's. He was just a kid. She should have known better, but that was Mom. She'd do anything for either one of us.

She was an amazing woman, and she was taken away from us way too soon.

Braden and I often wish she were here—that we could give her everything that our fortune would allow.

But then I wonder, if she *were* here, would we even have made the fortune?

If she'd been there when I was seventeen, would I have gone

down those paths best left untrodden?

That dark time.

Something I thought was resolved, but clearly is not—at least not as of three months ago.

This is a road I must travel alone.

Without Braden. Without my father. And certainly without Tessa Logan.

CHAPTER NINETEEN

Tessa

One of the male dancers heads to Skye, pulls her out of her chair, and leads her away from the table and onto the soft white sand.

Skye, who is normally shy around strangers and loves control, has apparently had one too many of her eponymous cocktails tonight. She gyrates along with the handsome man, sliding her hands over his broad shoulders and sculpted chest.

Several months ago, I might've been the first to take to the floor with one of these handsome men.

But I stay glued to my seat.

Kathy rises next, joining the men dancing.

She's single right now, having recently ended a short relationship with Braden's father. Bobby Black is a good-looking man, but too old for my tastes.

Seems like no man is quite to my tastes these days.

Except Ben Black.

I still can't get over the way he makes me feel—safe and secure.

But it's in my head.

He's the best man, and I'm the maid of honor, and I'm sure Braden told him to look after me.

I mean, why else would he plan a bachelorette party? That's certainly not the best man's job. It's not the job for any man.

Clearly… Because I told him no strippers. And these hot dudes dancing around?

Definitely strippers.

Although none of them have lost their trunks yet. I'm sure it's only a matter of time. The thought should bother me more than it does, which I suppose is a good thing.

Betsy and Daniela join the fun, and soon I'm sitting at the table alone.

I finish my champagne. Between that and the Skye cocktail I had earlier, I'm done drinking.

I won't be dancing, either. I'm happy to be the odd one out.

Until Skye pulls the guy she's dancing with over to me. "Tessa, come dance with us. This is Lucas."

Lucas is the best-looking one of the bunch. Smooth dark skin, muscles that could rival the best Olympic athlete, and a bald head. Normally I don't like it when men shave their heads, but it works on Lucas. He's fucking amazing.

"Why do you do this?" I ask him. "You should be walking a runway somewhere."

"Because I enjoy this, pretty lady." He grabs my hand and pulls me into a standing position.

I instinctively pull my hand away.

"Just try to have some fun, Tess," Skye says.

"Sure." *Deep breath.* I'll do anything for Skye.

I tentatively hold my hand out to Lucas again, and he takes it. He pulls me out onto the sand, and the man can move. I close my eyes, immersing myself in the reggae music. It's no salsa, but I like reggae.

Skye dances with us. She won't leave me alone unless I ask her to, and I certainly won't be doing that.

I dance for several minutes, leaving my hand in Lucas's.

His hand is warm and inviting, and after a few moments, I no longer fear his touch.

But his touch doesn't do anything for me other than that. As good-looking as he is, I'm feeling no arousal at all.

When the music stops and the band takes a break, I pull my hand away from Lucas. "Thank you for the dance," I say, and then I head back to the bar. I need some more water.

The night is warm, and the dancing made me sweat.

I feel a little exhilarated. Movement always does that. It helps when I'm feeling low. I shouldn't be feeling low, though. I had an amazing time at Dunn's River Falls, and then I had a great massage and mani-pedi.

I'm determined not to feel low. This is Skye's weekend, and I will not bring it down.

I head to the bar for my water, and the Jamaican bartender has been replaced with—

A sliver of recognition ignites at the back of my neck…and it feels…odd. Odd and definitely not good.

I've seen this man before.

He has fair skin, a strong nose. And something…

It's apprehension that's curling up my spine. Apprehension… and fear.

I pay no attention to it. I'm used to feeling this way around strange men. A gift from Garrett. The gift that keeps on giving.

But I feel like there's some memory lodged in the back of my head. Some memory that I can't quite grasp.

Something involving this man.

I cock my head, regard him. His hair is sandy brown, his eyes nearly the same color. He's pleasant looking, though not runway material like Lucas. Far from it, actually. Something about him is familiar...

But I can't place him. And I'm done trying.

"Have we met?" he asks.

"No," I say flatly.

I'm not in any mood to discuss the fact that he looks familiar. Not when the memory feels like it could be a bad one.

"What can I get you?"

"Sparkling water."

"Coming right up." He smiles at me.

And it's the smile.

The smile.

It's kind of snakelike, and I know I've seen it before.

Goose bumps erupt on my skin.

I take the drink he hands to me. "Thank you."

And I know this will be the last drink—alcoholic or not—I order tonight as long as that bartender is here. I take a seat back at the table. Betsy, Kathy, and Daniela are still dancing with the strippers.

"Hey, Tess." Skye sits down next to me.

"Are you having a good time?" I ask.

"The best. I honestly didn't expect you to get strippers. Or... scantily clad guys, to be more specific."

"Yeah, well...it's your big sendoff."

I'm not about to tell her I had nothing to do with it, that her future brother-in-law planned the whole thing. After I told him *not* to get strippers.

"They're so hot. I could dance all night. You know I don't

drink a lot, and I've lost count. I love Braden, and he's the only man for me, but…"

"God, you're not considering—"

She widens her eyes. "Oh my God, no. Never in a million years. I would never do anything to jeopardize my relationship with Braden. But I sure can look."

"Doesn't hurt anything to look."

Then I glance back at the bartender, my skin running cold again. "See that bartender?"

Skye glances over. "Yeah."

"You know him?"

She squints, looking closer. "No. He's kind of nondescript. Why? Do *you* know him?"

"There's something familiar about him." I frown. "Something…eerie almost."

"Are you sure you're not just flashing back to Garrett?"

"I don't think so. That guy doesn't look anything like Garrett."

She lays her hand on my arm. "I'm sorry this all happened to you, Tess. I should've been there."

"I'm glad you *weren't* there. You've been through your own stuff. At least I wasn't held at gunpoint."

Skye sighs, looking down. "It took me several sessions with my therapist to come to terms with that. I'm still not sure I'm over it."

When I think about Skye, how she must have seen her life pass before her eyes when a gun was pointed at her, I feel even weaker. Why is it taking me so long to get over something that wasn't nearly as devastating?

I was drugged, yes. Date raped, yes. But it wasn't like Garrett and I had never been together. It wasn't like I wasn't going to have sex with him anyway.

So why is this having such an effect on me?

My therapist says I shouldn't compare trauma, but it's hard not to. She also thinks there may be something in my past—before Garrett—that is contributing to mine, making it worse somehow. Something I've blocked out.

She may be right, but I've been going to therapy now for months, and we're no closer to figuring out what it might have been.

I'm done thinking about it now. How many times do I have to remind myself this weekend is about Skye and not me?

I've never been so fucking self-absorbed before in my life.

"Earth to Tessa…"

I snap out of my thoughts.

"So about that bartender…" Skye continues.

"He just looks familiar to me." A chill runs up my spine. "And frankly, Skye, he makes my skin crawl. There's just something about him that's not right. He doesn't have a Jamaican accent, either, so he's not from here. He sounded American."

"So? Maybe he moved. He lives here now, and he works here."

"But why?"

"Who *wouldn't* want to live here and work here? This place is a paradise."

She's right, of course. I need to stop thinking about it.

But something about him… Something's not right.

And it's driving me slowly senseless.

Maybe I need to give my therapist a call. It's too late now, but I can call her in the morning. She's really good about that. Taking time to talk to me when I'm not in a session. Most of the time she doesn't even charge me for it, which I appreciate.

I take a drink of my sparkling water.

Skye takes another long sip of her drink. "I just want to tell you again, Tess. This has just been wonderful. I can't thank you enough."

"You're welcome, Skye."

Sometime, after the wedding's over, I'll level with Skye. I'll tell her that Ben planned all of it. But I don't want to ruin anything for her right now. And finding out her best friend was too into her own self-absorption to plan her bachelorette party would ruin her evening.

Some best friend I am.

I take another drink.

I've had about enough of this party, but I should stay until the end.

Skye excuses herself and goes back to dance with the men and the other ladies.

And I realize what I've been reduced to.

Tessa Logan used to be the life of the party.

Because as a child, raised by devout Catholic parents, she was never allowed to be the life of the party.

As soon as I got out on my own in college, I let my hair down and enjoyed life to the fullest.

Carpe diem was my mantra.

But now?

I sit on the sidelines, looking in.

Knowing I don't belong.

And wondering if maybe…I never did.

CHAPTER TWENTY

Ben

The bachelor and bachelorette parties have ended, and Braden, Skye, and the others—along with the dancers—have retired for the evening. I'm sitting alone at the bar where the bachelorette party took place, nursing my third Wild Turkey of the night.

Or is it my fourth?

All I know is I'm feeling little pain, and that's the way I want it right now.

But even in this state, whenever I'm alone, the past comes haunting.

Fucking Dirk Conrad.

I wipe the thought from my mind. He's not going to ruin my weekend in Jamaica.

I don't want Dirk Conrad on my mind.

I don't want any of that shit on my mind.

Not this weekend, damn it.

Still…

As much as I've tried to forget, the memories are fresh. You don't forget being spattered with a man's blood. You don't forget the sight of human teeth in a fucking plastic bag.

You don't forget the sight of someone plunging a knife into a man's stomach.

You don't forget the gasping sound of a man taking his last breath.

And you don't forget the smell. The smell of death.

Not of rot. That comes later.

But death itself has a scent—a sickening, nauseating scent.

That's some serious shit that brands itself into you, becomes a part of you.

No matter what you do, how many drinks you have, how many women you fuck—that stays with you forever.

I shoot my Wild Turkey and push the glass toward the bartender. "One more."

The barkeep raises his eyebrows. "How many have you had, Mr. Black?"

"Does it matter? I'm paying premium price for it. Give me another."

I down it and push the glass toward him again.

"Mr. Black?"

"What?"

"There's a woman here—one of the bachelorettes."

"So?"

"I think I know her. A tall drink of water with dark hair, looks Latina?"

Tessa Logan. He's talking about Tessa Logan.

I absently curl my hands into fists. "What about her?"

"She's one hot piece of ass."

I rise then, grab the bartender by the collar. "You don't talk about her that way. You don't talk about any woman that way, but especially not her."

His eye twitches. "What do you think you're going to do about it?"

"I'll fucking bury you."

"We may not be in the U.S., but we still have laws here in Jamaica." He keeps his voice steady, despite the fact that I'm still holding his collar.

"Do I look like I give a damn about laws?"

"I know you don't." He smiles—fucking *smiles*. "In fact, Mr. Black, I know a lot of things."

Jesus fuck. Who is this guy?

"Enlighten me." I loosen my fist from his collar and let him go. "What do you think you know?"

"I know you're not the philanthropist you claim to be."

I scoff. "We give our fair share to charity, but I never claimed to be a philanthropist."

"I know you and your brother give to that food bank in Boston."

"That's because our mother used to take us there. We weren't always rich."

"Oh, I know that, too." He grabs a towel and wipes down the bar. "In fact...I know how you got your start."

"You don't know shit."

"You sure?"

Problem is that I'm *not* sure. Braden confided in me years ago about where the money came from to fund his first project. It came from Apple's father, Brock Ames. It was a payoff. But that's all over now. Braden took care of it, and every bit has been paid back.

But there was another infusion of quick cash that didn't come from Brock Ames.

It came from me.

"Does the name Conrad have any meaning to you?" the bartender asks.

Fuck.

I've had a lot to drink, but I've got to keep my cool. Keep my head.

"Can't say it rings a bell."

"I'm thinking it might." He gazes at my face, my chest, back to my face. "Though you might be a little drunk."

I poke him in the chest. "You get the fuck out of this resort."

"I don't work for you, Mr. Black. I work for the resort."

"Let's get one thing straight. You and I both know who's paying your salary this weekend. So get the fuck out of here."

"You sure that's what you want?"

I meet his gaze, glaring at him as I've never glared at anyone before.

Except that man, all those years ago.

I truly thought it was over until Dirk came to me three months ago.

But I knew then, and I know now.

It's far from over.

"Hey," the barkeep says, "I'd be willing to let bygones be bygones. I'll take whatever I know to the grave. *If* you put in a good word for me with the woman. The gorgeous one in black. I'm pretty sure I know her from somewhere."

"Fuck off." I grab my phone, make a call.

He'll be gone by morning.

CHAPTER TWENTY-ONE

Tessa

The moonlight glitters on the vast ocean, and I sink my toes into the sand, walking along the shore.

The party is over, and all the bridesmaids have retired to their rooms. Skye and Braden are no doubt having hot monkey sex in their suite.

But I'm not ready to go to bed yet.

I can't get that bartender out of my head.

He looks so damned familiar, and the feeling I get when I see him?

It's not a good one.

I won't be able to sleep, so there's no use going to my room.

My therapist uses hypnosis sometimes to relax me, and when she asked me what one of my favorite places is, I always told her the beach at moonlight.

So here I am, on the moonlit beach, and I'm hoping it will ease my anxiety.

The good news is I haven't had a panic attack since that night in the bar with Ben.

After I got drugged and ended up in the hospital, I was having them daily. So far, this is the longest I've gone without one, and even though that bartender has me on edge, the serenity of the beach and the waves swishing to the shore calm me.

I don't feel a panic attack coming on, and for that I'm grateful.

"Tessa?"

I turn at the voice I recognize.

Ben stands there, facing the ocean. In the moonlight, his dark hair glints with subtle blue highlights, and the stars cast sparkles over him.

I never would've believed he could be better looking, but the moonlight brings something more out in Ben Black.

Something beautiful...and dark.

Because darkness can be beautiful. I've always loved the darkness. Especially the moonlight on the beach.

It fills me with serenity.

Serenity I haven't felt in so long.

A serenity I thought was lost to me forever.

I almost forget that I'm pissed at him. "Thanks a lot," I say with sarcasm.

"For what?"

"I told you no strippers, Ben. And who should come prancing onto the beach? Four male dancers."

He drops his jaw, and his eyes widen. Is he truly shocked?

"What?"

"Did I stutter?"

"Tessa...no. I told the event planner to get topless dancers for the bachelor party. Only the *bachelor* party."

"She clearly didn't understand, then."

"Oh, God." He rakes his fingers through his thick hair. "I'm sorry. Are you okay?"

I nod. "You really didn't have anything to do with it?"

"I swear." He crosses his heart. "I'll take care of this. Heads will roll."

I look into his dark eyes. There's truth there. I believe him. "It's all right. The men were very respectful, and the ladies loved it."

"If you're sure."

"I'm sure."

He moves closer to me. The scent of alcohol is thick on him, but he doesn't act inebriated. "I'm surprised to see you out here alone."

"I understand how you might feel that way, but I feel safe here, Ben. Something about the ocean."

"It *is* relaxing," he says, "but I don't want you walking out here alone."

"Why? This is a private resort."

He looks at me for a moment, as if he wants to say something but then thinks better of it. "No reason. Just no woman should be walking alone after dark. You know as well as I do that women can be vulnerable."

I tense up.

Ben rakes his fingers through his hair. "Fuck... I didn't mean..."

"No, you meant exactly what you said." I cross my arms. "And you're right. I suppose I of all people should know that."

"Please... Don't let that curb your relaxation." He closes the distance between us, brushes a strand of hair out of my face. "You had a look in your eyes a moment ago, Tessa. It's close to the look you had at the top of the Falls today, but it was even more tranquil. A look I've never seen on you before."

"You haven't known me for that long."

"No." He frowns. "It is odd that we didn't meet until we started planning this trip. With Skye and Braden being together and all."

"I suppose that's partially my fault," I say. "I wasn't exactly the best friend to Skye when her relationship with Braden was blossoming."

"You weren't?"

"I felt kind of left out, to be honest. Unfortunately…that led me to things that…"

I say no more.

He knows anyway.

"I know my brother would feel absolutely awful if he thought he had anything to do with what happened to you. That he took Skye away from you."

I shake my head. "He didn't. It was all me. I was being silly and jealous and bratty. I see that now. I have no excuse for it. I could tell you that Skye and I have been close since freshman year of college, and that's the truth. I could tell you that we talked on the daily, and I was her fashion consultant—the few times I could actually get her to go out. That's all true, and it's true that I missed those things once she and Braden got serious. But she was still my bestie. There was no reason for me to react the way that I did."

He doesn't say anything for a moment. I'm sure he's weighing what to say so as to not offend me. Because I'm absolutely right. I was a brat, and we both know it. It was my behavior that led me to where I am today.

It wasn't my fault. I understand that. I had no idea that Garrett was going to be such an asshole. An asshole who would drug a woman.

The truly sad thing is that he didn't even need to drug me. I was infatuated with him—with his dark good looks, his love of dancing, his intelligence.

He didn't need to drug me to have sex with him.

But as I looked back at it in therapy, I came to understand that he was also conniving. He broke up with me, and I was heartbroken. Then he came back to me, and I was elated. Then he drugged me, and God knows what he did to me after that.

He didn't love me. He manipulated me, and who knows how many other women he violated in the same way?

He'll be sorry he chose me because I'll be the one to put him behind bars. He may be out on bail now, but there will be a trial, and he's guilty as sin.

I hate that he's out on bail right now, but I have a restraining order against him. He can't come near me.

Finally, Ben opens his mouth to speak. "No woman deserves what happened to you. It doesn't matter what you did or what you think you did. None of that matters, Tessa. This was *not* your fault."

"I know that." Doesn't change the fact that if I hadn't been envious of Skye's newfound love I probably wouldn't have put myself in the position to be harmed.

"Do you, though?"

"I do." I scratch an itch that springs up on the side of my head. "Objectively, anyway. Believe me, I've been over and over it with my therapist."

He smiles. "Good. I'm glad you're getting the help you need. Is there anything I can do?"

I look at him, then.

And for the second time, I feel the urge to touch him.

I reach forward, feather my fingers over his stubbled cheek.

It feels scratchy, but also…good. It feels good to touch another person. Another man.

He doesn't move. Doesn't try to touch me. He just lets me do what I want to do.

"You're such a good-looking man," I say.

"Thank you. You're a beautiful woman." He lowers his voice. "You're the most beautiful woman here."

My cheeks warm in the moonlight. It's nothing I haven't heard before.

I never minded it before, but these days it seems like a curse.

When a man looks at me now, all I feel is the glare of his eyes burning holes into my flesh.

But Ben is looking at me…and for the first time in a long time, I don't feel that.

I don't feel like he's burning two holes into me.

No. To the contrary, I *want* him to look at me. I want him to see me. Because I know he sees more than just my beauty.

He sees what I've been through, the haunting within me.

And though he may not understand, he's trying to. In his way, he's trying to help. He tried to help by taking the burden of the bachelorette party off of me.

He's a good man, and I'm glad he sees beyond my looks, but I'm more than what I've been through, and I want him to see *that* part of me too.

I drop my hand back to my side.

"You can touch me, Tessa," Ben says. "I don't mind."

I say nothing.

"Is there anything else I can do for you tonight? See you to your room?"

I resist the urge to lash out at him, to tell him there's more to me than some fragile woman who went through a tragic ordeal and nearly died.

"I'm not done walking yet."

"Then I'll walk with you. Because as I said, I don't want you out here alone."

CHAPTER TWENTY-TWO

Ben

Hell no, she won't be alone. Not after that asshole bartender threatened me. Tried to blackmail me. Does he have a clue what kind of security I have? He'll pay for mentioning Dirk Conrad and for trying to get Tessa handed to him on a platter.

Right about now, he's being escorted off the premises.

Fucking Dirk Conrad.

It's my own damned fault for getting involved with the likes of him in the beginning.

I think about what Tessa just said to me—about how she was feeling lonely and left out when Skye and Braden got serious.

We have that in common.

I got involved with Dirk in a stupid gang for similar reasons.

I was angry. Angry that I couldn't have any fun in high school. That I was expected to go to school, get perfect grades, and then go work with Braden and my dad. I felt left out of the fun of my senior year.

I wipe the thought away again.

Tessa needs my attention now. I won't let her walk alone.

But God…I itch to touch her. Hold her hand again like I did at Dunn's River Falls, but this time not to protect her.

Just to touch her.

I haven't been this attracted to a woman in a long time.

Braden would probably tell me I have a savior complex. That's not it.

I've never had a savior complex. Never in my life. That's Braden, not me. He felt so much guilt about what happened to our mother that now he wants to save everyone.

That's probably why Skye appealed to him so much. She didn't want to be saved. She was who she was, and no one was going to change her.

Including my brother.

To see them together is like seeing two interlocking pieces of a puzzle. He with his need and drive for control, and she with the same thing, except to a different extent.

"I'm perfectly safe here." Tessa's voice penetrates my thoughts.

I'm tempted to tell her that she's not. But I can't because that would just worry her.

"I'm sure you are," I say, "but I enjoy your company, so please let me walk with you."

"All right."

She begins walking then, her toes sinking into the wet sand.

They're polished now, a light pink. So are her fingernails.

Her hand felt so perfect in mine today. I want to take her hand so badly, but any move has to be hers.

So I'm surprised as hell when she turns to me and scrapes her fingers over my jawline once more.

If I could change that day fifteen years ago, I would.

But I can't. Tessa deserves so much better than I can offer. I can't bring her into my own house of horrors when she can barely face her own.

I close my eyes, ease my thoughts. Focus on this night. Nothing else.

Right now, I want to enjoy the soft touch of Tessa's fingers.

And think about how the rest of her would feel, naked, pressed against me.

I absently reach forward and glide my finger over her lower lip.

CHAPTER TWENTY-THREE

Tessa

"Your lips are so beautiful, Tessa…" Ben thumbs my lower lip, sending tingles down my spine.

Kiss me.

The words hover in my mind.

They make it from my brain, to my tongue, almost to my lips…

But I can't say them.

I can't bring them forth.

My body is so hot. In a different way than ever before. Does this mean these emotions I'm feeling for Ben are different? Or is it simply that *I'm* different from all of my experiences?

I don't know. I may never know. Does it even matter?

Kiss me.

Kiss me.

Kiss me.

Again only in my mind.

"So fucking beautiful," he says again. "I'd give my entire fortune to kiss your lips right now. If that were the cost, I'd gladly pay it."

I'm not sure what to say to that, so I say nothing. My heart thumps wildly, though. The thought doesn't frighten me. No.

It arouses me.

I want his kiss.

I want it so badly.

"But I'm not going to kiss you, Tessa. Not yet." He caresses the side of my face with his other hand. "When I kiss you, it's going to be a spectacular kiss. I'm talking rockets and fireworks. A fucking explosion, Tessa. The earth will move when we kiss for the first time."

I can't help the soft sigh that escapes my throat.

"Part of you wants it as much as I do. I know you do."

All I can do is nod, my lips trembling.

"I see it in your eyes, in those big, beautiful brown eyes that reflect something truly remarkable back at me."

"What's that?" I ask, willing my voice not to shake.

"You have a depth about you," he says. "A depth so great that I'm not sure I've seen anything like it."

Depth? I've never thought of myself as deep. I always thought I was kind of shallow. I rejected my parents' and grandmother's religion for boys and parties. I was into my looks, into my body. Obsessing over those ten pounds I thought I had to lose. Wanting fun, to live life day by day.

Carpe diem was my mantra.

Let your hair down was another.

"You say more things with your eyes," he continues, "than most people say in words. I see the pain reflected there. But I also see the pleasure. I see the good life that you've led. I see the memories. The memories of what life was before. They're still in there, Tessa. We both know that. We both know you can be whatever kind of woman you want to be. You're healing. Healing takes time. I should know."

He should know?

What has he healed from?

But the thought flees as he continues.

"I will never ever rush you, no matter how much I want you. And I do want you, Tessa."

His voice seems to drop an octave with those last words.

I do want you, Tessa.

"I never thought I could fall in love. It seems like every woman I've ever been interested in was focused solely on my money. But you're not like that, are you?"

I shake my head, still trembling.

Still trembling at his thumb on my lip.

"I could fall in love with you so easily. With that beautiful, haunted soul that I see behind those deep brown eyes."

I swallow audibly.

Kiss me.

The words again.

And this time—

"Kiss me," I say softly. "Please. Kiss me, Ben."

He leans into me, and I close my eyes—

But his lips land on my cheek. He pulls back as I open my eyes.

I raise my eyebrows at him.

"It's not the right time." He looks skyward, at the sparkling stars. "I wish it were. I want to feel those lips against my own more than I want to see the next sunrise. But it's not the right time, and you and I both know that."

CHAPTER TWENTY-FOUR

Ben

I take her hands.

They feel so perfect in mine.

I had to gather all of my willpower not to kiss her when she asked me to.

The words that came from my mouth surprised even me.

So much else going on...so why am I thinking about kissing Tessa Logan?

But when I look into her eyes, I know why.

Because she's beautiful.

And broken.

And for the first time in my life, I want to put someone's needs before my own.

The thought frightens me but also invigorates me.

She could be the one.

I'll have to move slowly, and I'm not used to moving slowly.

But slowly is the way I'll move now, because it's what she needs, and I've got other things that need to be dealt with in my own life.

The past coming back to haunt me.

The past that I thought was gone forever.

Dirk Conrad…

And whoever that asshole bartender is…

I need to make sure he never goes near Tessa.

"Tessa?" I say.

"Yes." She looks down at the sand. "I'm so sorry."

"For what?"

"For begging you to kiss me. That's not who I am, Ben."

I smile. "I wasn't offended."

"I didn't think you were. It's just…" She bites her plump lower lip. "You're right. It's not the right time."

"Tessa, I want to kiss you more than I want my next breath of air. I don't think that's any secret at this point."

She looks down again, and even though I can't see the blush on her cheeks in the darkness, I know it's there.

"We've got another big day tomorrow," I say. "Please let me see you back to your suite."

She nods then, her hands still in mine. We turn around, walk along the shoreline until we get to the point where she and I both left our shoes.

The beach is dark now except for the resort's security lighting.

The bar is empty, and that bartender—I don't even know his name—should be off the island of Jamaica by now.

At the very least, off this private resort.

Tessa stares toward the bar. "There was this bartender tonight…"

"There were a lot of bartenders tonight," I say.

"But there was one…" She rubs her upper arms as if to ease a chill. "He seemed familiar to me… Not in a good way."

I turn to her, gently hold her by both of her upper arms.

Surprisingly, she doesn't pull away.

"Tell me something, Tessa. Did you think you knew him?"

"I'm not sure. I don't have any recollection of him, but he seemed familiar."

"Was it the one with the light brown hair? Same color as his eyes? Large nose?"

She widens her eyes. "How did you know?"

"Just a hunch."

She meets my gaze, and her eyes look different. Not haunted as they usually are. No. This time, I see fear but also indignation.

"Do you know who he is?" she asks.

"I don't, but he won't be bothering you again."

She wrinkles her forehead. "It's not that he was bothering me."

"It's all right. I've had him fired."

She gasps. "Ben, why?"

"I had my reasons."

She breaks from my hold and turns away. "Not because of me, I hope. I would hate to be responsible for someone losing his job."

"No, Tessa. It had nothing to do with you. I didn't even know you knew the man until just now."

She calms down. "Okay. In all honesty, I'm glad he's gone."

"But you have no recall?"

She trembles slightly. "No. But I just had a feeling I knew him at one time, and it wasn't anything good."

Something about that bartender. Some connection to Tessa and to Dirk Conrad.

I'm not liking any of this.

I take her hand once more, and after we've both brushed the sand off our ankles and feet and put our shoes on, I lead her back into the resort hotel and see her to her room, which is right across the hall from mine.

Her lips are trembling slightly, and they're so full and so pink.

How I ache to kiss them.

But I hold myself in check.

I believe, at this point, she would accept my kiss.

But the kind of kiss I want to give her? She's not ready for that yet.

Instead, I kiss her cheek again, loving the texture of her soft skin against my own lips.

Then I take her key card from her, hover it over the reader on the door, open it, and watch as she walks in.

She turns back toward me. "Good night, Ben."

"Good night, Tessa."

She shuts the door, and I hear her click the deadbolt.

Then I enter my own room.

I fire up my computer, but the words are blurring.

Yeah, I had a lot of Wild Turkey.

I'll deal with all this bullshit another time.

I shut the laptop and go to bed, with visions of Tessa Logan's lips in my head.

CHAPTER TWENTY-FIVE

Tessa

I wake in the morning, and for the first time in a long time, I actually feel like getting up.

What I really want is a long talk with Skye, but I can't bother her. This is her weekend to spend with her fiancé.

I text Betsy instead.

Tessa: *You up?*

No reply. Just when I'm ready to give up, I see the three dots move.

Betsy: *Not yet. You need something?*

Tessa: *I was looking for a breakfast companion.*

Betsy: *Sure. Let's do it. I should shower first.*

Tessa: *I didn't shower. Just throw on a bathing suit and a coverall, put your hair in a bun. Meet me out on the beach.*

Betsy: *Breakfast on the beach? That actually sounds fab.*

Tessa: *Awesome.*

I throw my hair into a messy ponytail, put on a red bikini, and wrap a red-and-black sarong around me like a strapless dress.

When I walk out of my hotel room, I stare at the door in front of me.

Ben is behind that door.

Ben, who I asked to kiss me last night.

Ben, who I dreamed of.

Well…I'm not sure it was a dream. I know he was on my mind as I drifted off to sleep, and I didn't have a nightmare last night.

That's got to be a good thing.

I amble down the hallway and then down the one flight of stairs to the first level.

The kitchen is sounding with clatters, but I'm going to have my breakfast on the beach.

Ben arranged for servers to be available from six in the morning until midnight.

I find a cabana, grab two lounge chairs, pull them under the cabana, but then I change my mind and drag them back out under the sunshine.

Before Betsy arrives, a handsome server wearing no shirt approaches me. "Good morning, miss. What can I get you?"

"A cup of black coffee, please. And a plate of fresh fruit with two strips of bacon."

"Coming right up."

I'm glad I actually feel like eating. Fruit sounds good. Some succulent juicy fruit and a cup of strong coffee.

Betsy arrives, taking the lounge chair opposite me. "How are you doing, Tessa?"

I sit up. "I'm doing okay, Bets. But I need you to do something for me."

"Of course anything."

"Stop asking me how I'm doing. I need to stop ruminating."

Betsy smiles. "It's wonderful to hear you say that."

"Yeah. I feel like I've spent my life being self-absorbed. First when I left my parents' house. I was solely focused on me, all the things that had been denied me in their religious home. I was always focused on what *I* wanted to do. And now, after Garrett, I find I'm still focused on me. Only for a completely different reason."

"You have a pretty good reason this time, Tessa."

"But that's just it. It's *not* a good reason. I'm alive." I stretch out on the lounger and feel the sun's rays on my skin. "I'm on a beautiful Jamaican beach. My best friend in the world is marrying the man of her dreams. So I've been through something. I'm getting help, and today, for the first time in a while, I actually felt like getting out of bed, Betsy."

"That's wonderful," she says. "We should tell Skye."

"Absolutely not. If Skye shows up, I will tell her. But I refuse to make this weekend about me."

"It's funny that you say you're so self-absorbed, Tessa," Betsy says. "I've never thought about you that way."

"You haven't known me that long."

"It's not self-absorbed to want to live in the moment."

"Maybe not, but I wasn't content to just let Skye be happy with Braden. I made it all about me. About how I was feeling about the whole thing. And it led me to a place I never want to go again."

The server returns with my fruit plate and coffee.

"Good morning, miss," he says to Betsy. "What can I get for you this morning?"

Betsy eyes my plate of fruit. "I think exactly what you got her. But put a little cream in my coffee, please."

"Absolutely." His dark eyes twinkle at Betsy.

Betsy blushes as he walks away.

"So you think he's hot?" I say.

"Don't you?"

"I haven't seen a man on this resort who isn't hot yet."

Except for that bartender last night. He gave me the creeps.

The server returns with Betsy's food and keeps eyeing her. "I have a break in a few minutes," he says. "Would you like to take a stroll on the beach?"

Betsy bites her lower lip and looks at me.

I wave my hand. "Please, Betsy, go if you want to. I'm fine."

"You sure?"

"Absolutely."

"If you're sure you don't mind." She hops out of her lounge chair and smiles at the server. "How long is your break?"

"Only fifteen minutes. But it's a chance for us to talk a little." He holds out his hand. "My name is Manfred."

"Betsy," Betsy says with a smile. "Be back in a bit, Tess."

Betsy kicks off her flip-flops and takes the arm that Manfred offers her. And boy, is Manfred good-looking.

I have to smile to myself.

I'm actually looking at men as a pleasure for my eyes rather than something that can harm me.

Again I think about Ben and the fact that he wanted to kiss me.

As much as I wanted that kiss in that moment, I agree. It probably wasn't the right time.

Ben and I hardly know each other.

Which doesn't explain why my heart is beating like a snare drum when he walks toward me.

He looks luscious. His hair is damp, so he clearly just got out of the shower. He's wearing a flashy Hawaiian print shirt in green, gold, and blue, plus board shorts that match the blue on the shirt. His skin is lighter than mine, but he's got a good tan going and he looks fabulous.

He helps himself to Betsy's vacant chair, but he doesn't lounge. He sets his feet on the ground, facing me.

"You are just the person I was looking for," he says.

I cock my head and hold back a smile. "I am?"

"Absolutely. I have something you're going to love."

"I was having breakfast with Betsy." I glance down to the beach where she and Manfred are walking hand in hand. "She'll be back any minute. She went on a short walk with one of the servers."

"Yes, I see them over there. She looks a little smitten with him."

"Smitten?" I can't help a chuckle.

"Taken?" He laughs. "Horny?"

I shake my head. "He only has fifteen minutes for his break, so Betsy will be back soon."

"All right. We'll wait until Betsy gets back, and then you'll come with me."

"What did you have in mind?" I ask.

I'm almost hoping he'll say he wants to kiss me.

But he says something entirely unexpected.

"A cold plunge."

I pause, blink a few times. "What? You mean like in the ocean?"

He laughs. "No. The ocean water is certainly colder than the air, but I'm talking about a real cold plunge. In ice water. Water that's been chilled to fifty-five degrees."

I shrug. "Fifty-five isn't bad. It's like an early fall day in Boston. I can go out in jeans and a hoodie."

"But you're forgetting that water is colder than air."

"How does that make any kind of sense?"

"I could explain it to you, if I actually knew." He laughs again.

"Well, thanks for the offer, but no way am I getting into a tub full of fifty-five-degree water."

"Even after the hike up the Falls yesterday? Remember how invigorating it was?"

"Uh…it wasn't fifty-five degrees."

He gently takes my hand. "I think you'll like it, Tessa."

"I'll *like* freezing my ass off?" My teeth chatter at the thought even as the warmth of Ben's fingers makes me feel a jolt of pleasure. "I don't think so."

"Tessa"—his voice gets serious—"trust me on this."

I roll my eyes. "Yeah, right."

"I'm totally serious. Braden and I had one yesterday morning. We do it regularly."

"Does Skye do it with him?"

"Not that I know of, but Braden and I have been doing it for years. It's stimulating. But also, whether you can believe it or not, it's really relaxing."

"How in the hell is freezing your butt off relaxing?"

"First of all, you don't stay in that long," he says.

"How long do you stay in?"

"My record, as of yesterday morning, is eleven minutes."

I drop my jaw. "Are you kidding me? Eleven minutes submerged in cold water? You're nuts."

"Not all the way submerged, just up to your neck. Obviously you keep your head out so you can breathe."

I raise my hands in mock relief. "Oh, you're not going to make me put on an oxygen mask? Thank God."

"Trust me." He meets my gaze. "You *will* like this."

I sit up in my lounge chair and face him. "Look. I enjoyed the Falls. You were right about that, but somehow I don't think you're right on this one."

"You may not like it while you're doing it, but once you're done? I guarantee you'll love it."

"Not for eleven minutes."

"Of course not. For your first time, you'll only do three minutes."

"I'm not sure I can even take three minutes. How about three seconds?"

He smiles at me, and his hand twitches a bit. Does he want to touch me again? I honestly want him to. I can still feel his lips on my cheek from last night.

"I'm afraid you're on your own," I say. "Like I said, Betsy and I are having breakfast."

He eyes my empty plate where my fruit was. Then he stands and looks into my coffee cup, also finding it empty. "Looks like you're done with breakfast."

I gesture to Betsy's full plate and cup of coffee. "She's not."

"Her coffee is going to be cold by the time she gets back."

"Maybe." I wave to Betsy and Manfred. "But here they come."

"Thanks for the walk, Manfred," Betsy says.

Ben stands and offers Betsy her lounger back.

"Hi, Ben," she says.

"Betsy. Manfred."

"Good morning, Mr. Black. Can I get you anything?"

"Absolutely. A cup of your strongest black coffee, some scrambled eggs, bacon, and ackee and salt fish."

"Coming right up."

"Bring it in about twenty minutes," he says. "Ms. Logan and I will be back by then."

Betsy takes her plate of fruit and brings a slice of watermelon to her mouth. "Are you two going somewhere?"

"We are," Ben says. "We're going to go take a cold plunge."

CHAPTER TWENTY-SIX

Ben

"You're just the kind of guy we need, Black," Dirk says.

"You think, huh?"

"You've got brains *and* brawn. We need some brains."

"What the fuck for?"

"We're going to rob the convenience store," he says, "and you're going to help us."

I take another drag off my cigarette. "Yeah? Good luck with that."

"We don't need luck. Didn't I just say you were going to help us?"

I throw my butt down on the asphalt, stamp it out with the bottom of my steel-toed boot. "That's where you're wrong."

Dirk takes a step toward me. "You're in now. Because you know."

"Bullshit."

"I could kick your ass," Dirk says.

"You and what army?"

I've got five inches on him in height, and I'm just as muscled as he is. Of course, he's got Carlos and Jerry.

"Hey, man, I'm just thinking of you. I see that shack you live in with your father and brother. Everybody knows how hard you work. Wouldn't you like a little something for nothing for once in your life?"

My father's not the greatest father in the world, but he's no thief. He'd hate me even talking about something like this.

But damn…

It would sure be nice to have some extra money once in a while.

Stealing is wrong. I sure as hell know that.

So why the fuck am I actually considering this?

These three are losers. The kind who cut school half the time and smoke weed in the bathrooms the other half.

"So are you in, Black?" Jerry asks.

"No."

"You sure about that?" From Dirk.

It's not a threat. I could kick Dirk into next week, and we both know it. It's a simple question, one he expects me to contemplate.

So I do.

I clear my throat. "What are the details?"

"One a.m. tomorrow night. The place is open twenty-four-seven, but there's very little traffic that late on a weeknight. The guys and I have been staking the place. Between one and two is the best time."

"That doesn't make any sense. I would think between two and four would be better."

"Yeah, you'd think, but the truckers tend to come through around then."

I nod. I have no reason not to believe Dirk. He's been staking the place, and I haven't.

What I'm more concerned about is how the hell I'm supposed to be up at one in the morning. I'm so fucking tired after a day at school and then working that when I get home, I hit the sheets and don't think about a damned thing until my alarm rings at six.

And I start the whole process over again.

Get up, grab a bite, hit school, do homework during lunch, get home, grab a bite, hit the construction site, get home, grab a bite, hit the hay.

That's my damned life.

Granted, I'm sick to death of it, but these guys aren't thinking big enough. How much cash is there in a damned convenience store? A convenience store that probably has a security system in place because it's open twenty-four-fucking-seven?

These guys were never known for their smarts.

After all, they said they needed my brains.

"What if we change the plan a little?" I say.

"How so?" Dirk asks.

"How much money do you think they keep in the store?"

"About a grand," Carlos says. "My cousin works there during the day. He says they keep a thousand in the safe in addition to what's in the cash register at any given time."

"Yeah, a thousand dollars is more than any of us have ever seen," I agree, "but that's only two fifty each after we divide it. Is it really worth it? I mean, what is two fifty going to buy us? A week of groceries?"

"Or some good weed," Jerry says.

"Fuck no. If I help with this, not one of you is going to spend this money on drugs."

"I don't see how it's any business of yours of what we spend it on, Black," Dirk says.

Technically, he's right.

"If you want my help—and I've got a plan way better than yours—no drugs. Got it?"

"What are you thinking?" Carlos asks.

"I'm thinking there are better places to hit than a damned store that never closes. We can hit a place that's empty in the middle of the night. A place that has a hell of a lot more cash stashed away. I'm talking fifty grand at least, with absolutely *no* chance of getting caught."

· · ·

PRESENT DAY...

already took my plunge early this morning with Braden, but I'll do another so Tessa can see that it doesn't kill me.

We walk into the resort to the workout room, where Spencer is waiting for us.

"Mr. Black," he says. "There you are."

"Hello, Spencer. This is Tessa Logan."

Tessa holds out her hand.

Spencer shakes it. "Very nice to meet you." He rakes his gaze over her body, of course.

Everyone does. Men *and* women. It's beginning to irk me, even though I'm guilty of it myself.

"Ms. Logan and I would like to take a cold plunge."

"Yes. I've got everything ready as you instructed," Spencer says.

I take Tessa's hand, and together we follow Spencer through the gym, out onto the deck adjacent to the workout area.

"Fifty-five degrees?" Spencer asks.

"It's the only way I fly," I say.

Tessa is chewing on her lower lip. "I don't know, Ben."

"Try it for three minutes. You'll be amazed at how much better it gets after just the first minute. Spencer will tell you when the first minute is up, right, Spencer?"

"Absolutely, whatever you want."

"And I'm going to go first."

"Didn't you say you and Braden already did one?" she asks.

"Yeah, we did. We both went eleven minutes today. Braden, of course, was determined to not let me beat him in anything." I resist an eye roll. "But I don't expect you to do anything without watching me do it first, so I'll do five minutes this time, and you'll see how easy it is for me, and you'll have no problem with three minutes."

Tessa draws in a breath, and then, to my surprise, she removes the sarong tied around her chest, revealing an amazing bright-red bikini.

I suck in a breath.

I've seen her in a bikini before, but this one is scant. Her tits are nearly falling out of the top. And the bottom? It's a thong.

Oh my God.

Not something I expected Tessa to wear.

I unbutton my shirt and toss it on the back of a chair, right next to Tessa's sarong.

Spencer pulls the thermometer out of the tub and glances at it. "Good news for you, Ms. Logan. It's actually at fifty-seven."

She scoffs. "Like I'm going to be able to tell that it's two degrees warmer."

"You'd be surprised," Spencer says. "But since you've never done it before, no, you probably won't be able to notice."

"But I will," I say. "It'll be slightly easier for me."

Spencer holds up his stopwatch. "I've got the timer ready,

Mr. Black. Five minutes, you said?"

"Yeah, five minutes." Then I look at Tessa. "Watch me. I'll keep my eyes closed because I need to concentrate. All I need to do is breathe. Breathe and stay warm."

"You're not going to stay warm."

"No I'm not, but just watch me."

I close my eyes, draw in a deep breath, then shake my arms and legs to get ready.

Then I step into the tub, suck in a deep breath, and submerge myself up to my neck so that my chin is just touching the water.

Oh, coldness.

Sweet, sweet coldness.

I close my eyes and breathe in through my mouth and out through my nose and then in through my nose and out through my mouth.

Each time is different, and I do what feels right.

And though I know Tessa is there watching me, she flows from my mind, and all I do is concentrate on my breathing.

Five minutes is nothing, and Spencer's timer goes off before I know it.

I pop out of the cold tub, and Spencer hands me a heated towel.

Tessa shakes her head. "I don't know…"

"I'm certainly not going to force you," I say, "but trust me when I tell you that this will help you."

"Can you explain how?"

"I could, but I'd rather you try it first because I think you'll see the benefits once you do it. Three minutes isn't long, Tessa."

"How about one minute?"

"One minute doesn't really give you any benefit," Spencer offers, "because it takes one minute to get used to the cold."

"But you don't really get used to the cold," she says.

"No, not in the sense that you mean. You're not going to all of a sudden feel warm." I smile. "But you'll see what he means. And that minute will go by quicker than you think. If you want, I can have Spencer tell you when each minute is over."

She's chewing on her lower lip. "Maybe…" She steps toward the tub. She gazes at it, clearly contemplating.

"Honestly, ma'am, the more you think about it, the more difficult it is," Spencer says.

She darts him a look. "Fine. I'm done thinking."

She steps in the tub, and a shiver racks her body.

"Do it, Tessa. Do it. You can do this."

She breathes in deeply and then submerges herself up to her chin.

CHAPTER TWENTY-SEVEN

Tessa

I gasp for breath as the ice water covers my body.

"Easy," Ben says. "Regulate everything, Tessa. You can do it."

For some reason, it's important to me to show him that I can do this. Still, I'm not quite sure why he wants me to. But I trust him. I trust him enough to know that he thinks this will be good for me.

I gasp in another breath.

Then I hold it, force myself to hold it and breathe out slowly.

He said it was all in the breathing. I close my eyes, concentrate on my breathing.

My fingers feel...strange. The chill increases when I wiggle them, so I hold them still.

I'm not aware of anything else in my body, other than the fact that I'm freezing. So I breathe.

In, out, in, out.

Keeping my eyes closed, my breath steady.

Surely a minute has passed.

But Spencer said he would let me know when a minute had—

"That's one minute, ma'am. You're doing great."

One minute down, two to go.

And then no more thoughts.

I breathe, I breathe, I breathe...

I resist the urge to wiggle my fingers and toes, knowing now that it will increase the chill.

And I breathe, I breathe, I breathe...

In, out, in, out, eyes closed, nothing before me.

Nothing in my mind except breathing...

Breathing...

Breathing...

All thoughts, both good and bad, wiped clean away until my brain is a stark chasm of nothingness.

"And that's three minutes," Spencer says.

My eyes pop open, and my body pops up out of the water.

Spencer places a warm towel around my shoulders, and I hold it to me.

Warmth.

It's grand. But it will take more than a warm towel to ease the chill.

Still...

I feel...

Invigorated, almost, but not the way the Falls invigorated me.

No, this is different. This was almost...

Relaxing.

Ben is still wrapped in his towel and sitting on an outdoor sofa. He pats the seat next to him.

I sit.

Oddly, my teeth aren't chattering. Probably because it's so warm here in Jamaica.

"What did you think?" Ben asks.

I shake my head at him.

I'm not ready to talk yet.

I'm not ready to talk because I don't know how to describe what I just went through.

My mind... It was blank. All I thought about was breathing. Easing the chill.

I wait a few more moments until the warmth has eased the biting freeze.

"I think...I liked it."

A smile spreads across his gorgeous face. "Didn't I tell you?"

"It was... My mind was a complete blank, Ben." A tear rolls down my cheek as a swarm of emotion surges through me. "And my God... I don't think my mind has been a complete blank for a long time."

He smiles and wipes the tear away with his finger. "That's why I suggested it. It's forced meditation, Tessa. Your friends and your therapist can tell you all day not to think about something, and it's been my experience that only makes you think about it *more.*"

I can't help a slight chuckle as I sniffle. "That is *exactly* how it is."

"But when you're in a cold plunge, all you're thinking about is warmth. In order to get through it, you have to regulate your breathing, close your eyes, and concentrate. When you're trying to get warm, forcing yourself to regulate your breathing, nothing else can get into your head."

I look at him, then—really look at him. Beyond his handsome face and jovial personality. And inside of him I see something else.

He does this for a reason, too.

Perhaps everyone has demons of their own.

I smile at him. "When can I do it again?"

"Once a day is enough," he says.

"You did it twice today."

"I did, but only for a fraction of the time I normally do, and only to show you how to do it."

He's right. This isn't something you can just subject your body to constantly. But now that I know it can keep my mind blank, I want it again. And again.

"Once you're used to it, you can work up to five minutes. Maybe even ten. But only once a day."

"But we leave tomorrow."

"Tell you what." He grabs my hand. "You and I will have a date for a cold plunge at this time tomorrow morning. Before we get on the plane. Then, when we get back to Boston, you can come to my place and do one every day if you'd like."

"You have your own cold plunge?"

"I do. Braden lives in a penthouse, but I'm more of a suburb guy. Now, anyway. I have a house. I only recently moved there. I have my own swimming pool, my own cold plunge, and a full-time trainer who's also a massage therapist."

I roll my eyes. "Must be nice."

"I won't lie to you. It is. I grew up in poverty, Tessa."

Shock runs through me, and not from the cold plunge. "Poverty? I knew you had a modest upbringing, but…"

"Braden and I don't talk about it a lot, and he's managed to keep the gossip rags from getting the whole story. I'm sure he's told Skye, and Skye probably felt it was told to her in confidence, which is why you don't know. My father used to be an alcoholic, and then there was a fire."

"Yeah, Skye told me about the fire."

"We lost everything, and my mother had to take Braden and

me to a food bank to get food."

My heart bleeds for him in that moment. In my mind's eye, I see Ben as a beautiful little boy, hanging onto his mother's hand as she peruses the shelves at a food bank.

"I had a humble upbringing myself," she says, "but nothing like that. We always had good food on the table, warm clothes on our backs. Shelter over our heads. And there was always a little extra."

"You have a sister, don't you?"

"Yeah. Eva. She's two years younger than I am. She just finished college. It was her and my parents, and also my grandmother."

"Right." He smiles. "Teresa Maria. How did you come to be called Tessa?"

"From my father. He called my grandmother Teresa, so he called me Tessa to differentiate."

"You have an interesting look on your face," he says, "when you mention your grandmother. Just like when you told me about her before."

"Did I?"

"Yes… Those are happy memories for you."

"They are. My grandmother was my safe place back then. She still is, even though she's been gone for years. We had a connection that I don't share with either of my parents."

"I can see it when you talk about her." He looks away, staring out to sea. "I never knew any of my grandparents."

"Really?" I ask.

He nods. "They were all dead by the time I was born. Braden met some of them, but he was too young to remember."

That makes sense, of course. If Ben's grandparents had been alive, they probably would've been able to help the family keep them from living in poverty. That's what families do—help one another.

"Tell me more about your grandmother," he says.

It's funny. I don't talk about her that much. Even though she's such an integral part of me, I almost feel like talking about her would somehow taint my memory of her. I told Ben about her while we were sitting at the bar at Union Oyster House, and for some reason, I want to open up to him.

"She was an icon. I already told you about her altar, how she burned candles and incense when she prayed to the saints."

My therapist and I have talked about religion, about whether trying to get back into it would help me. We ultimately decided that it probably wouldn't because I left that part of my life behind with eyes wide open.

"Her altar, candles, and incense fascinated me when I was a kid. By the time I was nine or ten, I respected her very much, but I was no longer as fascinated by her candles and incense."

"Why not?" he asks.

"I don't know. I was older, I guess. I had just had my first communion, and—"

I stop abruptly.

My first communion.

That white dress. Those white panties.

God, I hate white panties. And I hardly ever wear white. Is this why?

And that bartender...

Images long buried flood my brain.

A white dress. White panties.

And an altar boy.

An altar boy with sandy brown hair and light brown eyes.

• • •

Fifteen Years Earlier...

"You look like a princess, little one," Nana says.

My communion dress was made special by a seamstress. She took measurements and everything. It's soft and shiny. Mommy says it's made of satin. It's the brightest white because white symbolizes purity.

"What's purity?" I ask Nana.

"It means you are a good girl, Tessa. It means your soul is pure."

I'm still not sure I understand, but I love the dress. It has fancy lace around the neckline and the hem, and the sleeves are short. I hate long sleeves. They make me itch. But my favorite part is the big bow in the back. I keep turning and turning in front of Nana's big mirror, trying to see it.

Nana smiles at me. "You're such a pretty girl, my Teresa Maria. You will break so many hearts one day."

"I don't want to break anyone's heart, Nana."

"Oh, but you will."

"What if someone breaks my heart?" I ask.

"Whoever does that will have your nana to deal with." She grabs my hand. "It's time to go to church."

I had to go to class to get ready for my first communion, where I learned all about the communion wafer and the wine and what they mean.

The church isn't far from our house, and we get there quickly. It's an old building made of gray stone. I told Nana once that I thought it looked like a castle, and she said that, in a way, it was.

Mommy takes me to the sacristy where the church ladies are preparing for the Mass. The other children who will get their first communion today are already there. There are four boys and three girls. My dress is the prettiest, I think.

She kisses my cheek. "Be a good girl, Tessa. This is such a happy occasion for all of us."

Eva tugs on Mommy's hand. "Why can't I have first communion today?"

"You're not old enough yet, bunny," Mommy says. "Let's go." She leads Eva out of the sacristy, looking over her shoulder and smiling at me.

Father Sam isn't here yet, but the church ladies smile at all of us and then leave the sacristy one by one with the altar scarves. Nana told me once that they're called liturgical clothes. They're always different colors.

The other kids and I are alone until an altar boy enters.

I don't know his name—I think it begins with a D, but I'm not sure—but he's tall with light brown hair, and his voice makes funny squeaks when he talks. I'm sitting by myself when he comes over to me.

"That's a pretty white dress," he says. "Come with me. Father Sam needs to talk to you."

"He does? Does he need to talk to all of us?" I glance at the others.

"He already talked to them. Come with me."

I swallow. "Mommy told me to stay here and wait for Father Sam."

"Father Sam will be here in a minute. He asked me to come and get you."

"Just me?"

"Just you."

I shrug. "Okay."

He takes my hand—his is clammy—and leads me to a small room—it's one of the Sunday school rooms, but there's no Sunday school because Mass is about to start.

"That's a pretty white dress," he says again.

I swallow. Something doesn't feel right. "Thank you."

"What are you wearing underneath it?" he asks.

"Underwear."

"Can I see your underwear?"

What a weird question. "I'm not supposed to show anyone my underwear."

"You have to if you want to get your first communion."

No one said anything about that. "Are you sure?"

"I'm sure. Father Sam would tell you, but he's not here yet."

I like Father Sam. He always shakes my hand like I'm one of the grownups.

"Okay." I lift my dress up, showing him my white panties.

"I have to touch your panties."

"Why?"

"Because it's part of what I do as an altar boy. Father Sam tells me I have to check the panties of all the little girls getting their first communion. It's part of the service."

My fingers twitch, and my tummy feels funny. I want to pull my dress back down. "No one told me about that part."

"That's because it's a secret. Didn't your grandmother tell you?"

"Why would she tell me if it's a secret?"

The altar boy gets a weird look on his face. Like he's a dog growling or something. "Your grandmother's a witch, Tessa. You know that, don't you?"

"She is *not*." I stomp my foot and let go of my dress, letting the satin fall back over me.

"She is. All those candles and incense she uses. It's part of her witchcraft."

"Witches are mean and wear pointy hats." I gulp, and I feel

like crying. "Nana's not a witch. You're lying."

"I'm not." He reaches toward me.

I back away.

"I have to check your panties, Tessa. Father Sam won't give you first communion if I don't."

I bite my lip.

"You're so pretty, Tessa," he says.

I like being called pretty. Mommy and Da say I'm pretty. Nana says I'm beautiful. But this is the first time someone other than a member of my family has said I'm pretty.

I like it. It makes me feel nice.

"Thank you," I say.

"Let me check your panties, and then you'll be ready for first communion."

I look around. "Where are the other girls? Are you going to check their panties?"

"I already did. You're the last one."

Did he? He must have done that before I got to the sacristy.

"Good girl. You stand still."

I obey him. He's older than I am, and I do want to have my first communion. So he'll check my panties, and then I'll go back to the sacristy and wait for Father Sam.

He comes toward me. "Hold up your dress again."

I do, covering my face with the skirt and squeezing my eyes shut. This is obviously something I have to do, so why does it feel all kinds of wrong?

He touches his finger to my panties and then slides his hand underneath. "Good. Now, whatever you do, don't make any noise. This is very important."

"Why would I make any noise?"

"Because sometimes it hurts when I check panties. But it's

all part of the process of your first communion. This is a secret between you and me and God. He'll never forgive you if you tell, and you won't get your first communion."

"And Father Sam?"

"Yes, he knows, but you can't tell him. You can't tell anyone, or you can't have your first communion. Do you understand?"

"Okay."

He slides his fingers underneath my panties and then between my legs.

And then he—

I gasp. Something is inside me. Inside a place I don't understand. And it hurts. It hurts so bad. It feels like he's cutting me with a sharp knife.

But I don't dare scream.

I don't dare say anything.

I want my first communion.

When he's finally done, it still hurts. "Take off your panties now."

"What?" I want to sob. Cry out. Beg him not to hurt me again.

"God needs your panties so you can have your first communion. Father Sam asked me to tell you."

He yanks the panties down, and I step out of them, staring at my shiny white shoes.

"Put your dress down now," he says. "And remember, this is a secret. This is a secret between you and me and God. He'll never forgive you if you tell, and you won't get your first communion. So pretend it didn't happen. In fact, say it now, Tessa. Say this didn't happen."

"This didn't happen," I gulp out.

"Good. Now run back to the sacristy, and wait for Father Sam."

• • •

This is a secret between you and me and God. He'll never forgive you if you tell, and you won't get your first communion.

The words plummet back into my mind as if they were uttered yesterday instead of fifteen years ago.

How did I forget?

How?

This didn't happen.

I remember my first communion. I remember taking the wafer, the wine—which tasted awful—and then turning around and seeing Mommy, Da, Nana, and Eva all watching me.

I remember all of that, so why didn't I remember that damned altar boy?

"Tessa?" Ben says. "Are you okay? You're shaking—are you not warming up?"

I swallow back the memory, rub my arms against the chills that aren't from the cold plunge.

I can't answer him. All I do is swallow and nod.

Once I'm warm, I excuse myself.

CHAPTER TWENTY-EIGHT

Ben

FIFTEEN YEARS EARLIER...

'm sick to death of my life. I don't trust Dirk and his cronies as far as I can throw any of them. But the convenience store? Really?

They're dumber than I thought.

Rob a place that never closes, that has security cameras everywhere? Not too bright.

A couple weeks ago, Dad sent me on an errand to a warehouse to pick up supplies. While I was there, I made a discovery.

Cash.

About fifty Gs total.

I found it stashed behind a piece of plywood covering the drywall on the far side of the warehouse where the two-by-fours are located.

I wasn't looking for it. The guy at the front desk knows me and lets me grab what I need if it's a small order. I wasn't in any hurry to get back on the job, so I took my time...and I found the cash.

Whether it belongs to the guy who owns the warehouse or one of the employees, I have no idea.

But it's there. I know it's there. And I know how to get into the warehouse.

I saw the clerk enter the lockbox code once when he was closing at the same time I left. I memorized the code. Not on purpose or anything. I have one of those brains. I remember things.

No one will be at the warehouse at night. We won't have to hold anyone up.

And I can sure use my share of fifty grand. The first thing I'm buying is a fucking case of beef jerky.

"Keep talking, Black," Dirk says.

"It's a warehouse in the industrial district. There's cash there, and I can get in."

"How?" Carlos asks.

"Does it matter?"

Dirk shakes his head. "Not in the slightest."

"We won't need weapons or anything," I say. "I'd say we should probably still wear ski masks, just in case, but I'm pretty sure there aren't any security cameras anywhere. It's a small warehouse where my father gets some of his supplies cheap. I've heard they might be black market."

"Stolen?"

"Maybe," I say. "I don't know. But they're cheaper than anywhere else." I lean in. "But here's the thing. If they *are* black market, no way will they call the cops if there's a theft."

"Sounds interesting," Jerry says.

"Interesting?" I scoff. "We score fifty times the cash with no chance of getting caught and you call that *interesting*?"

"I'm in," Dirk says. "When do we do it?"

I take another cigarette when he offers me his pack. He holds his lighter up, and I take a drag, lighting it. "Tonight," I say, blowing the smoke out. "We do it tonight."

• • •

Present Day...

Tessa headed straight to her suite after our cold plunge. The look on her face after we were talking about her grandmother...

It still haunts me, and I wanted to do something special for her, so I called the resort planner.

After a quick lunch with Braden and the other guys, after which they set out to play nine holes, I knock on Tessa's door.

She opens it, wearing a green T-shirt and gray sweatpants. Man, she makes anything look good.

"Hi, Ben."

"Did you bring any jeans with you?" I ask.

"Why?"

"Because I need you to put them on, along with the sneakers you wore on the plane."

She cocks her head. "What's this about?"

I beam at her. "It's a surprise. I'll wait here while you change."

"Ben, I kind of want to..." She sighs. "You know what? Yeah. Okay. Give me a minute." She closes the door.

I can't help smiling. She's going to love what's coming.

CHAPTER TWENTY-NINE

Tessa

"Oh my God!" I widen my eyes as Ben and I walk toward a beautiful stretch of beach.

We took a limo ride away from the resort, and Ben has been close-lipped about what he has in mind.

Before us stands a young man dressed in jeans and a white tee, and with him are…

I can't even believe I'm looking at such magnificent creatures.

Horses. Three horses. Two are shiny brown, and the third is golden with a white tail. A palomino. They're perfection, and for a moment, I forget about my first communion.

"Surprise!" Ben smiles.

"What's going on?"

"You said you love horses. So I got you horses!"

"When did I…" A smile spreads over my face. "When we were talking about Nana at the Oyster House. I told you how she used to read me horse stories."

"Right."

How sweet of him to remember. But… "Ben…" I return

his smile, but I shake my head. "I do love them. But I've never actually ridden one."

"Then we're even. I haven't, either. Come on." He reaches for my hand but doesn't take it.

Boldly, I grab his as we walk toward the man and the animals.

"You must be Mr. Black," the man says, holding out his hand. "I'm Cole, your guide."

"Nice to meet you, Cole. Call me Ben, and this is Tessa."

"It's a pleasure, Tessa. Ben here says he hasn't ridden before. How about you?"

"I haven't," I say. "Is that a problem?"

"Not even slightly. Hannibal here is great with beginners."

Ben widens his eyes. "Did you say Cannibal?"

Cole tilts his head back in raucous laughter. "No, Hannibal. With an H."

"Like Hannibal Lecter?" Ben furrows his brow. "Not feeling a lot better."

"Hannibal like my uncle Hannibal," Cole says. "And this is the gentlest horse I've got, so we'll let this lovely lady ride him."

Hannibal is the palomino, and his saddle is vibrant blue. "What kind of saddle is that?" I ask.

"It's waterproof," Cole says.

"Why would it need to be…" Then I glance at the sparkling blue water. "You don't mean…"

"Yes, that's exactly what I mean," Cole says. "We're going to ride along the beach and even go into the water." He hands me a life jacket. "Put this on."

"It's okay. I can swim."

"Sorry. Rules are rules." He hands one to Ben. "You too, Ben. Now, Tessa, let's get you mounted onto Hannibal here."

I swallow. "Okay. Let's do this."

"Place your left foot in the stirrup."

I breathe in deeply and slide my foot as instructed.

"Good," Cole says. "Now hold the reins in your left hand and the saddle with your right hand. Then gently swing your right leg over Hannibal's back and settle into the saddle. Make sure you're comfortable and balanced."

I laugh out loud. "I'm on a horse!" I look around, taking in the sights from the new vantage point.

Cole helps Ben onto one of the brown horses and then mounts his own. "All right! Let's start with a gentle walk along the beach. Keep your reins relaxed and look around. The horses know what they're doing. They won't start galloping away. You're perfectly safe."

Without me doing anything, Hannibal follows Cole and his horse. His movement beneath me is unsettling for a moment, but I get used to the sway of his gait quickly. Once I'm comfortable, I look out at the ocean—at the turquoise hue near the shore that darkens to a mysterious navy near the horizon. A fresh breeze, along with the light mist of saltwater from the crashing waves, drifts over me. Hannibal's mane flutters when the soft wind rustles through it.

Ben rides alongside me on his horse, Sunny. "Enjoying yourself?"

I can't reply for a moment. Words aren't adequate for what I'm feeling. I settle on, "Wow. Just...wow."

"Is this really the first time you've been on a horse?" he asks.

"It is."

"I think you're a natural." He smiles. "You move with the animal, as if you're one."

I glance over at him. He looks...uncomfortable. "You okay?"

"Yeah. Just a little bouncy for me."

Cole looks over his shoulder. "We're going to go into the water now. Are you both ready?"

"Yes!" I shriek.

Hannibal follows Cole and his horse to the shoreline, walking into the frothy waves.

"They love the ocean," Cole shouts over the sounds of the water. "They may get a little playful. Keep a gentle grip on the reins and you'll be just fine."

Hannibal adjusts his steps as he walks in up to his knees. I tighten my grip on his reins for a moment but then ease up, determined to enjoy every minute of this outing that Ben planned just for me.

The water swirls around us, and I almost feel weightless, as if Hannibal were a mythical winged horse and we could fly over the vast Caribbean Sea, all the way to the horizon.

Serenity fills me, and I look over at Ben. He looks anything but serene, but I don't laugh.

I simply gaze at him. At the man who planned something so special just for me.

The memories of my first communion that surfaced earlier are still there, but looking at the sheer magnificence of the natural world atop such a majestic creature puts things into perspective a bit.

And I feel okay.

I truly feel okay.

CHAPTER THIRTY

Ben

When we returned to the resort, Tessa thanked me profusely and hugged me. Actually hugged me. It was quick, but it was still a hug. Then she excused herself to shower the horsy smell away and get ready for tonight—the big dinner with all of the attendees present is tonight.

From what I understand, the women had the same meal that we had last night—jerk chicken with all the sides. Tonight, the entrée is curried goat.

Yeah, goat.

With sides of rice and kidney beans cooked in coconut milk, callaloo—which looks like spinach and is sautéed with garlic, onions, tomatoes, and Scotch Bonnet peppers—and fried cornmeal dumplings that are called "festival" on the printed menu.

"Goat, Ben?" Braden says to me, holding out the menu while he takes a sip of bourbon. "Really?"

I grin. "When in Rome..."

He simply chuckles and walks away to join Skye, who's with

Betsy and Daniela.

Tessa stands by herself, nursing a sparkling water. She's wearing a different black dress tonight and looks even sexier than last night.

Something is still eating at her. It could be the same trauma she's been struggling with, but I have a feeling it's something else. Something different.

Or I may be completely wrong. As much as I want to know Tessa, I really don't. At least not yet.

I approach her. "Hey."

"Hi, Ben. I can't thank you enough for today. First the cold plunge, and especially the horseback riding. It was all so... Just thank you."

"My pleasure." I resist the urge to touch her. "You doing okay?"

She takes a sip of water. "Why wouldn't I be?"

I shrug. "Just making sure."

"I got back to my suite after our excursion and found a string of texts from Skye. She wanted me to go for a massage with her."

"Sorry you missed it." I stretch my arms over my head.

"Don't be. I'm not."

I rub the back of my neck. I'm a little stiff from the horseback ride. "I haven't had time to get a massage here."

"Didn't you say you have a full-time massage therapist at home?"

I take a sip of bourbon. "Yeah."

She rolls her eyes. "You're so not the diva type."

I laugh, then. Erupt into laughter, actually. "You know so little about me, Tessa, but you're right. I'm not a diva. But do you know why I keep a full-time trainer and massage therapist at my home?"

"Because your life is so stressful?" she says, her tone a bit sardonic.

Oh, she has no idea. But that's not the answer I'm going for. I got over apologizing for my good fortune years ago. So I shake my head. "Because I *can*."

That actually gets a smile out of her. "I've had more massages this weekend than I've had in the last year."

"You only had one massage in the last year?"

"Yeah. I won a raffle at work—my old work—for a massage and facial. It was heavenly."

"Tell you what," I say. "You can come to my place whenever you want and I'll make sure you get a massage."

She shakes her head. "Right."

I gently touch her shoulder. "You're going to find, Tessa, that I never say anything I don't mean."

She cocks her head, this time not smiling. "So you were serious when you said you wanted to kiss me?"

Is she kidding? "Of course I was serious. I still am. But I won't until I'm certain you're ready for it."

She tilts her chin up slightly, moves a step closer. "What if I tell you I'm ready for it now?"

My cock reacts—whether to her nearness or to her words, I'm not sure. Probably both.

Her lips are pink and shiny and slightly parted. I could so easily slide my own over them, touch my tongue lightly to hers.

I lean toward her, licking my own bottom lip.

This is it. I'm going to kiss her. I'm going to kiss Tessa's beautiful lips.

Her eyelids slide closed, and—

"Dinner is served!" Braden's voice booms over a microphone.

Tessa's eyes shoot open, and I jerk backward.

Talk about killing the moment.

But it wasn't the right moment, anyway. The right moment will be when Tessa and I are alone somewhere. Maybe tonight under the moonlight on the beach as the waves crash to the shore.

I ache to grab her hand, but before I can, she walks past me and heads to the table under the cabana.

She and I are seated next to each other.

"Excited about the goat?" I ask.

"Not even slightly."

Our appetizers are already in front of us—Jamaican patties. They look kind of like small turnovers, and they're filled with ground beef and spices. They're savory and delicious. The servers fill up wine and water glasses as chatter ensues among the party.

When the servers arrive with domed dinner plates, I inhale. The curried goat has a sharp and spicy aroma, and I find myself looking forward to trying it.

Just as Tessa's plate arrives and the server removes the dome, her phone vibrates between us on the table.

"It's my sister," she says with a huff. "Why would she be calling me here? She knows—" Then her eyes widen. "Excuse me, please. I should take this."

"You want me to come with you?" I ask.

She shakes her head as she rises, already putting the phone to her ear. She disappears into the hotel.

Worry gnaws at me, but I take a bite of the curried goat anyway once everyone is served.

It's...good, actually—the goat has been slow cooked and is incredibly tender. Garlic, onion, and coconut are all apparent in the flavor. It's similar to beef, but with an added gaminess.

Minutes pass. My plate is half empty, and Tessa hasn't returned.

Skye, who's seated on my other side, touches my arm. "Where's Tessa?"

"She got a phone call from her sister."

"Eva? That's strange." She rises. "I'm going to check this out."

I finish my curried goat and a glass of Malbec, and they still haven't returned. I steal a glance at Braden.

He gives me a slight nod.

That's my cue to go see what's going on. He's the host of tonight's shindig, so he can't very well leave. Though he'd leave in a minute if Skye were the problem.

Skye and Tessa are nowhere to be found, so I head up to Tessa's room across the hall from mine.

I knock.

No response.

I knock again. "Tessa? Skye?"

The door opens, just a crack, and Skye stands there. "I need to go talk to Braden. Can you stay with Tessa, please?"

"Of course. What's going on?"

Skye wipes a tear from her eye. "Tessa's dad had a heart attack. He's in the hospital, and it doesn't look good."

My heart plummets to my stomach. "Oh my God."

"We need to get her back home to Boston as soon as we can. So I need Braden to get the jet—"

"Skye, I'm on it." I grab my phone. "The jet is here, so we should be able to get out right away."

"The problem is," Skye says, "if they take Tessa back tonight, will they be able to get back here in time to take to fly us all back tomorrow?"

"I don't know. I guess you could all leave later in the day. I'll see if I can find a commercial flight for Tessa, but that will only work if it leaves within the next couple hours. I'll go with her. Tell Braden to get the driver ready."

But as I check my airline apps, I find there are no commercial flights available at this time of night to fly from Montego Bay to Boston.

"Damn it."

"What?" Skye asks.

"Nothing available. We're going to have to use the jet if we want to get her back as soon as we can."

Skye nods. "I'll tell Braden. If we have to leave later tomorrow or stay another day… That's fine for Braden and me, but what about the others?" She sighs.

"Captain Rogers can get the jet right back in the air as soon as Tessa and I land," I say.

"What about FAA hours?" she asks. "The flight from Montego Bay to Boston can take up to five hours. The captain will max out."

"The co-pilot can fly back."

"Yeah, but both of them will still need a break for twenty-four hours before—"

"Skye, we'll work it out." I grab her shoulders. "We have other pilots. We can fly someone down here tomorrow morning, and you'll get out in time. Please. This won't be an issue."

"You're right, of course. I'm just…" She rubs her temples. "This is just the worst. It's the last thing Tessa needs right now. She loves her family."

"I know. Where is she?"

"In the bedroom. She's…not in a good place, Ben."

"Which is why I'm flying back with her. She shouldn't be alone."

"Are you sure?" Skye asks.

"I've never been more sure of anything," I say.

Skye leads me out of the sitting area and into the hallway. "Go tell Braden what's going on, and I'll stay here and help Tessa get packed. Do you need to pack?"

"All I need is my wallet and my phone," I say. "But I'll grab a few things quickly, and then I'll go see Bray."

Skye nods again, and I leave, heading into my own suite across the hall.

I travel light anyway, so it doesn't take me long to grab all my stuff and throw it in my suitcase. Once I'm ready, I leave the suitcase outside my door and go back to the dinner, where I grab Braden and pull him aside.

"Fuck," he says after I give him the lowdown. "Just what she doesn't need right now."

"I know. But we got through the bachelor and bachelorette parties. You and Skye can stay and enjoy yourselves. I'll take care of the pilot situation. And Tessa."

"Yeah, sure." He gives me a quick hug. "Thanks, bro. I owe you one."

Except my brother owes me nothing. Because it's becoming increasingly clear to me that I would do just about anything for Tessa Logan.

CHAPTER THIRTY-ONE

Tessa

The jet lands in Boston in the middle of the night, and Ben's driver meets us at the airport and transports me straight to Mount Sinai, where my father is.

After checking in with the volunteer on duty, Ben also accompanies me up to my father's room in the ICU.

I haven't checked in with my mother since we landed. I was afraid to. Afraid I'd get bad news.

We wait in front of the elevator. I tap my foot on the glistening white floor. "For God's sake!" I curl my hands into fists. "Where's the fucking elevator?"

Ben looks around. "We can find the stairs. It's only three floors."

"Yes, please." I feel better when I'm moving.

Just standing here doing nothing, waiting for damned—

Ding!

Finally the mirrored elevator doors part, and I rush in, Ben behind me. The doors close, and slowly—so damned slowly—we ascend. When the doors slide open, I rush out—

But a young man in dark blue scrubs walks into the elevator at the same time, carrying a tray of something. He collides with me and—

"Now look what you did!" he exclaims as what look like packages of gauze and bandages thud to the floor.

I stand, mouth agape, unable to form words.

"She did nothing," Ben says. "Don't you know it's courtesy to wait until people get off the elevator before you get on? Come on, Tessa." He grabs my hand. "Are you okay?"

"Yeah, yeah. Except, no. No, I'm not." Tears spring to my eyes.

"He's an asshole," Ben says.

"What if he was trying to get to a surgery?"

"He wasn't. It's the middle of the night, and even if he were, he wouldn't be using the regular elevators. This isn't your fault."

I gulp, following him through the hallway, reading the numbers on the plaques by the hospital rooms.

And when I get to—

I gasp.

The room is empty.

I rush out to the nurse's station. "I'm looking for my father, Daniel Logan. Where is he?"

The nurse widens her eyes. "You're his daughter? I thought he only had one."

"I was out of town. I got here as soon as I could. Where is he? Where's my mother?"

She smiles weakly. "I think you need to talk to your mother, my dear."

My heart is racing as if I've just run a marathon, and my mind… My mind…

The nurse's face blurs in front of me. Ben's strong arm

steadies me, and my vision clears.

The nurse's face reveals nothing.

She knows nothing, of course.

Oh God, oh God, oh God…

"Tessa," Ben says calmly, "you need to call your mother."

"It's the middle of the night."

"I know, but she knew you were on your way, and she needs to know you're here."

But my mother doesn't pick up. It goes straight to voicemail.

This is Carlotta Logan. I apologize for not being able to take your call. Please leave me a message.

"Mommy, it's me. It's Tessa. Where are you? I'm here at the hospital. Where is Da?"

And then my phone clatters to the hard, tiled floor of the hospital hallway right outside the room where my father is supposed to be.

My mother is walking toward me, tears streaking her face.

"Mommy!" I run to her.

She cries into my shoulder.

"Mommy, where's Da? Tell me what happened?"

She sniffles on my shoulder. "I'm so sorry, Tessa. Your da… He didn't make it."

The world spins, then. The room spins. Everything spins.

My mother becomes a blob that is glommed onto me.

She doesn't even look like my mother.

I look up to the stars, to the heavens—but of course I see only the drywall in the hospital ceiling.

My body chills, as if pins are prickling me, daggers slicing through my heart.

My da…

My daddy…

My father…

"He's with Nana now."

The words come from somewhere. I believe from my mother.

Nana wasn't his mother. She was Mommy's mother. But she loved Da. She thought he was the best thing that ever happened to Mommy.

She finally lets go of me—but I still don't see her. Her face is a blur. All I see are the tears running down it. As if water is just coming from somewhere other than her deep brown eyes.

"It was a massive coronary," another voice says. "We did all we could."

"But I talked to Eva. And to you… When did I talk to you?"

"Tessa, that was hours ago."

Right. I was in Jamaica. Then on the plane. Then Ben's car.

Ben.

Where is Ben? He was here.

And then I see him.

He's standing a few feet away from me, keeping his distance, letting me be.

And then he's all I see. His height, his potency, the way he fills up the room with his presence.

Everything falls around him, and he's all that's standing.

He *is* strength.

I turn away from my mother and fall into his arms.

• • •

Time passes in a blur, and the next thing I know, I'm lying in a bed.

It's not a familiar bed.

"Mommy!" I cry out.

Someone comes to me, sits on the side of the bed. Strokes my forehead. "It's okay, Tessa. You're safe."

That's not Mommy's voice.

I sit up. Ben Black is there. "Where am I?"

"I brought you to my house. I didn't want you to be alone. Your mother and sister are here as well, in different guest rooms."

"This isn't your room?"

"Of course not. I'd never be so presumptuous."

He looks down at me, and his face is so handsome and caring in the sunlight streaming in through the window. How much time has passed? I have no idea.

I feel so empty. So much emptier than any other time in my life. Even when I woke up in the hospital after what Garrett did to me. Even after remembering what happened at my first communion.

This is worse. A thousand times worse.

I wasn't violated this time, but I lost so much more than what Garrett took from me.

What Garrett and the altar boy took from me, I can heal from. I can get back.

I can never get my da back.

"You need anything?" Ben asks.

"I should go to work."

"It's Sunday, Tessa."

I shake my head to clear it. "Sunday? I don't… It was late Saturday night when we flew from Jamaica."

"Yes, and we arrived in the middle of the night, Sunday morning."

"And we went to the hospital."

"Yes."

"And I was too late, Ben." Tears fall from my eyes. "I was too late to see my da. I was too late to tell him how much I love him."

Ben rubs circles into my back. "He knows, sweetheart."

I jerk at the term of endearment. "Don't call me that."

"I won't. I'm sorry."

I wipe a tear with my finger. "I don't mean it that way. It's just…that's what Garrett called me."

"All right." He pulls me into a hug against his hard, warm body. "How about if I just call you Tessa?"

"Of course Garrett called me Tessa, too. But it's my name, and he won't take that from me." I sniffle. "And damn it, he won't take sweetheart from me, either. So you know what? If you want to call me sweetheart, go ahead."

"It's all right." He strokes my hair. "I don't need to use that one. We'll find one that works for both of us."

"Do you think you're ready to kiss me now?" I ask.

He lets go of me and rises, rubs his hands through his hair. He turns for a moment but then turns back toward me, meeting my gaze. "You know I've been ready to kiss you for a long time, Tessa. But now is not the right time."

"I disagree. Now is the *perfect* time."

He closes his eyes, almost as if in pain. "If you only knew what you do to me."

I stare at him. At the anguished twist in his handsome face. "If it's anything like what you're doing to me right now, then I *do* know, Ben. Please. I *need* you. I need that kiss."

He sits back on the bed. "A kiss from me is not a substitute for the loss of your father."

God, more tears are coming. I choke them back. "I know it's not. You really think that I think *anything* could make up for that?"

He pushes my hair back over my forehead. "God, you're so beautiful."

"Then kiss me. Please."

"I want to. I want to so badly. But our first kiss, Tessa, isn't going to be like this. It's not going to be an escape from something. And it's not going to be a substitute for something."

"I'm not seeing it as any of those things."

"Tessa, mere days ago, you jerked away at my touch."

"Stop treating me like I'm some fragile glass figurine that will break if you touch it. That's not what I need."

He shakes his head. "You're not fragile. You're strong, Tessa. So very strong."

"Not strong enough." I gulp. "I need that kiss, Ben. I can't even describe how much I need it."

He cups my cheek. "I'll hold you. I'll bring you breakfast in bed. I'll draw you a warm bath."

"Or a cold plunge?"

"Or a cold plunge. Whatever you need. But I can't kiss you yet, Tessa."

"Why not?"

His gaze darkens. "Because if I kiss you, I won't want to stop with a kiss. I'll want to do things you may not be ready for."

"Maybe I *am* ready."

He comes near me then, grips my shoulders. "Are you ready for everything, Tessa? Because once I kiss those lips, I'm going to want to rip your clothes off, suck on your gorgeous tits, suck all the juice out of your pussy, and then I'm going to fuck you hard. Hard and fast and raw. Because *that's* how much I want you."

I jerk backward at his words.

He stands abruptly, rakes his fingers through his hair. "Fuck. I'm so sorry, Tessa. Those words should have never come out of my mouth. Certainly not today, after what you've been through. Probably not ever." He sits down. "Can you forgive me?"

I reach out and caress his cheek. His expression is so tortured, so full of anguish. He's hurting for me. But he's hurting for himself, too, and that's why he lashed out.

"I can forgive you," I say. "And you're right. I'm not ready for that."

But I want to be.

Because all those things he just described? I want them. From him.

Only from him.

"I *can* stop with a kiss," he says. "I learned self-control a long time ago. But that's not even the point. I want our first kiss to be perfect, something you'll always remember, and if I kiss you now, it will forever be tainted with grief for your father. Plus, something's still bothering you. Something about that bartender in Jamaica. Something…" He rubs his forehead. "I can't kiss you yet, no matter how much we both want it."

CHAPTER THIRTY-TWO

Ben

Tessa, Eva, and their mother, Carlotta, go home to Carlotta's house later that day.

I brought them to my place because it was closer to the hospital, and I wanted them secure.

Sherlock drove them home, but I didn't accompany them.

Tessa needs some space.

She's as strong a woman as I've ever met, but she's struggling with so much, and all I can do is think about her—think about getting inside of her beautiful body, not only because I want to desperately, but also because it would ease some of my own suffering.

Fucking Dirk Conrad.

But I can't blame him.

No. I have only myself to blame for getting involved with that stupid gang of lowlifes, anyway.

I knew better, but I did it anyway. I did it to rebel against my life.

My hard fucking life.

Never in a million years did I consider that there was something better out there. That Braden, Dad, and I would someday never want for anything.

That idea wasn't even on my radar back then. I was thinking about all the beef jerky I could eat and some money to take a girl out the way she deserved for once.

It wasn't until four years later, when I was twenty-one and Braden was twenty-four and we met the Ames sisters, that we were able to get our business off the ground and market Braden's invention.

Nothing can be proved.

Even then, I was smart enough to take every precaution we needed to take.

In fact, I was the brains behind the whole thing.

I had to be. The other three were fucking idiots.

But when push came to shove, it *was* all my idea.

A man lost his life.

Sometimes, when I look down at myself in the shower, I see not drops of water sliding down my body but rivulets of blood.

And I remember…

I remember all the blood…

* * *

FIFTEEN YEARS EARLIER…

"What the fuck did you do that for?" I demand.

"You said this place would be empty, Black. You fucked us all over."

I thought it *would* be empty. Just a warehouse where my father bought supplies at rock-bottom prices that had a big stash of cash behind some loose drywall.

I don't know who it belonged to or where it came from, but I didn't care. If it had been legally obtained, no one would be hiding it.

So I figured, what the hell? Rather than a grand from a convenience store safe, I had an easy mark worth so much more.

I knew how to get in and out of the warehouse, and no one knew *I* knew about the cash.

So we went for it. None of us had guns, or any other weapons, for that matter. At least that was our agreement beforehand.

But Dirk—he had a switchblade.

I didn't know about it. Carlos and Jerry might have known, but I didn't.

And…someone else was in that warehouse. Why? I don't know, but he was there.

When the man came at us—big and burly—Dirk went crazy.

Pulled out a switchblade and ran at him, stabbing, stabbing, stabbing…

And the blood.

The spattering blood. From his chest, from his mouth…

All over my face, my arms, my clothes.

All over my fucking shoes.

The blood, the blood, the blood…

But I held steady.

Carlos threw up, and Jerry looked away for a minute.

I gulped it all down.

It isn't the worst thing I've ever seen.

No.

When I first saw my mother's face after she was burned, flesh and skin dripping from her.

What I'm seeing now? Blood spurting out of this big, burly dude?

It doesn't look nearly as bad.

What the hell were you thinking?

The words hover at the back of my throat, but I can't bring them forth. I can't bring anything forth.

I can't even scream, the way Carlos is shrieking like a little girl.

Damn, damn, damn...

Finally, I pull Dirk away.

"We need to get the fuck out of here," I say.

"You said nobody would be here." Dirk's voice is robotic.

"I know what I said. But we have to get out of here *now*."

"Who is that guy?"

"I have no idea. He doesn't work here that I know of. He may have been trying to rob the place, same as us. Fuck, Dirk, he didn't have a weapon. What the—"

"My God... The money..." Jerry starts picking up bills.

"For Christ's sake," I whisper harshly, "leave it."

"Are you fucking kidding?" Carlos wipes the puke from his mouth and bends down to help Jerry.

The two of them scramble to pull the money together and shove it in the duffel bag I brought.

I don't help them, but I'm damned sure going to take my share.

Dirk is covered in blood. It doesn't show on the black hoodie he's wearing, but it's all over his jeans.

"Take a look at yourself," I say to him. "Did any of your blood get mingled in with this guy's? Did you nick yourself with that knife?"

"Hard to say. There's blood all over me."

"There's blood all over all of us, but did you nick yourself at all?"

"I don't think so. I don't feel anything."

Of course he doesn't feel anything. None of us do. We're all fucking numb right now. Our survival instincts are in overdrive.

This went so, *so* wrong.

"We can't leave it here," I say.

"The hell we can't."

"No, we can't. We have to…get rid of it."

· · ·

Present Day…

t.

I said *it*.

I called a human being *it*.

Because he was no longer a human being. He was a corpse.

Just the thought…

Despite looking away at first, Jerry knew exactly what to do. Made me wonder what kind of home he came from.

The victim turned out to be an escaped convict with no family, so no one really mourned his loss.

He disappeared into thin air.

When his photograph showed up on TV, I recognized him.

He wasn't an it.

He was a man.

A man whose life was cut short.

Largely because of me.

CHAPTER THIRTY-THREE

Tessa

Da's funeral is held in our church—the one made of gray stone that I used to tell Nana looked like a castle.

"In a way, it is," she told me.

I never asked her why she said that because my first communion was later that day.

I didn't talk to Nana about the saints much after that.

She'd often ask if I wanted to sit with her at her altar, the way I used to, and pray to the saints and to the Blessed Mother, but I always said no.

Something held me back after my first communion.

Now I know what it was.

How had I blanked the altercation with the altar boy out of my mind? I haven't had a chance to talk to my therapist about it. I've been busy dealing with Dad's passing.

Our next session will be a big one.

Mom, Eva, and I sit in the front pew along with Dad's brother, Uncle Josh, and Mom's two siblings, Uncle Miggie and Aunt Lily. In my hand, I clutch a small silk bag holding the pearl from the night Ben and I ate at Union Oyster House. Somehow, it helps.

I don't want to look at the black lacquer casket covered with the white pall and sitting near the altar, but I can't force my gaze away. Da is in that coffin. My da.

Except *not* my da.

Only his body.

His body that's been filled with embalming fluid and dressed in his Sunday best.

I swallow back the nausea.

I nearly lost it during the entrance procession. Why a Catholic funeral has to be such an event is beyond me. I need to say goodbye in my own way.

The priest, Father Johnson, offers scriptural readings and prayers and then gives a short homily about my father. For the first time in forever, I listen to the words spoken in a church.

"We gather here today to remember and celebrate the life of Daniel Logan, devoted husband to Carlotta, loving father to Teresa and Eva, and brother to Joshua. When we mourn the loss of a loved one, it is our faith that provides solace and guidance. Dan's life was a demonstration of the strength of his faith, and his journey was marked by love, devotion, and unwavering belief in the teachings of our Lord."

I don't know Father Johnson. I've never seen him before, but he seems to know my father well. As a child, I often heard him say to my mother, "It's in God's hands now, Carly." He'd give his pain and suffering over to God so easily.

Something I can't do. Don't want to do.

Murmurs of *Amen* surround me, but I can't bring myself to say the word.

"I'd like to invite Dan's brother, Josh, up to say a few further words."

My uncle, who looks a lot like my father—same brown hair and blue eyes—rises and walks to the altar.

"Thank you, Father." He looks at us in the front row. "Carly, Tessa, Eva, family and friends. Today, we gather here to remember my dear brother, Dan, a man of unwavering faith and a source of inspiration for all who knew him. As we reflect on his life, I can't help but recall some of the wonderful and humorous moments we shared together.

"You see, growing up with Dan wasn't just about learning the catechism. It was also about learning the art of mischief. Dan had a unique talent for finding adventure in the most unexpected places. I remember one time, when we were kids, we decided to sneak into the church pantry and sample some of the communion wafers. We thought we were being discreet, but Father Doug caught us red-handed. He gave us a lecture we'd never forget about respect for the Eucharist. Dan, being Dan, turned it into a life lesson about the importance of our faith."

My uncle's words hit me with the force of a blow to the head. I remember that story. Da told me about it before my first communion. I never thought about it again after…

I never thought much about my first communion again.

Not until now.

What if I had remembered what happened with the altar boy? What if I'd told Mommy and Da? Would Da have lost his faith? Or would he have put it in God's hands? Would he have confronted the altar boy? Would he have—

My uncle's voice interrupts my racing mind.

"As we mourn his passing, we remember Dan not just as a devout man but as a loving husband, father, brother, a loyal friend, and someone who could find joy and laughter even in the most challenging moments. He showed us that faith isn't just about seriousness. It's about finding joy in the journey, even when the road is rocky.

Those words. It's almost as if Da is saying them to me. I can even hear his voice inside me.

It's about finding joy in the journey, angel, even when the road is rocky.

"May his soul rest in eternal peace. Amen."

"Amen."

This time I say it, and I remember Da for how he was. His humor, his faith, his love for me, Mommy, and Eva. Even for Nana. She was Mommy's mother, not his, but he loved her so much.

Communion follows.

It's been ages since I took communion. Not since high school. And now that I recall what happened before my first communion? I don't want to have anything to do with it.

But the Eucharist meant a lot to Da. He always said it reminded him that though he was imperfect, he was still able to commune with God by taking a meal with Him.

So I walk to the altar, following Mommy, and I take the wafer and the wine.

For Da.

I do it for Da.

I'm forever grateful when the service is over.

Except now comes the most difficult part.

Watching as my father is lowered into the ground.

CHAPTER THIRTY-FOUR

Ben

I steer clear of Tessa after the Mass. Only family and close friends go to the gravesite. Braden and Skye are going, but I choose not to. I'd go if I thought it would help Tessa, but she and I haven't had hardly any communication since she went to stay at her mother's, and that was nearly a week ago. I've texted her a few times to check in, and her responses have always been short and polite.

Instead, I have Sherlock drive me to Tessa's mother's neighborhood, and we wait in the car for the family to arrive back from the burial for the wake.

I sit in the backseat, going through email after email, when one catches my eye. I don't recognize the email address, and I'm ready to send it to spam when I see the subject line.

I haven't forgotten.

Chills skitter over my flesh as I open the email.

It's me, Black. Remember when I said you'd get something in the mail a couple months ago?

I remember, all right. I didn't sleep all night and watched the mail at home and at work like a hawk for the next week until I was convinced Dirk had been bluffing all along.

There's no evidence. We made sure of that at the time.

I continue reading.

I decided to wait. Bide my time.

Time's up, Black.

My blood turns to ice.

CHAPTER THIRTY-FIVE

Tessa

We have the reception at our house after the burial. Watching my father's body being placed under ground for all eternity was excruciating. I wished Ben were there, and a small part of me wished for faith—that belief that Da is still with us, enjoying eternal life with our Father in Heaven.

But my faith is gone. Obliterated, beginning with an altar boy at my first communion.

Aunt Lily and the church put together a feast for us. Mostly Mexican food. Even though Da wasn't Mexican, that was the food he loved the most.

Braden and Skye are here, of course, along with Betsy and several of my friends from my old job. I haven't been with Black Inc. long enough to make new friends. In fact, I haven't been back to work since before Jamaica. Luke was great about giving me time off for bereavement.

Of course, that's no doubt due in part to the fact that I was a special hire by the Black brothers themselves.

I sigh.

One good thing has come out of all this.

I haven't given Garrett Ramirez a thought.

Until this moment.

Ben is here, talking in the corner of the living room with Betsy, Braden, and Skye, but every now and then, he looks over at me. I haven't seen him smile, though.

Of course not. A funeral reception is hardly the place for a smile.

Mom, Eva, and I are sitting on the couch together, and people are lined up to talk to us and pay their respects.

My eyes have been watery all day, but I've kept my composure.

"Daniel was such a wonderful man," a young woman I sort of recognize says to me.

"Thank you. Yes, he was."

"I hope you have a lot of good memories to get you through this trying time."

I force a smile. "We do. He was a great father."

She takes my hand. "I'm so sorry for your loss."

"Thank you."

I repeat that conversation—or a variation thereof—so many times I lose count.

In the meantime, parishioners, guests, friends, and relatives nosh on the feast my aunt prepared. I love my aunt's cooking—she makes the best enchiladas—but my stomach is a void.

I've been forcing myself to eat bland things all week—oatmeal, rice with a sprinkle of salt, plain pasta with butter.

Even my staples of bacon and Ben & Jerry's haven't sounded good to me since Da died.

I didn't get to say goodbye.

I didn't get to hold his hand and tell him I love him.

"He knew," Mom has assured me.

I know he knew, and I know he's been worried about me since the Garrett situation.

He never approved of my leaving the church, of course, but still he loved me, was devoted to me.

I've tried looking up to the heavens to talk to him—to tell him that I'm okay—but it feels all wrong.

We were a traditional Catholic household, and my father was definitely the head of the family. My mother never worked outside the home except to volunteer for school and church activities.

Will she have to get a job now?

So many unanswered questions that we haven't even allowed ourselves to think about because we're mourning.

I haven't brought these issues up with my mother, but I'm wondering… Will I have to move back in with her? Help her make ends meet?

I'll do it if I have to.

The old Tessa? Man, would she have balked at that.

This Tessa, though… This Tessa will do her duty. Do what she has to do to take care of her mother. It will be my penance for not being here to say goodbye to my father.

I know better than to think that way, of course. I was in Jamaica with Braden and Skye, celebrating their impending nuptials. I'm Skye's best friend, and that is where I was supposed to be. Plus, my father had no history of heart issues. We had no idea he might have a massive coronary and not make it.

He was strong and fit, though my mother's Mexican fare was filled with dairy and meat fat.

All these thoughts go through my head as the same words come out of my mouth again and again.

Thank you for being here. I appreciate you being here. Yes, he was a wonderful father.

When the receiving line has finally dwindled down, I rise and turn to my mother. "I've got to get out of here for a minute."

My mother nods. "Go ahead, Tessa. You too, Eva. Uncle Josh and I have got this."

My mother is so strong. Her husband—her life mate—was taken from her, but she's concerned about me.

My mother and father had their share of knock-down dragouts over the years, but they had one rule. Never go to bed angry. Not once in the entire time I lived with them do I remember them not sleeping together in the same bed.

And they never did go to bed angry.

Even when they were up until the wee hours of the morning—as Da used to say—they would find some common ground, and then they would go to bed.

I look around my house. Remnants of Nana are still here, her figurines of the Blessed Mother and her crucifix.

All I could think about—especially after Nana passed away a few years after my first communion—was getting the hell out of this house so I could live a life. Not be bound by my mother and father's strict rules.

I wasn't even allowed to date until I was seventeen. And then, I had to parade my dates into the living room where they were subject to interrogation from both my mother and my father.

It almost wasn't worth it.

So when I got to college, I went a little wild.

I lost my virginity the first week, and I never looked back. When Skye and I got close, and I found out we were exact opposites, I was always the one who made her go out, forced her to dress less conservatively.

And what do you know?

She was the one who snagged a sexy billionaire.

I smile at the thought.

It was ridiculous that I felt so envious of Skye's relationship with Braden. She's checked in with me every day since Garrett, twice a day since my father died.

All this, when she should be focusing on her upcoming wedding.

It's four weeks from today, at a posh hotel in downtown Boston.

No expense has been spared for the future Mrs. Braden Black, of course.

I walk to the kitchen and then outside in the backyard. The skies were gray during the burial, and now it's raining, so I'm alone, which is what I'm after.

I don't care about the rain. It feels good—kind of reminds me of the cold plunge.

Ben and I were supposed to do another cold plunge Sunday morning last week, but of course that didn't happen. We ended up flying home in the middle of the night.

My black dress is getting drenched, but again, I don't care.

I relish the pelting of the drops as I look to the gray sky, trying to feel my father.

But I don't feel Da.

I feel…Ben.

He's texted me a few times since Da died, but other than that, he's left me alone. Given me space.

It's not like we're in a relationship or anything.

But feelings are growing within me—feelings I never thought I'd have again, despite Garrett and my recently resurfaced memories of the altar boy.

Feelings that—if I allow them to take hold—I'm not sure how to deal with.

What happened with Garrett is still so much a part of me, and now, dealing with the loss of my father plus the recovered memories of my first communion, I'm not sure I'll be ready to have these feelings for a long time.

But the feelings don't seem to care about any of that, because they're here. They're here every time I think about Ben. Every time I look at him.

Every time I remember the feel of his lips on my cheek.

Every time I think about the conversation we had about how he wanted to kiss me, but it wasn't the right time.

Was he right?

More likely his brother told him to stay away from me. Although from what I know about Ben Black, he wouldn't let anything—including his powerful older brother—keep him from something he wants.

And what about me?

Why am I thinking about Ben Black kissing me when I'm trying to talk to my father in the pouring rain?

Ben was right to refuse to kiss me that day at his house, right after Da died. I can't fall into the pit of proving I'm alive by having hot monkey sex. I had enough of that in college and afterward—all the way up until Garrett.

The rain helps me, and soon I'm dripping wet. A chill runs through me, so I turn and—

I gasp.

Ben stands there, clad in his black suit and gray tie, which probably cost a fortune, and he's getting pelted as well.

"I saw you out here," he says. "When the rain got stronger, I figured I'd better check. You okay?"

"I think that's a loaded question, and we both know it."

He frowns. "You're right. I'm sorry. Of course you're not

okay. You just lost your father."

"At least I've had something to keep my mind on," I say with a sigh.

He takes a step closer. "You want to talk?"

"Not especially. I'm so over talking right now. If I have to say, 'Thank you so much for coming. Yes, he was a wonderful father,' once more, I may explode."

He glances back to the house. "People are starting to disperse. Let's get you inside."

I look up to the sky, letting the drops pummel my face. Then I turn and look at Ben. "I don't I want to go inside."

He touches my cheek. "You're soaking wet, Tessa."

I hold my hands out, look up to the sky once more. "So what? Since when does being soaking wet matter? I kind of feel like I need to be rained on right now."

"Do you want to tell me why?"

I smile to the clouds. "I've had an amazing life."

"Had? You're twenty-five years old, Tessa. The majority of your life is still ahead of you."

"I don't mean it that way." I put my arms down and turn to him. "I mean I had the best dad in the world. He was strict for sure. Both my parents were. But they loved me unconditionally. When I fucked up—and I fucked up a lot—they always forgave me. Of course, they punished me, but they did everything because they loved me. And then what did I do? The minute I could leave their house, I threw away all of the good values they taught me. I threw my faith to the wind, gave my virginity to the first guy who asked."

"Tessa, everyone rebels a little bit when they leave home."

I turn back to face him. "Did you?"

He shakes his head. "I did it *before* I left home, and my God, you have no idea."

I look down. "I didn't appreciate what I had."

"Of course you did." He moves another step closer. "You kept a good relationship with your mom and dad, didn't you?"

"Yeah, I did."

"You had to find your own way. Everyone does. There's nothing saying you can't go back to your religion if you want to."

"Except I don't really want to."

"And that's okay, too."

"Mommy and Da were so disappointed when I left the church."

"But you're you, Tessa, and they both still loved *you*."

I smile weakly. "Yes, they did."

"See?"

I close my eyes, images appearing in my mind. Of my brown-haired and sparkling-eyed father hoisting me up and playing rocket ship when I was a little girl. Helping me decorate Christmas cookies when Mommy and Nana made them. Holding me and letting me cry into his shoulder when Nana passed away, telling me, "Da will always be here for you, Tessa. Always."

And when I spent my first weekend at home after college. His face lit up when he saw me, and he captured me in a huge bear hug. And then he asked me the dreaded question. I inhale a deep breath. "I remember one time when I was home for the weekend, I went to Mass with Eva and my parents. My father asked me if I'd been going to Mass at school, and I lied to him. I told him yes."

Ben chuckles lightly. "I don't know of any kid who hasn't lied to his parents."

I open my eyes. "But that's not the thing. He looked at me, looked me directly in the eye, and said, 'Don't you ever lie to me again, Teresa.'"

"So he knew."

"He did. He had some sort of sixth sense when it came to me lying. And he didn't berate me about not going to Mass. What was more important to him was the lie."

"It sounds like he was an amazing father."

"He was." I sniffle, holding back a light sob. "He really, really was. I was closer to him than to my mother, to be honest. I was probably closest to Nana, my mother's mother, but when she passed away, my father became my rock."

"Tessa…"

I meet his gaze.

"Please, let's go inside."

I shake my head.

Tilt my chin upward. *Do you think you'll ever kiss me?*

But the words don't make it out of my mouth.

Ben moves toward me, closer, as if in slow motion.

And Ben—strong, handsome, wonderful Ben—touches his lips to mine like a gentle stroke of a watercolor brush.

I part my lips, and fireworks shoot through me.

I've never waited so long for a kiss, never wanted a kiss so badly, and this kiss lives up to every expectation I had.

He slides his tongue between my lips, slowly at first, but then he deepens the kiss. Our lips cling together, and my breath catches my throat.

He cups both my cheeks.

A face holder.

I love a face holder.

The kiss lingers, and my nipples harden, my pussy pulses.

Feelings I never thought I'd have again, and I'm having them from a mere kiss.

Perhaps it's because I've anticipated it for so long.

It's perfection.

Such perfection.

Just the kiss...

Nothing else matters.

Not anything.

As the rain falls, the drops tumbling over us, for the first time in a long time—maybe since that last time I scrambled off Nana's lap before my first communion—all is right with the world.

CHAPTER THIRTY-SIX

Ben

I said I was waiting for the right moment.

Turns out the right moment was in her mother's backyard, after her father's funeral, while raindrops are pummeling us.

She parts her lips, and I dart my tongue between them. A soft sigh leaves her throat and vibrates against me. The kiss is gentle at first, exploratory, until—

Tessa wraps her arms around my neck and deepens the kiss. Shivers course through me—from the rain or the kiss?

It's the kiss. This fucking spectacular, perfect kiss.

Our lips slide together, and the sensation is electrifying.

Yes, the perfect time. The right moment.

The perfect kiss.

She pulls back a few minutes later and gasps in a breath.

I slide my finger over the contours of her cheek and jawline and then over her bottom lip, which is swollen from our kiss. "You okay?"

She simply nods, grabs my hand, and leads me back into the house through the double doors that lead to her mother's large kitchen. Before we enter, though, she stops me.

She smiles at me, drops of rain catching on her lashes. "You were right, Ben. The earth moved." She grabs my hand and pulls me through the doors into the kitchen.

I inhale the spicy and robust scent of the Mexican food. I haven't eaten anything, and my stomach responds with a growl.

"Tessa!" Mrs. Logan says, entering the kitchen. She's a beautiful woman, but her eyes are sunken and sad. "My goodness, what were you doing out there? I thought you had gone to your room. You're soaking wet."

"I'm fine, Mom," Tessa says as we drip all over the black-and-white tile floor. "You remember Ben."

I hold out my hand, water dripping from my sleeve. "How are you holding up, Mrs. Logan?"

"As well as can be expected, I guess." She turns. "Lily! I need some towels in here. A lot of towels."

I look into the living area. "Looks like the reception is about over. Only a few people left, so I should be going."

"Can you stay?" Tessa asks.

I chuckle, wanting so much to pull her into my arms, but her mother is standing right there. "I kind of need some dry clothes."

"Then..." She turns to her mother. "Would it be okay if I went back to Ben's place with him?"

Tessa's Aunt Lily—who looks a lot like Mrs. Logan but with some gray in her hair—enters the kitchen, bearing two large towels and hands one to each of us. I dry off my face and hair, but there's not much I can do about my black suit. It clings to me.

Did Tessa really just ask if she could come home with me?

Does she know what will happen between us if she does?

Perhaps she does know, and that's why she wants to come.

"I have to talk to Ben about some work," Tessa continues.

"Can't that wait until tomorrow?" Mrs. Logan asks. "Or Monday, when you're actually at work?"

"Your mother's right, Tessa," I say. "You should stay here."

"I'll walk you to your car, then," Tessa says. "I'm wet anyway."

Two or three people are scattered in the living and family rooms, but most of the mourners have left.

Sherlock is outside waiting. I signal to him not to bother getting out of the car in the rain.

Tessa grabs my hand. "Thank you."

"For what?"

"For being here. For talking to me. For that kiss."

I smile, caressing her cheek. God, her skin is soft as silk. "It was the right time."

"It was." She looks up to the sky. The rain has subdued a bit. "It was the perfect time."

I stroke the back of her head. "I'd like to kiss you again, Tessa. I think you know that. I think you know I'd like to do a lot more than kiss you."

She nods, a raindrop landing on her eyelash. I gently flick it off.

"Would you like to have lunch tomorrow?" I ask.

She smiles, her cheeks blushing pink despite the chill of the rain. "I think I'd like that."

"I'll pick you up around noon here. You'll still be here, right?"

"Yeah. But then you can take me back to my place. I already told my mom I'll be going back, since it's so much closer to work. Aunt Lily and Eva are staying here with her."

"Awesome." I touch my lips to hers. Sparks jump all over me. "I'll see you tomorrow, then."

I get into the car, and as Sherlock drives away, I look through the rain-spattered window at Tessa, her fingers touching her lips.

. . .

Sunday afternoon lunch with Tessa turns out to be brunch. When I pick her up at noon, she says she is hankering for some scrambled eggs with bacon. I take her to the Plaza Hotel's Sunday champagne brunch, which goes until two o'clock.

I'd actually entertained the idea of bringing her to my place and making her lunch, but then I figured it was too soon.

That kiss yesterday in the rain…

She was so beautiful with the rain and the tears sliding down her cheeks. Tormented and haunted, yet so damned beautiful.

When she tilted her chin, I knew it was the right time.

I'm surprised when she takes a sip of the champagne that our server poured for her.

"Do you like champagne?" I ask. "You didn't drink it on the flight to Jamaica."

She sets her flute down. "I do. I had some for the toast at Skye's bachelorette party. And I had a Skye cocktail. Other than that I haven't had a lot to drink since…"

I nod. I'm not going to make her say it.

"I can't thank you enough," she goes on. "The party was perfectly executed. Even the dancers."

"Again, I'm so sorry about that."

She shrugs. "I know, and it wasn't my thing, but Skye and the others loved them. Anyway, thanks for planning everything else. It all came together so well."

"Tessa, I was glad to do it. You were obviously struggling, and I wanted to help."

Her brown eyes sparkle. "Do you save every damsel in distress you come across?"

I smile. "Can't say that I do."

"Then why did you help me?"

I pause a moment. Then, "Because it's my brother's wedding. I wanted these parties to be perfect."

Her lips turn down just a bit.

Is she disappointed in my response?

Because the truth of the matter is while my response is accurate, I also wanted to help *her*. She knows this, but it won't hurt me to say it again.

"I also did it for you," I continue. "I've been drawn to you since that first time we met to have a drink and plan the parties. The more I get to know you, the more I want you. I dream about doing more than kissing those lips of yours, as you know. I wanted to kiss you that first night I met you, Tessa. That first night when you were scared of your own shadow."

"Why didn't you?"

I smile. "Normally, when I feel like kissing a woman, I do it. I know the signals. Of course, I misread the signal once. Got my face slapped."

She drops her jaw.

"But you wouldn't have slapped my face."

"Probably not."

"You also weren't ready for a kiss that night."

"Absolutely not," she echoes. "I was beginning to wonder if I'd have to wait until my deathbed—" Her eyes go wide as a look of horror crosses her face. "Oh my God. I can't believe I just said that. My father just died, and I'm not... I don't want you to think..."

I reach across the table and pat her hand. She doesn't pull away.

"I don't think anything of the sort, Tessa."

She frowns. "It's odd, really. I'm devastated about my father's loss, of course. I miss him horribly, and I wish I had been able to see him one last time. But I'm actually feeling better than I have in a month. What does that say about me? What the hell kind of person am I?"

I shake my head. "I'm not a therapist, but I'd say you're pretty normal. Your father's death got your mind off of the trauma you've experienced. In a way, it's helping you heal."

"That doesn't make any sense."

I shrug. "Like I said, I'm no therapist. It's just a theory."

We're silent for a few minutes, until—

"So…is this a date?" she asks blatantly.

I laugh lightly. "I think so."

"Good." She smiles.

And it's about as genuine a smile as I've ever seen on her face.

"So you want to date me?" I ask.

She blushes but doesn't break our eye contact. "I didn't think I'd ever want to date anyone again, but yes, Ben. I think I would like to date you."

"Then we'll continue taking it slow."

She narrows her gaze. "What if I don't want to take it slow?"

"Baby, I don't want to take it slow, either." I grin. "Trust me. I've had all kinds of images in my head about all the things I want to do to your luscious body. But I'm going to wait until you're fully ready to experience them because I want your mind in that game."

"Will you at least kiss me some more?" she asks coyly.

"Guaranteed."

She smiles and takes a bite of her frittata. She's eaten more today than I've ever seen her eat, including on the island when we were inundated with gourmet food.

I flake off a piece of my salmon and bring it to my mouth. The flavor of the capers explodes across my tongue. Then, without thinking, I raise my glass of champagne. "To...whatever this is."

I regret the words as soon as they leave my mouth. I know *exactly* what this is. I'm interested in Tessa—more interested than I can remember being in any woman *ever*.

She probably needs more time to heal, and she may not be ready for what I want to do to her.

And with the way my life is going right now...

I don't have any business entering into a relationship.

Not until I deal with Dirk Conrad once and for all.

...

FIFTEEN YEARS EARLIER...

"We're going to need some pliers," Jerry says.

"Pliers?" I shake my head. "What the fuck for?"

"We're going to have to pull his teeth out."

Green acid crawls up my throat. "You can't be serious."

"We'll get rid of this body," Jerry says, "but there's still a chance it may be found. If it is, forensics will be able to identify him by his dental records."

"Jesus Christ," I say. "How the hell do you know all this? What the fuck are you into, Jerry?"

Jerry scowls at me. "Just get me some pliers. This is a construction warehouse. There are tools here, right?"

Yeah, there are tools here. Pliers. I know exactly where they are. Numbly, I walk through the aisles until I find what I need.

I bring the pliers back and hand them to Jerry. "This is all you, man."

Jerry takes the pliers, looks them over. "One of you shine

your phone on his mouth, and another one of you needs to hold his head."

Oh. Fuck. No.

I've done all I'm doing.

Dirk holds the guy's head while Carlos shines the flashlight from his phone on the dude's teeth.

I want to turn away, but this is a train wreck.

A train wreck, and I'm caught right in the middle, about to be smashed by two boxcars.

Jerry pulls the poor guy's teeth out one by one, so deftly that I'm pretty sure this isn't the first time he's done such a thing.

Damn, he probably pulls teeth out of animals for sport or something.

Why the hell did I get involved with these idiots?

"We need a tarp or something," Carlos says.

I scout out the warehouse once more, but I don't find any tarps. I've got one in my truck, though, which I was stupid enough to drive here. "No tarps in here," I say when I return, "but I've got one in my truck. I'll be back."

I sneak to my truck, grab the tarp quickly as I look around, and walk back into the warehouse.

Only to find the other three crawling on the floor.

"What the hell are you doing?"

"Dildo brain there"—Carlos points to Dirk—"dropped all the teeth when Jerry handed them to him."

"Come on, Black," Dirk says. "We've got to find all of them."

"You've got to be kidding me," I say under my breath.

I join the others on the concrete floor, searching for human teeth. Yeah, that's what I'm fucking doing.

When we've grabbed them all, Carlos counts them. "Twenty-seven," he says.

"A human being has thirty-two teeth," I say dryly.

"No shit?" Dirk says.

"Uh…yeah. Basic human anatomy. Did you sleep through health class?"

Did I really just ask that question? Of course he did. If he was even there.

"Not if he had his wisdom teeth removed," Carlos says. "Who doesn't have their wisdom teeth removed?"

"I haven't," I say.

"My brother did when he was eighteen," Dirk says. "Twenty-seven is probably all of them."

"Even with his wisdom teeth gone, we're missing one," I say.

"We searched every fucking crevice," Dirk says. "The dude only had twenty-seven teeth. Maybe one got knocked out."

Dirk has a point. This lowlife could have easily lost a tooth in a fight. Or to a nasty-ass infection.

"All right," I say. "We've got to get the fuck out of here." I look around. "What the hell do you plan to do with this body anyway?"

"Throw it in the bay."

I gulp down puke again. "Jesus Christ."

"We need your truck to do this, Black," Dirk reminds me.

I'm in too deep to bow out now. "Fine. We're going to get rid of the body, and then the three of you are going to help me scrub my fucking truck. After that, I don't want to see any of you ever again."

"Fine by me," Dirk says. "Once we divvy up this cash, we'll all be set for a while."

I'm not sure I even want my share, but I'll take it. I'll take it in case this thing blows up and I end up in prison. At least I'll have something to leave for Dad and Bray.

I didn't kill the guy, and I didn't pull out his teeth.

But I found the pliers and gave them to Jerry, and that tarp wrapped around the poor sod is mine. We have to transport him to the bay in my truck.

This is so fucked up.

What the hell was I thinking?

One thing's for sure—I will never stray again.

I will do my duty. I'll go to school, get good grades, do my work after school and on weekends. Contribute to my household.

I'll be the good son.

The best damned son ever.

CHAPTER THIRTY-SEVEN

Tessa

Ben looks so handsome today. He's wearing jeans and a white-and-blue striped button-down shirt, the sleeves rolled up.

I ended up going to Mass this morning with Mommy, Eva, and Aunt Lily. I didn't want to, but I didn't want to disappoint my mother. Not after everything else. When we got back, I packed up my stuff, and I was ready when Ben's driver picked me up for lunch.

"So you're sure you're ready to go back to your place?" Ben asks.

I nod. "I have to. I didn't go running home to Mom's after Garrett."

Though my mother did stay with me for a week. I don't need to tell Ben that. He probably knows anyway because Skye knows, which means Braden knows.

"All right. I'll take you back there, we can dump your stuff, and then what would you like to do for the rest of the day?"

"You don't have to take care of me for the rest of the day," I say.

"Who says I'm taking care of you? Maybe I'd like to spend the day with you. We could take a walk. Go to the zoo."

I smile when he says that. "I *love* the zoo. I love all animals. Da used to—" I sniffle a bit. "He and I both loved the zoo."

"You sure you're up for it?"

I don't even think before I nod. "I am. It may just be the perfect place to finalize my goodbye to him."

"Perfect." He smiles. "It's a date, then. I happen to love the zoo too."

I take another bite of my egg casserole. It's not as good as my mom's, of course. She spices hers up with chile pequin.

My dad always used to joke that he never ate good food until he met my mom. His mother didn't like to cook. My mom's Mexican food is just delicious.

Before we went to Jamaica, I decided I wanted to learn to make all of my mother's delicious recipes, even though I've never been much of a cook, except for guacamole.

Her recipes are my comfort food. I'd like to be able to make them for myself when I need them.

And I also want to cook them for Ben.

Ben, who is now more than just a friend.

More than just a date.

The thought doesn't frighten me.

Mere days ago, it would've had me running, but now?

Now I want it.

I want another kiss.

And I want more before this day is over.

I smile, thinking about how I'm ready, when Ben's phone buzzes. He glances at it next to his plate, and his lips twist into... not a scowl, exactly, but not anything good.

"I'm so sorry," he says, rising. "I have to take this."

"It's okay." I attempt a smile.

Once he's gone, I start to shiver. Tremble. Am I going too fast?

Because I've gone too fast before, and I ended up paying for it.

• • •

SEVERAL MONTHS EARLIER…

I knock on Garrett's door to surprise him with margaritas and homemade guacamole.

When the door opens, my smile drops from my face. Before me stands a blond woman…wrapped in a towel.

The pitcher of margaritas drops from my hands, and the glass breaks on the concrete stoop. The guacamole follows, making a big green mess.

"Who the hell are you?" I demand.

She smiles. "Not sure that's any of your business."

I brush past her. "Garrett! Where are you?"

Garrett scrambles out of the kitchen wearing nothing but a pair of boxers.

"You've got to be kidding me," I say.

Garrett freezes. "Tessa, this isn't what it looks like."

"Really?" I let out a humorless laugh. "So you weren't just fucking that woman?"

"Well, yeah, but… It was nothing. Just a hookup from an app. Lolita—"

I drop my jaw. "Lolita? You're kidding, right?"

"It's her name."

"Unbelievable."

Anger courses through me, hitting me right at the back of my neck. But heartbreak will follow. I really liked this guy. We had a lot in common—or so I thought.

I raise my eyebrows but then lower them. I don't need *him* thinking he just broke my heart. I thought we had something going. I told him no when he asked for anal, but I let him do everything else he wanted.

"It's just a hookup. I didn't think you and I had anything serious. This doesn't change anything between us."

I sigh. "I guess I just thought—"

"Try not to think too hard." He comes in for a kiss.

I keep my lips sewn shut.

He pulls away and frowns. "So that's it? You're going to punish me for being honest with you?"

"Punish you?" I shake my head. "It's her or me, Garrett. You have to choose."

"But we're supposed to meet for a late dinner, remember?"

Yeah. The late dinner. I was going to surprise him with homemade guac for an appetizer before we went. The homemade guac that's now all over his stoop.

I cross my arms. "Fine. Choose. Or I'm out of here."

He narrows his gaze. "I don't like ultimatums, Tessa."

"I don't like giving them, but you need to make your choice, Garrett. Lolita or me."

"But I just met her. It's nothing—"

"Are you not hearing me? I said choose."

He glares at me. "Fine. I choose the one who isn't making me choose. I choose her."

I turn and walk out of his house. His concrete stoop is full of broken glass and ruined guacamole. It's my favorite pitcher, but I'll live. I leave the mess, choking back sobs.

When I get home, Rita clamors for attention at my feet. I grab her and hold her to my heart. "You love me, don't you, Rita?"

She scrambles out of my arms. I grab my phone and call Betsy.

"Bets?" I say, when she answers. "Get dressed. We're going clubbing."

. . .

I need to work on Betsy's wardrobe. She's a pretty girl, but she insists on wearing baggy dresses when she's got a killer body. Still, she looks great tonight with her hair pulled away from her face in a headband and a flowing burgundy mini dress. For once she's wearing clunky sandals instead of military boots.

Once we're at the club, we head to the bar and squeeze into a standing space. I order two margaritas and down mine before Betsy takes her first sip.

"Ease up, Tessa," Betsy says to me.

"I'm good." I nod to the bartender.

He's new here, and he's a treat for the eyes—blond hair, green eyes, and muscles that go on for days. Plus a huge tattoo all over his forearm. It's a bird of some sort.

He waves at me. "Be with you in a sec."

I simply hold up my margarita glass. Universal language for give me another, and quick.

A moment later, he's got my margarita, and he slides it to me with a smile. "You want to try something stronger?" he asks.

"Stronger than tequila? You mean a shot, right?"

He gestures to the end of the bar. "Meet me over there."

Betsy's still nursing her drink and watching the dance floor, so I wander to the end of the bar. The bartender grabs my hand and takes me behind the bar to a small room where boxes of liquor are stored.

He holds out his hand. In it is a small light-blue pill.

"If you're having a bad night," he says, "this will get you out of your funk."

I pick up the small tablet and examine it. The word SKY is etched on it.

Sky. Give it an E and you've got my bestie. My bestie who's put me on the back burner for her billionaire boyfriend.

"What is this?" I ask.

"It's the answer to your shitty night," he says. "It's ecstasy."

I place the pill back in his hand. "I'm not interested in drugs. I'm sure I can't afford it, anyway."

"This one's on the house, gorgeous. If you want more after that, you come to me. My name's Nick."

"No thanks, Nick."

"You sure about that?" He drops the pill back into my hand. Sky.

The word on the pill seems to be a message to me.

Take the damned pill and get over yourself. Get over Garrett. Get over Skye.

Get over your pathetic life. Swallow it all down.

"All right, Nick." I pop the pill into my mouth and swallow it. "Thanks."

"If you want more, you know where I am." Then he stares into my eyes. "But keep it between us, okay?"

"Yeah, of course. Since it's illegal and all."

"My employer looks the other way," Nick says, "but the cops won't."

"Got it." I turn.

He tugs on my arm.

I look over my shoulder. "Yeah?"

"Whoever made you feel shitty isn't worth it, you hear me? If

I didn't have to work tonight, I'd be all over you."

I give him a weak smile. A bartender who takes his job seriously but who also deals drugs. Interesting.

"Thanks," is all I say. Then I turn to find Betsy.

I spy her on the dance floor with a tall guy wearing glasses.

Just as well. I watch the dance floor and check my phone intermittently. I'm not sure how much time has passed when a guy approaches me.

"You want to dance?" he asks.

He's dark-haired and handsome. "Sure." I follow him to the dance floor, waving when I catch Betsy's eye. We dance through two songs, and then I excuse myself to get some water.

But first, I need to pee. I head to the bathroom, take care of business, and then check myself in the mirror—

A piercing shriek echoes through the restroom.

It's coming from me.

My reflection in the mirror…

It was me. But I had two red horns coming out of my head.

I grab hold of the counter and look again.

Back to normal, thank God, but my head is swimming. I don't feel like me at all.

Until I do.

In fact, I feel more like me than I have in a long time, maybe ever. I'm damned giddy, and I can't wait to get back on the dance floor. I wash my hands quickly and don't bother checking my makeup because I don't care. I just want to dance.

I leave the bathroom and force myself through the crowd and back on the dance floor, grabbing the hand of the first man I see.

"Excuse me!" A woman grabs the man's hand back. "He's with me."

I should apologize, but I don't. The guy I was dancing with

previously—I never got his name—grabs me and twirls me into an intricate salsa dance step that I easily follow.

And I dance.

Soon it's just me on the floor, surrounded by bright moving lights. Some of the lights have eyes and some have noses. Some actually try to talk to me, but I ignore them.

And I dance.

I dance and dance and dance and dance.

One of the lights is talking to me. It's a red light, but I don't understand the words. They're just flashes as I dance.

I dance and dance and dance and dance.

Fewer lights, then.

Fewer still.

The red light is next to me. We're moving. But I'm not dancing.

I'm in a bed.

But not my bed.

. . .

"Tessa, thank God!"

My head hurts, like someone's driving a knife into my brain. Where the hell am I?

"Can you hear me?"

"Yes, for the love of God. Stop shouting, Betsy."

A sigh *whooshes* from Betsy.

"Where am I?"

"You're in my bedroom."

I look around. The sun is streaming through the window and forces my eyes shut. Yeah, this is Betsy's place. But why am I here? And how did I get here?

"You were really fucked up last night, Tessa." Her voice wavers.

Last night. Garrett. Betsy. The club. The margaritas. The bartender.

And the ecstasy.

The little pill that said Sky.

"Oh, shit," I say. "I took ecstasy last night."

Betsy's eyes go wide. "You did *what*?"

"I was feeling... Garrett dumped me, and Skye and I..." I bury my face in my hands. "Our friendship is a mess. God, what was I thinking?"

"It's okay. You're going to be okay."

"Thanks for having my back, Bets." I rub the throbbing in my temples. "God, I feel like shit."

"I've got some tea. I'll get you a cup."

"God, no. Just some water."

She nods, walking toward the door.

"Betsy?"

She turns. "Yeah?"

"Don't tell anyone about this, okay? Especially not Skye or Garrett."

CHAPTER THIRTY-EIGHT

Ben

"What the fuck do you want?" I grouse into the phone after leaving Tessa at our table.

"Come outside." Dirk Conrad's tone is low and menacing.

"I'm having brunch."

"I know where you are. Come outside."

"For Christ's sake. You're not getting anything out of me, Dirk. This is ancient history, and I don't give a rat's ass if you're struggling. This isn't on me. It's all on you."

I end the call.

I have the best security money can buy, but cell phones are never solely private. I don't want him saying anything else through those lines.

I walk outside the Plaza and look around.

He strides toward me, wearing low-hanging jeans again, a New York Yankees cap on his head. A gold bracelet sparkles on his wrist, seeming out of place. "Let's walk."

"I'm in the middle of something."

"This won't take long."

What the hell? I may as well see what he wants now. He'll probably try blackmailing me again, which didn't bode well for him the first time. He claimed something would come in the mail, but nothing ever did. That was months ago, and he really thinks I'm going to fall for this again?

There's no evidence. We were very careful—thanks to Jerry and his knowledge of how to dispose of a body.

Poor fucker. He was an escaped convict, and no one went looking for him, but still...

I sure never meant for it to happen.

Dirk and I walk together for about a block before I stop. "I'm not going any farther. Tell me what you want here and now."

"I hear you met my brother."

I wrinkle my forehead. "I don't think so."

"David. At your brother's bachelor party. He was the bartender you had dismissed."

I clench my jaw as tension threads through my body. Is he fucking kidding me? This can't be happening. The man who wanted Tessa. Who upset Tessa. I glare at Dirk. I suppose there was a slight resemblance. Christ. I want to lunge at Dirk. Take him out for good. "Figures he was related to you, since you're both assholes and all."

"Turns out he has a past with someone you care about."

"I doubt it."

"That lovely young thing you're dining with." He grins.

An invisible crow pecks at the back of my neck. "Why don't you tell me what you think you know right now?"

"That's for her to tell you. I'm here to show you something." He reaches under the collar of his shirt and pulls out a chain. On it is some kind of—

The salmon in my stomach threatens to come back up. "What the fuck?"

He fiddles with the chain, moving his fingers in an almost sensual way. "I probably don't have to tell you what this is. Because if you remember, when we yanked that motherfucker's teeth out all those years ago, we couldn't find one. It was easy enough for me to get the rest of you to believe that the derelict was missing a tooth, but he wasn't."

I look closely at what Dirk has dangling around his neck. "You are one sick bastard."

"I'm a sick bastard who knows how to keep insurance. This happens to be that poor guy's cuspid."

A cuspid. One of his canine teeth—a tooth that can easily be disguised as something else. It's not like he could wear a human molar around his neck with four roots hanging down.

"You're disgusting."

"Funny thing about teeth," Dirk says. "They can identify people."

"Dental records can identify people, you moron. One tooth isn't going to do anything."

"I don't know. There might be DNA in here."

"You're fucked up. That tooth is fifteen years old."

"Still, I have it. This is my insurance policy, Black. You're going to have to pay me off, or I'm going to the cops."

I don't for a minute believe him. If he had that poor fucker's tooth this whole time, he'd have crawled out from his snake pit before now. At the very least, he'd have sent me evidence of it three months ago when he threatened to. This is some other person's tooth, and I don't even want to consider how Dirk might have gotten it.

I close the short distance between us but resist grabbing his collar. We are out on the street, after all. "You're the one who killed him. Or have you forgotten that little fact?"

"No, I haven't forgotten that fact, but I figure you'd rather pay me than go down with me."

"If you and I go down, so do Carlos and Jerry."

Dirk shrugs. "Jerry's already in the slammer, as you well know," he says.

He's not wrong. I've kept tabs on all of them since I had enough money to do so.

"And Carlos is long gone," Dirk says. "I'm figuring you're smart enough to pay me off rather than have the both of us go down."

"I'm done with this conversation." I turn and then look over my shoulder. "Don't contact me again."

"Meet me in an hour." He shoves a business card in my hand. "This is the address. Come unarmed."

"Are you fucking kidding me?"

"I'm not kidding you. That pretty woman you've got in there with you? I happen to know someone—and it's not my brother—who wants her out of the picture. Someone who's willing to pay me a lot. So if you don't meet me, I'm going make sure that happens."

This time I don't hold back. I lunge toward him, reach forward to grab his collar, but then think better of it once more.

It's Sunday afternoon in downtown Boston. Certainly not as busy as it would be on a weekday, but there are lots of witnesses nonetheless.

"You leave her out of this." My jaw is clenched, my whole body throbbing with the need to mutilate this fucking bastard.

Dirk chuckles coldly. "I thought that might get to you. I've been watching you for the past couple weeks, and my brother was watching you in Jamaica. Seems you've been paying a lot of attention to a gorgeous young woman. So I did some digging, and I found out a certain man is out on bail for reckless endangerment and rape."

"She has a restraining order. He goes near her, he goes back to jail."

"She may have a restraining order, but that won't stop him. Because you see, I filled his head with some...information."

"You mean lies?"

"Does it matter?"

I look at the card in my hand. "Fine. I'll fucking be there."

"Good. See you in an hour." He walks away, the human tooth still dangling around his neck.

Before I head back to the Plaza, the first thing I do is call my security company to get someone on Tessa right away. Then I do a quick internet search.

"Fuck," I say out loud.

DNA *can* be extracted from a tooth. In fact, dental tissues such as enamel, dentin, pulp, and cementum have the advantage of being resistant to physical and environmental degradation and are an excellent source of DNA. I still don't believe the tooth belongs to that escaped convict, but damn... If I'm wrong...

I head back into the restaurant. I've got to put on my game face.

"Is everything okay?" Tessa asks. "You were gone a while."

"Just a business deal that's driving me slowly insane." I pull out my wallet and throw enough to cover our brunch plus a generous tip onto the table, trying to still my racing heart. "But I have some bad news. I have to go to work this afternoon. I won't be able to take you to the zoo after all."

The crestfallen look on her face breaks my heart.

"I'm so sorry."

"It's okay. I understand. Maybe I'll…"

"You want me to take you back to your mom's?"

She shakes her head. "No, I can't keep crawling back to my parents' house. It's not the same now, anyway, with my father gone."

"I know, but it's only been a week, Tessa. If you need more time with your mom—"

She holds up her hand. "I don't. I'm okay, Ben. Just take me back to my place, and we'll do the zoo another time."

"You can count on that."

• • •

I instruct Sherlock to take Tessa home. No way am I having him drive to this place. This is between Dirk and me, and he has no idea of the kind of security I have watching me at all times.

However, I turn off my security for this.

This is something I don't want anyone to know about. And if my security team—who I trust implicitly, of course—finds out I'm meeting with Dirk, that means more people will know, and I don't want that.

The address is for a warehouse on the south side of town, eerily close to the warehouse where our crime took place fifteen years ago.

Not the same one, though.

I have the cabbie drop me off about two blocks away and then wait for me.

I throw a couple hundred-dollar bills in his lap to show him I'm serious. "Double that if you wait."

"Not a problem, sir."

I walk, then, the two blocks to the warehouse, to the address on the card Dirk gave me.

I'm going to finish this once and for all.

CHAPTER THIRTY-NINE

Tessa

Sherlock drops me off at my place, and I head up.

I won't be getting another kiss from Ben tonight after all.

It's early in the day yet, about two p.m.

I sigh.

The zoo seemed the perfect place to feel Da one last time, but I know something else that will be nearly as perfect. I'll make one of Mommy's recipes—Da's favorite food in the world.

I'll cook for him. I'll cook for me.

I have to go to the market. I grab my mom's recipe for cheese enchiladas, which is my favorite. It was also Da's favorite.

I grab my purse and walk to the nearest market. It's Sunday, so they will close soon, but I make it just in time. Mommy's red sauce requires a bunch of different ground peppers, but I can't find them all. Regular chili powder will do, laced with a little cayenne.

Corn tortillas, cheddar jack cheese, and lettuce, onions, and tomatoes for toppings. And for the sauce? Chili powder, cayenne, garlic, onion, cumin, tomato paste, and water with flour for thickening.

I grab everything I need, and then, on a whim, I also grab the ingredients to make caramel flan, one of my mother's signature desserts.

I didn't expect to buy so many groceries, and as I load my two reusable bags, I realize how heavy they are for the walk back to my place.

But that doesn't matter, as my step is light, and I'm excited.

I'm going to make enchiladas and flan for Da and me.

I smile.

And Ben.

I'm going to invite Ben over for dinner.

He may not be able to come, since he had to go to work, but I'm going to invite him anyway. And if he can't make it? I'll eat and have leftovers.

What's important is that I feel like eating.

My enchiladas won't be as good as what Aunt Lily made yesterday as part of her feast for Da's reception. But that's okay.

These are for Da and me. If Ben's available, I'll invite him over to share them. But I need to remember to do good things for myself, too. I'm important.

I get back to my place, and I'm gathering the ingredients together when my phone rings.

It's Skye. She's checking in as usual.

"Hi, Skye," I say into my phone.

"You doing okay today, Tess?"

"Yeah, I am." I walk through my kitchenette into my small living area. "I know this makes no sense at all, but I actually feel better than I have in a long time."

"Tessa?" Skye's tone is concerned.

"I know. My father. I'm going to miss him terribly, and I hate the fact that I didn't get to say goodbye in person. But we had a good relationship, Skye, even after I left the church. He knows how much I loved him and cherished him. I can't imagine what life's going to be like without him, but for some reason I feel like cooking today."

"You?"

"Hey, I can cook."

"If you call packaged ramen and Lean Cuisines cooking."

"I eat that stuff because I don't have time to cook most of the time," I say.

She scoffs at me.

"Okay, fine. I'm lying. I do make killer guac, though. I need to hold onto my roots, Skye. My dad is gone. It was so unexpected. What if the same thing happens to my mother? I need to learn how to cook. Cook all of the Mexican favorites from her side of the family, and even some Irish stuff for my dad. I'm starting today. Because I feel like it. I'm going to make some cheese enchiladas."

"Sounds yummy. I'd invite myself over, except Braden and I already have plans."

"Actually, I'm going to invite Ben."

Skye gasps. "Are the two of you—"

"No, not really. He's only kissed me once. Yesterday."

"At your father's funeral?"

"At the reception, actually. I was standing outside in the rain, and it was…"

I almost don't want to tell her because it was so perfect. If I tell her, if someone else knows, it'll be tainted in some way.

"Ben… He…kissed you?"

"Yeah."

"Just a kiss?"

"Yeah. I'm not even sure he was ready for that much, but the timing was perfect."

"That's very un-Ben-like."

"Meaning?"

"He moves quickly, Tessa."

"Not with me, apparently, which works out fine."

I stop talking for a moment. Does that mean he's not actually interested in me? Am I imagining it?

No, of course not. I can't be imagining it when he made such a point about wanting to kiss me but waiting for the right time.

"Tess? You still there?"

"Yeah, I'm here. He and I had lunch today, actually, but he got called into work. So he probably won't be able to come over to sample my mediocre enchiladas anyway, but I thought I'd invite him."

"First of all, your enchiladas won't be mediocre. Genetics alone should see to that."

"I've helped my mom in the kitchen many a time," I say, "but I've never actually made them myself."

"You want me to come help you? I don't have to meet Braden for a few hours."

"No, that's okay. For some reason, it seems really important that I do this myself."

"I understand. If you need anything, you know where I am. Day or night. I will always answer the phone for you."

"I know, Skye. Thanks."

I return to the task, whipping up the sauce. I mix together some butter and flour to make a roux, and then I add the chili powder until it's good and thick. I add water slowly, continuing to whisk as it boils and thickens.

Once that's done, I take the corn tortillas, dip them in the sauce, and fill them with cheese, folding them over and placing them in an oblong pan. When they're done, I pour the remaining sauce over all the enchiladas and top them with more cheese.

Then into the oven they go.

And I realize I haven't called Ben.

I decide to text him instead.

Tessa: *Hey. I hope your work is going well. I'm making enchiladas if you'd like to come over for dinner. I'm making flan, too.*

I set my phone down and wait for the ding of his return text.

And I wait.

And wait some more.

He's probably in a meeting. But on a Sunday afternoon?

Of course he could be. This is Black Inc. You don't get to be a billionaire without working all hours of the day, all days of the week. They do business all over the world. It's already Monday morning in China and Australia.

That's okay. If he can't make it for dinner, I will eat enchiladas to my heart's content.

Because I have an appetite now.

Just like I had an appetite this afternoon for lunch.

So odd, given that my father is gone.

But that was a week ago, and yesterday's funeral helped me say goodbye to him.

It also helped me realize that life is fragile and short.

And I don't want to spend one more second of it feeling sorry for myself or giving Garrett Ramirez any kind of control over it.

The robust aroma of the melted cheese starts to fill my small kitchen. I find my mom's recipe for flan, and I begin to assemble the ingredients.

Flan is a custard dish, which means eggs and milk. I'm

beginning to mix it together when my phone finally beeps.

I grab for it so quickly that I actually drop it onto my tile floor.

I pick it up and sigh in relief. The screen is intact.

Ben: *Sure, I'd love to. How about around six?*

Tessa: *Perfect.*

I pull the enchiladas out of the oven, cover them in foil, and put them in the fridge. I'll resume baking them later.

But I can still make the flan.

I find myself smiling and humming Mommy's old Mexican folk tunes as I pad about my kitchen, cooking for Ben Black.

Cooking for a man.

A man who...

A man who I think I might be able to love.

CHAPTER FORTY

Ben

I stare at the warehouse for a timeless moment, at the shadows cast over it by the afternoon sun. I draw in a breath.

I have to deal with this and put it behind me once and for all.

Especially if I want to make something work with Tessa.

I walk in, shoulders back, head held high. I'm not nervous so much as uneasy. He's got nothing except a tooth, which could belong to anyone.

"Right on time." Dirk gives me a snakelike smile.

I look around. "We secure here?"

"Sure."

Which means we're not. He doesn't have the resources to make sure we're secure. Good thing I don't have any tech on me. I case the small warehouse—and it is small, reminiscent of the warehouse where this shit took place fifteen years ago. Is this another black market warehouse?

"Where'd you find this place?" I ask.

"Does that matter?"

"Sure as hell matters to me. I don't like being forced into a corner."

"So you admit I've got you?"

"I admit nothing." I look him up and down, from the Yankees hat to the scuffed-up work boots on his feet. "You're probably wired. Or you're trying to record me on your phone. None of it will work, because none of it is admissible in court."

"Maybe I'm working for the cops."

"You think I didn't already check that out?" I scoff. "What I don't understand, Dirk, is why you're pushing this. You stand to lose a lot more than I do."

"There are worse things than spending the rest of your life behind bars. Free food, shelter, clothing for life."

I regard his gold bracelet. "You don't look like you're doing so poorly."

"Only because I'm good at stealing." He smirks. "Also, if I'm in prison, I don't have to support those bitches who had my kids."

"Nice. You screw them and then don't want to deal with the consequences. You ever hear of a condom, dumbass?"

"Fuck off."

"I'd be happy to." I turn to leave.

"You're not going anywhere."

Is he armed? Probably. He told me to come unarmed. Which I didn't, of course.

I look him straight in the eye. "Did you ever think of putting all that pent-up energy to use doing something good instead of something criminal?"

"That ship sailed a long time ago, Black. For both of us."

I shake my head, stepping toward him. "That's where you're wrong. That ship didn't sail. You fucking killed a man, Dirk.

You. Not me. Not Carlos. Not Jerry. Maybe we're accessories, but the actual murder? That's on you."

"Don't forget whose idea the whole thing was in the first place," he reminds me.

As if I could. But I don't say this. Instead—

"I haven't forgotten. It was *your* idea."

"The fuck are you talking about, Black? I didn't even *know* about that warehouse."

"And I *did*?"

I'm playing a dangerous game, and I know it. Indeed, it *was* my idea to rob the warehouse, only because I knew there was a stash of cash there. Someone else apparently knew as well and got there first.

To his detriment. The poor fucker got killed by Dirk. Got his teeth yanked out by Jerry.

Wrapped up in my tarp.

After we stashed the body in the Boston Bay, I went back to the warehouse early in the morning and I scrubbed away every drop of blood I could find.

I was ready to put my share of the money back, but ultimately I decided not to. Why the hell should Jerry, Carlos, and Dirk get paid out and not me?

Dirk knows none of this. After that night, I told those three never to speak to me again.

They never did.

"It was self-defense," Dirk says.

"He didn't pull a gun on you."

"Maybe he did."

"You're a fucking moron, Dirk. Don't pull that shit with me. I know the truth. It was all your idea, and you needed me to come because I had a truck."

He curls his hands into fists. "Fuck you, Black. It was my idea to hold up the convenience store. The warehouse was *your* idea."

I shake my head. "You're wrong. Why are you lying?"

"Why are *you* lying?"

Easy. I'm lying because Carlos is in Mexico and Jerry's in prison, so the only people who can corroborate Dirk's story are a convict and a guy who's not in the country.

I'm using my brain, which is what I should have done fifteen years ago. But I was being a dickhead back then. A fucking spoiled little rebel who didn't want to pull his share of the weight in the household.

I was being a prick and a stupid ass. If I could take it all back, I would.

But I can't. So I've got to get Dirk the hell off my back. Problem is? Sounds like he doesn't have anything to lose.

He doesn't mind going to prison and dragging me down with him.

I have great attorneys. There's no body. There's the tooth around Dirk's neck, but I've got people who can make quick work of that.

No, it's only my word against Dirk's. And without a body, no charges will be filed against either one of us.

He doesn't seem to know that, however. It's almost like he *wants* to go to prison.

I'm the one with something to lose. I'm Ben Black, and there will be publicity I sure as hell don't want.

Worse? Braden and my father will never forgive me.

Can the business survive it? Maybe. We have enough of a fortune to last more than ten lifetimes, but shit like this is what brings companies down.

So I have to deal with this myself, and it ends here and now.

"You want to go to the cops? You want to go to my brother, my father? Go for it, Dirk. I don't fucking care."

"Are you forgetting about this?" He pulls the tooth out from his collar again.

"Who gives a rat's ass? It's been fifteen years. No one will even know where to start looking for the person that belongs to."

"What if I know where the other twenty-seven are?" he asks.

I blink. "You don't."

"Maybe I do."

He's lying again, because *I'm* the one who took care of the fucking teeth. No way was I going to trust any of those three to do it. Each day, I put one in the trash and took it to the dump.

Those teeth are scattered far and wide in landfills at this point.

But I can't say that. I'm in the middle of trying to convince him that this was all his idea.

"You know what, then? Like I said, go for it. I'm sick and tired of these fucking games, Dirk. We're thirty-two years old now, and I've got a damned good life. The fact that you screwed yours up is not my problem."

"I think it is." He plays with the tooth around his neck. "I want ten million, Black. Unmarked bills, and I promise you'll never hear from me again."

"You made that promise to me once three months ago, yet here you are."

"Yeah? You didn't pay up then."

"You didn't send me anything like you said you would. Clearly you thought better of blackmailing me then. So what the hell are you doing now?" I drop my gaze to his neck. "If you had that tooth three months ago, you would have rubbed my nose in it then."

He shrugs. "Turns out I didn't need the money as bad as I thought I did. I figured it was better to wait, and I'm glad I did, because now you've got something that my brother and I both want."

Rage curls at the back of my neck. "Don't you fucking dare go near her."

"Seems I can kill two birds with one stone. I can get that tall, sweet thing, let my brother have his way with her, and then give her to Garrett Ramirez to dispose of."

My hands clench into fists as full-fledged rage sweeps through me, landing at the back of my neck. "Don't you fucking dare go near her."

"She's alone right now. At her place, isn't she?"

Why did I leave Tessa alone there? I called to get security on her, but—

I stalk forward, ready to pummel the smirk of his ugly face. "If you harm one fucking hair on her head, I'll—"

He raises his hand. "Shut the fuck up, Black. Ten million, and this all goes away."

"You're not getting a fucking penny from me."

"Then I guess I have to go to Daddy and big brother."

I meet his gaze, my own darting daggers at him. "You know what? Fucking go for it. Do whatever you want. They'll be angry, yeah. But in the end, blood is thicker than water, and you'll get what's coming to you." I grab him by the shirt, yank the chain off his neck, and throw him to the concrete floor of the warehouse.

"You give that back, you son of a bitch." He rises, rubbing his behind.

I dangle it right out of his reach. "I didn't want to do this, but I think I'll have to invoke the age-old finders-keepers rule."

"You didn't find it. You took it."

"Potato po-tah-to," I say. "I've got better things to do now. Do *not* contact me again."

CHAPTER FORTY-ONE

Tessa

The flan is out of the oven and cooling. I place sugar and butter in a small saucepan to make the caramel sauce, and once the flan is set, I'll refrigerate it and apply the sauce later.

Ben is coming.

I decide to take a shower, and then on a whim I paint my fingernails and toenails.

I had a manicure and pedicure in Jamaica, but I haven't done this myself since...

Since before Garrett.

I wiggle my toes, looking at the light blue color.

I've missed this.

I've missed doing the silly things girls do—painting my fingernails and toenails, getting excited about a new guy.

It feels...

It feels *good*.

Part of it will always be tainted by what Garrett did. About what happened before my first communion.

And I'll always miss my father.

But my heart still beats.

And I want to make the most of this life.

I dress in a pair of baggy jeans—boyfriend jeans as Skye calls them. But I like them. I like them because I can pair them with a tight top—today a skintight blue camisole that matches the color I painted my fingers and toes.

The contrast of the loose boyfriend jeans and the tight camisole looks good. Sexy, even.

Funny. I haven't dressed to entice a man in a long time. Sure, I wore a bathing suit in Jamaica, but that was because I was in Jamaica. I was on the beach. That's where you wear bathing suits.

I could've bought a one-piece for the trip, but I don't like one-pieces. I hate how you have to take the whole thing off when you need to go to the bathroom. It's a pain, and for that reason alone, I've always preferred two-piece suits.

My hair is clean and glossy, and I'm tempted to wear it down, but instead, because I'm cooking, I pull it up into a high ponytail to keep it out of my face.

When I look in the mirror, the person looking back at me finally looks familiar.

I'm back. I may not be completely healed yet, but I'm here. I'm me. And I'm cooking for a man I'm interested in. A man who has only kissed me once.

I need another kiss.

Old Tessa wore a lot of makeup. I was big on the smoky eye and lots of contour. Tonight I choose not to do that. I keep it to some lip stain and some blush with just a touch of mascara.

That's it.

And I still see me.

I'll never be the Tessa of old. Experience has changed her.

But I don't have to be sad-and-depressed Tessa, either.

I can be a new Tessa. New Tessa doesn't need to hide behind makeup. New Tessa appreciates her own natural beauty.

Satisfied, I leave the bathroom, keeping my feet bare. The combination of tight camisole and boyfriend jeans works well with bare feet, especially when my toes are freshly painted.

I head to my kitchenette, pull the enchiladas out of the refrigerator, remove the foil, and slide them into my preheated oven.

I wish I'd had time to make homemade refried beans, but I didn't. That's a twenty-four-hour project, starting with letting pinto beans cook on low in a slow cooker overnight.

So I cheat. I open a can of refried beans, throw them in a pot over the stove, and add some salsa, mixing until they're heated. Then I place them in a ceramic dish, shred some cheese on top, and slide them in the oven with the enchiladas.

I couldn't find any good-looking avocados at the market, so no homemade guacamole tonight. But I did put together some pico de gallo with a jalapeno added for spiciness, which I'll serve with tortilla chips.

Rita shuffles around my feet. I pick her up. "Hello, Margarita." I kiss her little head. "Any other time when I made this meal, I would be making your namesake cocktail."

Margaritas.

Rita.

Saint Rita. The patron saint of something that speaks to me now.

I know Ben likes Wild Turkey, but he *did* drink a margarita in Jamaica the first night.

I wish I had some Wild Turkey...

I don't, but I do have the ingredients to make margaritas. It may not be what Ben wants, but it's been so long since I've had a margarita, and I think I'd like one.

The Skye cocktail in Jamaica was quite good, but not as good as a margarita.

I put Rita down. "What the heck?" I say out loud. "Let's make some margaritas, Rita."

I take my bottle of reposado from the small cupboard above my refrigerator and grab several limes out of the fruit drawer. Sugar and triple sec are next.

I halve the limes and juice them until I have one full cup of lime juice.

Then I grab my blender and mix everything together.

I'm a purist. I don't drink my margaritas frozen. I mix them, and then I shake them over ice in a cocktail shaker.

That makes them cold but doesn't dilute them.

But I wait. I'll shake them once Ben gets here and then—

Rita barks at a knock on the door.

"He's here, Rita!"

I pad to the door in my bare feet, and I open it.

And Ben—gorgeous Ben—comes right in.

Before I know it, he grabs my face, and he touches his lips to mine.

CHAPTER FORTY-TWO

Ben

God, her lips.

As soft and sweet as I remember. Even more so. My cock responds, aching in my jeans.

I pull back, ending the kiss before it even starts.

Tessa widens her eyes, her lips still parted and glistening from the kiss.

She looks beautiful. She's dressed in a sky blue tank top that hugs her curves—and her nipples are hard against the fabric.

Her feet are bare, and it's incredibly erotic.

I want to throw her up against the wall and fuck her into it. I want to fuck her in the shower, on the couch, on the dining table, on the kitchen counter, on her bed, on the floor, against the wall. Especially after the day I've had.

But I can't. I have to behave myself. I have to do this thing right.

"Sorry," I say.

She pulls away, smiling. "I don't think I was complaining."

"I had a shitty afternoon, Tessa, but that's not your fault." He caresses my cheek. "I should have come in, said hello first."

"I'm sorry you had a bad afternoon." She hugs me and presses her cheek to my chest. It feels so good, so comforting, and so… "You want to talk about it?"

"Not particularly." I inhale. "Something smells amazing in here."

She waves toward her small kitchen. "I know we just had Mexican food yesterday at my father's funeral, but I felt like cooking my mother's recipes. Which is odd, because I'm not a cook and haven't made anything for myself since…well, before Garrett."

I hold back a wince at her mention of Garrett. I'll have to pay a visit to the little leech, make sure he and Dirk's brother stay far away from my woman.

My woman?

My God…

I've only kissed her, and now she's my woman?

I'm fucked in the head. So fucked in the head that I'll protect her at all costs. I'll bulldoze Boston to the ground if I have to.

Fuck. I rake my fingers through my hair. I've never felt this way about any woman before. Hell, I've never felt this way about any*one* before.

I breathe in. "I love Mexican food. I can eat it seven days a week."

"I'm glad, because I made it from my favorite of my mother's recipes. Cheese enchiladas with homemade red sauce."

I inhale again. "It smells amazing."

"Come in. I've got some chips and salsa set out. And I made margaritas."

I can't help smiling at her. Not my favorite, but for Tessa I'll happily drink battery acid.

"I know it's not Wild Turkey but—"

"Tessa, a margarita sounds delicious. Normally I don't go for the sweeter drinks, but with Mexican food, it feels right."

"I haven't made margaritas in a long time." Her lips tremble slightly. "I haven't drunk a margarita in a long time."

"You told me it's your favorite drink."

"It is." She kneels and scratches her dog behind her ear. "I named Rita after a margarita."

I smile. "That's so adorable."

"I don't know about adorable, but I think I'd like to have a margarita. Jamaica was the first time I drank anything alcoholic since…well, you know. I felt like I wanted one tonight."

I follow her into her small kitchen. She pours the margaritas into a shaker. Then she strains them into two lowball glasses with salted rims and hands one glass to me.

"Cheers," I say, clicking my glass to hers.

"Cheers," she echoes and takes a sip.

I smile then because what I see is pure sunshine and goodness. Tessa's face lights up like downtown Boston during the holidays.

"Good?" I ask.

"So good." She licks a few grains of salt from her lips. "The salt, and the tangy sweetness of the lime, and the smoky tequila… I really forgot how much I love margaritas." She sighs. "I seem to have forgotten a lot of things."

"You'll remember." I take a sip. The lime and salt are tangy on my tongue, and the tequila has a bite that I like. Much better than the one in Jamaica. "This is delicious. What kind of margarita mix did you use?"

She scoffs. "Margarita mix? That stuff's awful. I make my own simple syrup, and I use the juice from fresh-squeezed limes. I use reposado tequila, and I also use Cointreau instead of a cheap triple sec. If I'm really feeling excited I use Grand Marnier, but I don't have any."

"I can honestly say this is the best margarita I have ever tasted."

"I imagine it's one of the *only* margaritas you ever tasted."

"Now that's not true. When I was young, I preferred sweeter drinks over straight bourbon." I stop abruptly.

Not a great time to think about when I was young. Tonight can't be about anything except Tessa and me.

"Are you okay?"

"Yeah. But I don't want to think about my younger days right now."

In fact...

What I want is to kiss her again.

I take another sip of the margarita, and then I set it down on her small counter before taking hers out of her hand and setting it beside my own.

I cup both her cheeks. "God, your skin is like silk."

She moves her hands upward, covering mine with her own.

Then she parts her lips.

I wait.

I wait for her to say something.

But she doesn't.

So I kiss her.

I kiss her, and the sweetness of her lips infuses me, takes me to a place where everything is okay.

She doesn't resist, not at all.

So I deepen the kiss.

I touch my tongue to hers, swirl it around, tasting every part of her mouth.

She tastes of lime and sugar and tequila and salt.

But she also tastes like Tessa. A sweetness that doesn't come from the margarita.

A sweetness that's all her own.

She moves her hands from mine and wraps her arms around my neck, pulling me close to her.

I'm already hard, and our bodies are touching, so she can feel my arousal.

But it doesn't seem to bother her.

We kiss, my heartbeat becoming rapid, my need transforming to pure yearning.

All that energy—the tension that has been inside me since my meeting with Dirk—I let it go in this kiss.

I move my hands from her face, grip her shoulders, slide one hand into her beautiful hair, and pull the band out of her ponytail, letting her hair flow around her shoulders.

Then I grasp a handful of it, yanking her head back as I break the kiss, trailing my lips over her silky neck, kissing her, moving my lips to her ear, and tugging on her lobe.

"Tessa…" I growl into her ear.

"Ben…" she replies on a soft sigh.

"I…"

"I know," she says. "Me too."

I'm not sure she knows what I mean. What I mean is that I need her. I want her. I *ache* for her right now.

I want to fuck her into next Tuesday. My cock is hard as granite and yearns to be set free.

All this time I tried to go slow, not kissing her until the time was right—yesterday in the rain.

God, it was so right.

And now I want it all. To sink into her lush body and lose myself.

But no.

She cooked me an amazing dinner.

I can't… I can't…

"It's okay," she says. "Please. I want to."

I turn her around so she's facing her counter, my bulge hitting her lower back.

"Be sure, Tessa," I whisper against her neck. "Be sure, because if we start this, I'm not going to want to stop."

"I'm—"

The kitchen timer clangs.

"Crap," she says.

"What is that?"

"The enchiladas. They're done."

I move away from her, chuckling. "Saved by the bell, so they say."

She turns around, swallows, and meets my gaze. "I don't think I wanted to be saved that time, Ben."

I lean against her kitchen counter. "It's not a bad thing. It will give us both a chance to cool off. You went to the trouble to make dinner, and I plan to enjoy it."

She smiles. It's a weak smile, but a genuine smile. Different from the other weak smiles I've seen on her beautiful face lately.

She grabs a couple of potholders and pulls two pans out of the oven.

"Cheese enchiladas and refried beans," she says. "They'll need a few minutes to cool."

I inhale the spicy and robust aroma. "Smells delicious."

She picks up her margarita and takes a sip. "I hope so. I've never made these without my mom's help. Like I said, I'm not really a cook, other than a killer guac. But I felt like making my mom's recipes today."

I squeeze her arm. "Probably because you're missing your dad."

She nods. "He loved my mom's Mexican food. He said he could eat it every day."

I pick up my margarita and drain it.

"You want another?"

"No."

She frowns.

I hold up a hand. "No, it's not that I didn't like it. I just don't want to have more than one drink tonight. I want to have all my faculties about me, because when I kiss you again, Tessa, I want to be fully aware of everything I'm doing. I don't want a buzz to keep me from enjoying our time together."

She smiles again. It's weak but genuine. "Okay. Have a seat." She motions to her small table where two place settings are set.

Glasses of water are already poured, and she picks up my plate, serves me some enchiladas and a glop of refried beans, and sets it back down. She serves herself and sits down across from me. She closes her eyes for a few moments, then opens them.

"Dig in," she says.

"Were you…praying?"

Her cheeks blush a bit. "Yes and no. I already told you I left my parents' religion long ago, but I like to always express gratitude before I eat. I've gotten out of the habit, but it seems more important than ever now that I express gratitude for everything I have. I want to remember that no matter what struggles I'm having, my life is actually pretty darned good, and I'm grateful."

"Your heart still beats," I say softly.

"Yeah." Her brown eyes are warm as she looks at me. "You told me that on the plane going to Jamaica."

"I did." I pick up my fork and look down at my plate.

"Something I have to remind myself of a lot. Especially lately."

"Something going on?"

I smile. "No. Everything's fine."

I can't burden her with my problems. I could make them go away in an instant with money, at least for now, but then they'd only come back to haunt me again.

I have to figure out a better way.

"Tell me more about your religion while you were growing up," I say.

She lifts her eyebrows. "Are you sure you want to hear more about that?"

"You look surprised."

"I am. You don't seem the religious type."

"I'm not, but I find it interesting. I told you we went to church on Christmas and Easter before my mom passed away, but that was about it. I believe in a higher power, but I don't follow any particular religion. So yeah, I'm interested."

"My parents were very devout Catholics," she says. "They were both raised in religious families. Irish Catholic and Mexican Catholic. And then there was my grandmother."

"Oh?"

"Yeah. I told you about her altar. She studied all the saints, taught me a lot about them. But there was also a mystical side to her religion. She used to say it was Santeria."

"I'm not sure I know what Santeria is."

"I've never quite understood it. It literally means 'the way of the saints.' Her mother—my great-grandmother—was Cuban, and she practiced Santeria, but what Nana did was really Catholicism with some mystical stuff thrown in. She sought personal relationships with God and the Blessed Mother and the saints through prayer mostly, but also through some divination.

But she didn't worship other gods." Tessa smiles. "I remember one time she thought the remnants of enchilada sauce on her plate was an apparition of the Blessed Mother."

"You mean the Virgin Mary?"

"Yeah. I thought Da was going to pee himself right at the dinner table, he laughed so hard. Nana didn't speak to him for twenty-four hours after that. But she loved my father. Absolutely adored him. She forgave him." Tessa laughs, but then her face twists slightly. "I haven't thought about that in forever. His humor was so much a part of him. I miss him so much."

Her laugh pleases me, but I feel the pain of her missing her father. "I know. I'm sorry."

She shakes her head. "I'll be okay. He'll always be here." She places her hand over her heart. "But anyway, Nana didn't indoctrinate me into religion or anything, but she and I were very close. When I was little, I thought it was really cool to watch her light her candles, pray to the saints, do her rosaries."

Her stories warm me. "I'm glad you were so close to her."

"Yeah. I never really knew my grandparents on my father's side. They both died when I was quite young."

"I'm sorry to hear that."

She shrugs. "I suppose you can't miss what you never had. Anyway, my grandmother was always my safe space. When I sat on her lap, no harm could come to me."

"And you were named after her."

"Right. Teresa Maria."

"It's a beautiful name."

"I always kind of hated it." She chuckles. "Even though I loved my grandmother who also had the name. But I like the nickname I got—Tessa. It was different and unique. I've never known another Tessa in all my years of going to school and in being in the workforce."

"It *is* unique." I gaze into her eyes. "And it's beautiful. It suits you."

She looks down, her cheeks turning a beautiful rose. "Thank you."

I finally take a bite of enchilada. The flavor explodes on my tongue—the creaminess of the cheese, the smoke and spice of the sauce, and the subtle sweetness of the corn tortilla. "My God," I say. "This is delicious."

"Better than Aunt Lily's at the funeral?"

"Doesn't even come close."

"Aunt Lily uses this exact recipe," she says. "But she was cooking for a large crowd, and that's different."

I take another bite, relishing the deliciousness.

"I have flan for dessert," Tessa says.

I nod.

But I already know what I want for dessert.

CHAPTER FORTY-THREE

Tessa

The way he's looking at me...

I've seen that look in a man's eyes before. Many times, of course.

He wants me.

And for once, that fact doesn't frighten me.

It arouses me.

I want him to want me.

I'm ready for him to want me.

Because I want him, too.

If possible, I want him more than I've ever wanted a man before.

When both our plates are clean, I swallow, gathering my courage. "We could have our dessert later."

"Are you sure?" he asks.

I nod a bit hesitantly—not because I'm actually hesitant, but because this is Ben Black. The billionaire extraordinaire who could have any woman on the planet. Can I measure up? *Will* I measure up?

Old Tessa wouldn't have concerned herself with such thoughts. She would have let her hair down and seized the day.

"Say it, Tessa," he commands. "Say you're sure. Say you want me to take you to bed."

I gulp down my last bit of apprehension. "I'm sure, Ben. I'm very sure. I'm feeling things with you I wasn't sure I could ever feel again."

His lips are on mine then, and the kiss is feral. So raw and untamed, and I welcome it.

I melt into him, into the kiss, into everything this represents. Not just the first time with a man I'm attracted to and who I think I might love, but the taking back of my body. Of my heart and soul.

This is Ben. Kind Ben who won't harm me. Who'll be with me every step of the way.

And there it is… That familiar tickle between my legs that I felt for the first time in what seemed like forever when Ben kissed me under the rain.

I let my hands wander over his broad shoulders, into his silky dark hair. He groans against me, a humming growl that I feel more than hear.

Ben's aroma of leather and spice mingles with the scent of the Mexican food. He tastes of all three, his tongue like velvet against mine as our lips slide together in a kiss that is ferocious in its intensity.

Have I ever been kissed like this? Have I ever wanted a man this much?

Mere weeks ago, I didn't think I'd ever want a man this close to me again.

But then Ben…

Sweet but commanding Ben, who refused to kiss me until the

right time, who told me what would happen if he'd kissed me that night on the beach…

That's going to happen now…and I want it.

I want it so much.

He breaks the kiss with a smack.

Disappointment surges through me. "Ben?" I say tentatively.

"I want to go slow with you, Tessa, but I—" He shakes his head. "I need you. I need to fuck you, and I need it now."

I absently touch my finger to my lips, tender and swollen from our passionate kiss.

Ben's eyes—they're both on fire and haunted at the same time.

"What is it?" I ask.

"I have no business being here, asking this of you." He threads his fingers through his hair.

I close the distance between us, cup his stubbled cheek. "You have every business being here. I invited you. I want you here. I want *this*."

He grabs me by my waist and pulls me into him, the bulge in his jeans grinding into my tummy. "I'm giving you this one chance, Tessa," he says. "If you ask me to leave, I'll leave. But if you don't, I'm going to fuck you. And it's going to be hard and fast. It won't be pretty. But it *will* be consensual, I assure you."

His words travel into my ears and straight between my legs.

I've had pretty fucks. Lots of them. Right now I want Ben. I want to be with him, but I also want to give him what he needs.

"You deserve better," he says before I have a chance to reply. "So tell me to leave, Tessa. Tell me to leave, and I will."

I look into his burning brown eyes, into his soul.

Something torments him, and it's not just how much he wants me in this moment. That's part of it, but there's more. Much more.

"Take what you need from me," I say. "Please, Ben. I want this as much as you do."

He inhales deeply. "I want to give you what you need, and I can't right now."

I look him right in his beautiful and tormented dark eyes. I want more than anything to ease his pain. Whatever is haunting him, I want to be the one to erase it. "What I need is what *you* need. I swear it."

His mouth comes down on mine once more.

Everything. This is everything all at once. The feel of his tongue entwined with mine, the robust flavor of his mouth, the fullness of his lips, the spicy scent of him.

And the bulge.

The bulge showing how much he wants me. How much he needs me.

That part of a man I thought I might never want to see or feel again.

I want to see and feel it more than I ever have.

He slides one hand over my breast, cupping it, thumbing the nipple underneath the fabric of my camisole.

Sparks skitter under my flesh, and I nudge against his bulge, grinding.

He groans another growl into me, and then he breaks the kiss, his eyes on fire. "Bed," is all he says.

I lead him to my small bedroom, to my unmade bed.

He pulls the cami over my breasts, letting them fall free, and he sucks in a breath. "Fuck. So damned beautiful."

Warmth spreads over me as he unbuttons his shirt, revealing his hard chest, perfect pecs, and abs with just a smattering of black hair over them. I take my lower lip between my teeth, and I gawk at him. Simply gawk. It's nothing I haven't seen before. I saw him shirtless in Jamaica. But in this moment, he's mine.

All mine.

No one else is looking upon this magnificence except for me.

"Still sure?" he asks, his voice low and husky.

"God, yes."

He cups both breasts, staring into my eyes. "Fuck. I need you so much."

I fall against him, literal putty in his hands. "Then take me, Ben. Please."

He unsnaps and unzips my jeans and thrusts his hand inside my panties. "God. You're soaked."

My feet are bare, and I wriggle out of my jeans until I'm standing only in my purple panties.

He slides his fingers under the waistband and glides the panties over my ass and hips, and I step out of them.

He rids himself of his shoes and socks and then undoes his belt and jeans in rapid succession.

When he stands before me, his massive cock jutting from his thick black bush, I gulp.

He's so beautiful, and I want—

But before I think any further, he grabs a condom out of the pocket of his jeans and sheathes himself, and in another second, I'm on the bed, and he's inside me.

CHAPTER FORTY-FOUR

Ben

Fuck.

She's so tight, a perfect fit.

I stay inside her sweet cunt for a few timeless seconds before I pull out and thrust back in.

Thrust, thrust, thrust...

Hard, hard, hard...

Soft moans fly from Tessa's throat.

I should do more for her...

I should suck on those gorgeous nipples...

Eat that delicious pussy...

Give her one, two, three orgasms...

And I will.

Just not now.

Thrust, thrust, thrust...

Until—

"God, yes," I groan, spilling into her.

And with my climax, I release the horror of this day.

Or I try to.

For when the contractions cease, and I move off Tessa, relaxation sweeping through my body...

I find it's all still there.

The memories of what I did all those years ago.

Dirk, the tooth, his threats about his brother and Tessa.

Everything I thought might miraculously go away.

It's all still there.

I lie for a moment, my arm over my forehead, and I berate myself.

She gave me permission, but I shouldn't have done this. I should have taken my time with her. Made love to her the way she deserved. Made her feel as important as she truly is to me.

Instead, I fucked her. I took care of my own needs first.

Now I feel like river scum.

I turn to her. "I'm so sorry, Tessa."

"For what?" she asks, her voice soft and forgiving.

"Your first time after... It shouldn't have been like that."

She kisses my neck. "You told me exactly what you were going to do, Ben, and I said okay. This isn't on you."

"It's not on you, either."

"It's on both of us. You told me what you needed, and I told you to take what you needed."

"But you—"

She reaches forward and quiets me with two soft fingers over my lips. "Please. It's okay."

Such overwhelming emotion grips me. It's...intense. And foreign. And so, so deep and powerful. It's rage at the thought of what Dirk wants to do to her. Fury at Garrett Ramirez for doing it. Sheer wrath at any threat against her. And fucking madness at the thought of any other man ever frightening her or touching her or even looking her way.

And at the same time, it's tenderness. Warmth.

Fuck.

It's that moment when everything in your fucked-up life seems clear as day because you've found the one person you're meant to be with.

It's *love*.

I caress her cheeks, her jawline. I kiss her neck, the tops of her breasts. She's so lovely, flushed from the quick fuck, and despite what she's been through—her assault and drugging, the death of her father—she put my needs ahead of her own.

This is a woman I can no longer live without. Tessa. She's the one.

When I move backward, look into her gorgeous eyes, she smiles at me.

All is still good. Thank God.

I play with her nipples using my lips and my fingers, relish in her moans and sighs.

"Now, Tessa," I say, "I'm going to love you the way you deserve."

CHAPTER FORTY-FIVE

Tessa

I let out a whimper of loss when Ben rises from the bed. He disposes of the condom in the wastebasket, and then he returns, looking me up and down with wide eyes.

"My God," he says, rejoining me on the bed. "You're the most beautiful woman I've ever seen."

"You're the most magnificent man I've ever seen."

He rubs his cheeks against my breasts, the stubble making me tingle. "I'm going to suck on these tits, Tessa. Then I'm going to suck on that sweet pussy until you come so hard you're going to beg me to stop."

His words ignite me with more passion. "Please..." I beg.

He kisses my mouth first—a deep and passionate kiss with the same urgency as before, yet it's slower and softer this time. Our mouths stay together for moments upon moments as I undulate beneath his hard body, arch my back, and lift my hips, searching, searching, searching...

When he breaks the kiss, I'm both saddened and gladdened. I miss his lips on mine, but I want his mouth other places.

In fact, the power of the ache I feel for him frightens me a little.

But I move past it—pretend I'm in the cold plunge where my mind is a blank.

I don't want past experiences tainting what Ben is about to do to me, and I won't let them.

He squeezes my breasts, stares at them for a few moments, tugs on my nipples. I writhe against him, letting the feelings possess me, shield me from what haunts me still.

This moment is all that matters.

When his lips clamp around one nipple, I moan at the feeling that courses through me. The want, the need, the sheer yearning. No one has touched me with such a combination of rawness and gentleness as Ben does.

He sucks on one nipple while toying with the other with his deft fingers, tugging and twisting gently at first, and then not so gently.

"Yes…" I say on a sigh.

"So beautiful," he says against my nipple. "So perfect."

When he drops the nipple from his lips, I let out a whimper. He meets my gaze. "You have the most succulent nipples I've ever tasted, Tessa."

I close my eyes, arch my back.

"Oh, no," he says. "You keep those eyes open. I want you to watch me devour this pussy of yours. I'm going to eat you raw, Tessa. I'm going to eat you until you don't know your own name."

He trails kisses down my abdomen and then spreads my legs.

He closes his eyes and inhales.

"My God, you smell good. Like a ripe peach. Will you taste as sweet?"

I can't wait for you to find out. But the words come out only as a soft sigh.

He opens his eyes. "You're so beautiful. So plump and swollen and wet for me."

He parts my legs farther and slides his tongue over my slit.

"Ah!" I cry out.

He stops, looking up at me, his chin glistening.

"It's okay," I say. "Please, Ben. Stop second-guessing yourself. Stop second-guessing *me*. I want this."

He smiles slyly and dives back into me. He nibbles on my clit for a few seconds and then slides his tongue into my pussy.

I arch my back, bend my legs until my feet are flat on the comfy bed so I can grind against his stubbled face. It's a good burn.

He feasts on me, and with each slide of his tongue, each nibble of his lips, I glide closer, closer, closer…

Until—

"My God, Ben!"

He thrusts a finger into my pussy, and I catapult over the cliff and soar over a gorgeous blue sea of ecstasy.

The climax caresses me like a hug while also shattering me as if I've been struck by a lightning bolt.

"That's it," his voice says from somewhere inside my bubble. "You come, Tessa. You come for me. Only for me."

My walls contract around his finger as he moves it with deft precision inside me, over and around and finding that perfect spot that sends me reeling once more.

"Have you had enough yet?" he asks against my flesh.

But I can't form the words to answer him, and he continues, jolting me into yet a third orgasm.

I'm not sure I've ever had a third before.

I'm not even sure of my own name at this point.

I'm lost.

Lost in an ocean of paradise.

All thoughts cease... Only pleasure... Rapture... Euphoria...

And the perfection of what I'm feeling.

When I come down, Ben eases his finger from me, climbs up my body, and kisses me, our flavors mingling on our tongues.

I sigh.

Still perfection.

•••

SEVERAL MONTHS EARLIER...

"Ugh," Skye says to me. "Why do I even try?"

"Because it's good for you." I pull my body upward from my perfect downward dog.

Skye and I are doing okay. I've been a bitch about her and Braden, but after that incident with the ecstasy, I'm feeling better about everything. I hate drugs. I always said I'd never try them.

And I never will again. Not ever.

Skye sighs. "I do love yoga, and yeah, it helps with stress and all that, but the fucking downward dog!"

"It's tough for some people."

"That's what you always say."

I give her a playful punch on her shoulder. "And I'm still right."

Skye laughs. We're both panting and sweating after a hot yoga class.

She grabs a towel and wraps it around her neck. "I need a shower."

"See you in the steam room," I say.

Skye nods and heads toward the locker room. I take a long

drink from my water bottle and then grab a clean towel to sponge off my face.

"Hi, Tessa."

I jerk.

It can't be.

Garrett? At a yoga studio?

No way.

And of course he looks like a god in his muscle shirt and shorts.

"I assume you're not here for yoga," I say.

"I was watching the class from outside the room," he says.

"Stalking?" I can't help saying. Since I left him at his house with Lolita, he's been calling and leaving messages, which I've been ignoring.

"No." His gaze darkens. "Waiting for you. I know you and Skye always do yoga here on Saturdays. You told me, remember?"

"I remember a lot of things," I mumble.

He reaches toward me. "Tessa…"

I slap his hand away. "What do you want, Garrett?"

He breathes in. "God, it's hot in here."

"We just had a hot yoga class. It's supposed to be hot." I walk out of the studio, and he follows me. "What is it?" I ask again.

"I just wanted to say I'm sorry and that I won't be bothering you anymore. If you tell me no this time, I'll never bother you again."

"Okay."

"I really am sorry." He reaches toward me again, but he doesn't touch me. "I'm not seeing Lolita anymore. It really was just a hookup."

"Okay," I echo.

God, he looks so good. I hate myself for still wanting him.

"I made a huge mistake, choosing her. Please, let me make it up to you. Have dinner with me tonight."

Everything in me says I should tell him to fuck off. To get the hell away from me and never come near me again.

Except—

"Fine. All right. I'll have dinner with you."

A grin splits his handsome face. "Awesome! I'll pick you up at your place at seven. Wear something sexy." He gives me a quick kiss on the cheek and leaves the gym.

I take my towel, go to the locker room, and shed my sweaty clothes for another towel. I'm feeling equal parts giddy and shitty. I breathe in the steam, letting the humidity and the eucalyptus scent relax me.

"You in here, Tess?" Skye's voice.

"Over here." I take a long drink from my water bottle. "You're not going to believe this."

"What?" she asks.

"I just ran into Garrett."

"In the ladies' locker room?"

I chuckle. "No. After you left the yoga studio, he walked in."

"Garrett? At yoga?"

"He was wearing a muscle shirt and jock shorts. Fuck, Skye, he looked amazing."

"Uh-oh."

"Right? Anyway, he said he was waiting for our class to end so he could talk to me."

"Ugh. Stalker much?"

Ha. I said the same thing when he arrived. "No, he just said he's sorry he's been bothering me, and if I tell him no this time, he'll leave me alone."

"So what did you tell him?"

"I told him…" I look away from Skye, camouflaging myself in the steam. "I'd have dinner with him tonight."

Skye breathes out slowly. "Tessa…"

"Well, it's not like we said we were exclusive, right?"

"Right. You're right."

"I've missed him."

"Why don't we find you another guy?"

"I'm not getting on a website, Skye."

"That's not what I mean. You want to meet Braden's brother?"

"Ben Black?"

"That's the one."

"Is he available?"

"As far as I know."

I inhale a breath and let it out slowly. "No, I don't think so. I mean, thanks for the offer, but I hate fix-ups."

"Okay." Skye shrugs. "Let me know if you change your mind."

"To be honest, I'm still hung up on Garrett."

"I know. Or you would have told him to fuck off."

I sigh. "You got that right. So I need a favor."

"Of course. Anything."

"I need you to come to dinner with us tonight."

Skye bites her lip. "I'm so sorry, Tess. I made plans with Braden."

I sigh.

"I'm sorry," she says again.

I cross my legs and look away. "I'm always going to play second fiddle to him, aren't I?"

"No, but I wouldn't break plans with you if he asked me to, either."

I gulp down the rest of the water in my bottle. I'm not being fair, and I know it. "You're right. You have better things to do than be my babysitter."

"Maybe…" Skye scratches her chin.

"Maybe what?"

"I could check with Braden. Maybe we could join you guys for dinner and then—"

I hold up my hand, waving steam in my face. "No. Don't worry about it. I just…"

"What?"

"If I don't have a chaperone I'll end up in his bed."

"Be your own chaperone."

I roll my eyes. "That's such a Skye thing to say."

"And needing a chaperone is a Tessa thing. Black and white. If you don't have someone else there, you'll sleep with him. There's no middle ground." Skye shakes her head. "You're so much like Braden sometimes."

Skye has told me this countless times—that I see everything in black and white. No middle ground. Because I'm a mathematician, all I see is right and wrong. "I am?"

"Yeah. He says he doesn't accept anything as absolute, but in his way, he does."

"What do you mean?"

"He just has his own ideas, and nothing will sway him."

"He sounds more like you than like me," Tessa says.

"He's a lot like me in other ways. I'll grant you that. But that's not even my point." She grabs my hand. "My point is you don't need a chaperone. You *can* control yourself."

"Yeah. You're right. It would just make things easier."

"Life isn't always easy."

"Fuck," I say. "You sure got that right."

. . .

My eyes shoot open.

That last date with Garrett. The date that led to…

How, after my conversation with Skye, I was sure I could control myself…and I would have, if he hadn't drugged me.

In that same conversation, Skye asked if I wanted to meet Ben.

If only I'd said yes, I could have avoided all of the trauma… and ended up where I am now.

In bed with Ben snoring softly next to me.

In bed with the man I love.

CHAPTER FORTY-SIX

Ben

Waking up next to Tessa Logan feels all kinds of right. I sneak out of bed as the light streams into her bedroom and illuminates her luscious body. I grab another condom out of my jeans, return to bed, and spoon up against her, my cock hard as a rock.

"Baby…" I whisper.

"Mmm…" she softly moans.

I kiss the soft flesh of her tan shoulder, ease my cock between her ass cheeks. "This okay?" I ask.

"More than okay," she murmurs.

I slide into her pussy.

This is how I should have made love to her last night—slowly, sweetly, taking all the time to see to her pleasure before I took my own.

But last night…

Yesterday…

No.

Won't think about that now. Won't let any of that taint my

time with my girl.

Because she *is* my girl.

I'm in love with her. She's not ready for it, and neither am I. But I fucking love her with every bit of my heart and soul.

"Feels good," she mumbles.

"God, does it." I slide out and in again, relishing how perfectly she gloves my cock.

"Don't we both have to go to work this morning?" she asks.

"I'm the boss."

"You're not *my* boss."

"I'm your boss's boss." I pulse into her, releasing with a grunt.

I stay inside her until she moves away and turns to face me. "I'm not going to play that game. I'm not going to be the employee who's fucking the boss and gets away with everything. You'll get a full day's work from me every day, Ben. I swear it."

"Easy." I move her gorgeous dark hair off her forehead. "I'm kidding. But there's plenty of time. Plenty of time for me to take care of you, too."

She squirms out of my arms and off the bed. "You took plenty good care of me last night. But if I don't get moving, I'm going to be late for work."

"Okay, okay."

"And you need to get ready, too. Anyone who has to miss taking me to the zoo on a Sunday afternoon is obviously swamped, so get moving."

Thud.

Reality is back in full fucking force.

I wasn't working yesterday afternoon. I was dealing with Dirk Conrad. That tooth he was wearing around his neck is still in the pocket of my jeans.

I grab my jeans to get my phone. Damn. It's dead.

"Tessa!" I yell into the bathroom.

"Yeah?"

"I need to plug in my phone."

"There's a charger on my nightstand and another in the kitchen," she calls back.

I glance at the nightstand. Tessa's phone is plugged into the charger, so I walk, still naked, out to the kitchen, find the charger, and plug in my phone. Then I return to the bedroom and join Tessa in the shower. I'm used to a much larger space, but the closeness seems apt for Tessa and me.

She smiles. "I was hoping you'd join me."

"How could I not?" I stroke her wet hair. "You're at your most beautiful in the water, Tessa. Whether it's Dunn's River Falls, or taking a cold plunge, or in the rain where I kissed you. Water brings out the most amazing beauty in you. It's like you were a mermaid in another life."

She smooths shampoo onto her scalp. "I never dreamed of being a mermaid," she says, "but I used to dream that I could fly."

I move my hands to her head and begin massaging the shampoo through her gorgeous hair. "Did you? I'm pretty sure I've had that dream, too."

"My therapist said it's a common dream for children."

"Is it?" I work the lather through her long hair and then turn her toward the shower water to rinse. "I'd like to know all your dreams, Tessa."

"The best one just came true." She rinses the last of the suds from her hair and turns to me, water dripping off her long lashes the way it did in the rain.

I cup her cheeks. Her hair is a sleek wet curtain clinging to her shoulders and neck.

I want to say the words.

Must say the words.

"I love you, Tessa."

She drops her jaw.

"I know it's too soon. I know it makes no sense, but I love you, Teresa Maria Logan."

She opens her mouth, but I gesture her to stop.

"Don't say anything. I don't expect you to say it back to me. But it's important that you know how I feel." I kiss her forehead. "I love you so damned much, Tessa. When I first laid eyes on you, I lost a piece of my heart. I don't want it back, not ever."

She melts into me, and the shower pelts us.

When it becomes lukewarm, I turn off the water and leave the shower, handing Tessa a towel.

I look away as she dries off, toss my used towel onto a rack, and enter her bedroom to put on my clothes. I have to get to the office for a meeting at ten. I keep several spare suits and accessories ready at the office. I'll need one today.

After that...I need to talk to Braden.

I need to finish this Dirk Conrad thing once and for all, and it's high time I tell my brother what's going on. He should hear it from me.

He should have heard it from me fifteen years ago.

Tessa leaves the bathroom and stares at me. "Are you leaving?"

"I have a meeting to get to." I kiss her quickly on the cheek. "We'll talk later."

"But Ben, I want to tell you—"

"Later, baby. I love you."

I leave her standing in her towel, staring after me.

I want to hear the words from her ruby lips, but I fear once I do, I won't have the strength to do what needs to be done.

CHAPTER FORTY-SEVEN

Tessa

"I can't believe it, either," I say to Skye on the phone a few minutes later. "He told me he loves me, and then he just left."

"And you wanted to say it back?"

I sigh into the phone. "I did, Skye. I know it's soon, but I've never felt this way. Ben helped me help myself. He... He's special."

"That I can believe. His brother is pretty damned special, too."

I can hear Skye's smile through her voice. "He is. You both saved me that day."

"Tess..."

"No, you did. And after I was so unfair to you, asking you to change your plans and have dinner with Garrett and me."

"Well, if I had—"

"Don't go there. We both know why it happened."

"I hope he rots in prison," Skye says.

"Me too, but he's the least of my concerns. Right now, Ben is off to work without knowing that I love him back."

"That does seem odd. Most men want to hear it back once they say it."

"Right? I don't get it." I sigh. "I need to get dressed and get to work. I worked all of two days at this new job before I took off for Jamaica and then asked for another week of bereavement leave."

"I hear your boss is a tyrant, too." Skye laughs. "But seriously, Tess, I'm happy for you. Truly. You deserve everything good."

"I wasn't sure I'd ever feel the same after Garrett, but I had such a nice time with Ben in Jamaica, and he didn't so much as kiss me, Skye. Then my dad…"

"I know, Tess. I'm sorry."

"It's almost like he left me all his strength. I know that sounds silly."

"I don't think it sounds silly at all," Skye says. "Losing him helped you to remember who you are. Not that losing him was a good thing."

"I know exactly what you mean," I say. "And it makes perfect sense to me. Thanks for the chat, Skye. I've got to get to work."

"You want to have lunch today?" she asks.

"I'd love to, but I'm planning to work through lunch. I want them to know I'm serious about this job and didn't get it just because I'm in love with the boss."

I dress quickly in a narrow black skirt and white blouse, and I'm putting on my black pumps when someone knocks at my door. Rita goes berserk.

"Coming!" I yell.

I pick up a squirming Rita and look through my peephole.

And I gasp.

• • •

"No... Stay... Please..."

"I'm out of here. I have an early morning meeting."

I hold the vodka bottle. Where did it come from? I'm not sure. I'm not naked. Just my bottom half. Just...

He's a blur. It's Garrett, I think. He's leaving. The blur is leaving, and I'm on the floor holding a bottle.

Didn't mean to do it. Wasn't going to. Don't even remember some of it. The room goes black for a moment.

I try to stand when the light returns. Dizziness sweeps through me. And I feel... I feel...

Phone?

Where's my phone?

Skye should have been here with me. She let me down. My bestie let me down. She's too wrapped up in her billionaire boyfriend.

Bladen Brack.

Baden Back.

No.

Braden Black.

Phone. I crawl toward the couch where I left it, pick it up. *Skye. Skye. Skye.*

I call Skye.

"Hey, Tess."

"Skye?" My voice sounds squeaky.

"Yeah? Are you okay?"

"Not even slightly." I choke back a sob and then—

A-choo! A sneeze rips from my mouth. My allergies have been killing me lately. I'm on all kinds of herbal crap for them. Echinacea sometimes helps, but not today.

"What's the matter?" Skye asks. "Why are you crying?"

"Damn these allergies," I say. "I need you. Please."

"Okay, okay. Calm down. What do you need?"

"It's Garrett. I… I slept with him."

"Okay."

Okay? It's not okay. Why would Skye even *say* that? I'm not even sure why I did it. Why it happened. "Why couldn't you come to dinner with us? You knew what was going to happen."

"Tess, I—"

"I needed you tonight."

"Okay, okay. Calm down." She pauses a moment. "Where are you? I'll come to you."

"At my place. He left, Skye. He fucked me, and then he left."

"Did you ask him to stay?"

"I did. He said he had an early meeting in the morning. But tomorrow's Sunday." My whole body heaves. "He lied to get out of spending the night with me. How could I have been so stupid as to let him in my bed again?"

"Are you drinking?"

I sniffle and glance at the bottle of vodka. "A little."

"Tell me you didn't take anything else. Please."

She's thinking of the ecstasy. The pill that said *Sky*. Damn Betsy, anyway. I told her specifically not to tell Skye. "No. Not yet. But I'm a mess. Can you come over?"

"Yeah. Sure. I'll be there as soon as I can. Hang in there, okay?"

"Thanks, Skye."

"No need to thank me. Get hold of yourself, and I'll be there soon." She ends the call.

I stay on the couch. Can't move. Or don't want to move. But I find my leggings and force them over my legs and ass. Don't want to have my ass hanging out when…

I don't feel right. I know where I am. Who I am. But some of it is so fuzzy, and I feel…sick. Really sick.

Rita nudges me. I pet her soft head.

Then a knock, and Rita runs to the door barking. I swallow back nausea, gather my strength to rise, walk to the door, and open it.

It's Skye. And she brought Braden, of course. The two of them are joined at the fucking hip.

"Hey," I say weakly. "Hi, Braden."

"Hello, Tessa." Braden walks straight into my apartment. "What can we do for you?"

"Braden…" Skye begins, scooping up Rita and closing the door.

"Have you eaten?" Braden asks.

Right. He's talking to me. "I had dinner with Garrett."

He picks up my nearly empty bottle of vodka. "How much of this have you had?"

"Braden…" Skye again.

"A few shots," I reply.

At least I think I did. I don't even like vodka.

Skye grabs Braden's arm and steers him out my door, whispering something to him. Probably something lovey-dovey.

Skye closes the door and turns to me. "Sorry about that."

"It's okay. I'm sorry to ruin your evening."

"You didn't."

She's lying, but I love her for it. I love my bestie. Except when I'm angry with her. Except when—

"Come on," Skye says. "Spill it."

I sigh. "It's so stupid. I went and fell in love with the jerk."

"That's not stupid."

"Why couldn't I meet a man like Braden? He treats you with

so much respect and love."

"Have you forgotten he dumped me a couple weeks ago?"

"No. But things seem fine now."

"They're good, but it took a lot of work on both our parts. I even started therapy to get to the bottom of everything."

"I know." I shake my head. "I guess I just want more than Garrett wants to give me right now."

She grips my shoulders. "So you're not in the same place. That doesn't have to be a bad thing. He did come back to you, and he's willing to be exclusive."

"That's what he says, anyway."

"Do you think he's lying?" she asks.

"I don't know. He could be. After all, he lied about having an early meeting tomorrow."

"Are you sure?"

"It's Sunday, Skye."

"Braden has meetings during the middle of the night sometimes. We flew out to New York early on a Sunday morning that one time so he could deal with some kind of contract in China."

Yeah. I remember that well. She neglected to cancel our shopping date, and...

God...I can't go there right now.

"So maybe he has a breakfast meeting with the boss," Skye continues. "Or a racquetball date or something."

"Then that's what he should have said. But what he actually said was 'I have an early meeting tomorrow.'"

Skye frowns and looks around the room. "It's too late to order pizza. How about I run across the street to the convenience store and grab a few pints of Ben & Jerry's?"

I smile, even though the thought of ice cream makes me want

to hurl. "Would you?"

"I absolutely would. As long as you promise no more drinking. Alcohol solves nothing."

"I know. I know."

"This isn't like you, Tessa."

I sigh again.

"Are you really in love?" she asks.

Am I? I feel something. Intense attraction. It's similar to how I've felt before when I've been in love. Or thought I was. "I think so. I realize I haven't known him very long."

Skye shrugs. "You've known him as long as I've known Braden, and we're in love. Sometimes you just know."

"And sometimes one person feels something the other doesn't."

Skye shakes her head. Her two heads. I don't feel so well.

"Tessa, you're a catch. We both know it, and so does Garrett."

"I'm not sure he does."

"Then honestly? He's not worth it." She grabs her purse. "I'll be back in a flash. Dump the rest of that." She nods to the vodka bottle.

"Yes, ma'am."

Once she's gone, I take the bottle to the bathroom and dump the tiny bit that's left in the toilet.

Then I slide to the tile floor and—

"Oh, shit."

The convulsions start in my stomach and rise. Acid, bile, vodka, everything putrid…

It all comes up and out into the toilet bowl…

My head… Spinning… The toilet goes blurry… And… And…

Darkness.

...

PRESENT DAY...

"I know you're in there, Tessa," Garrett Ramirez says. "There's someone here who wants to say hello."

The man with Garrett on the other side of the door is the bartender from Jamaica, the one Ben got fired.

He holds up something white. "Recognize these, Tessa?"

Rita scrambles out of my arms, and I lean against the wall for support. My heart is racing, and the familiar tingle of panic hits my fingers.

No. Fucking. Way.

That's why that bartender looked so familiar. He was the altar boy. The one whose name began with D. David. I remember now. David Conrad. My first communion. He took my panties, and he—

I gulp back the nausea that threatens to make its way up my throat. What kind of sicko keeps a little girl's panties?

Must focus. Must stay strong. Can't panic. Won't panic.

"You two get the hell away from here. I have a restraining order against you, Garrett. I'm calling the cops."

"You might want to talk to your new boyfriend before you do that," Garrett says. "Because if you call the cops, things could get real dicey for him."

My new boyfriend? Ben? How do they even know about Ben?

Right. Jamaica. The bartender he got fired. Of course.

The urge to protect Ben swarms through me, overruling my own panic and fear, and in a flash I'm a lioness, ready to strike.

"Get out of here right now," I demand.

"You going to sic your ferocious little dog on us?" Garrett

says, laughing.

What a fucking creep! How did I ever think I was in love with this asshole? I didn't even understand what love was.

I couldn't date until I was seventeen, and I went wild in college. All those physical feelings were new to me, and I mistook them for love.

Every single time, I mistook them for love.

Not anymore. What I feel for Ben goes so far beyond anything I thought I felt for Garrett or anyone else. We didn't get physical right away, which was my MO before.

We didn't…

He wouldn't even kiss me.

And now that we've been together? I know how much better the physical is when the emotion is also present.

My God…

Both of these men took something from me. David stole my innocence, and Garrett stole my spirit.

My innocence may be gone forever, but my spirit has been restored. Ben helped me with that. He showed me what's important. What I have to fight for.

Myself.

David and Garrett may have both taken something from me that was not theirs to take, but I can survive.

I can thrive.

My heart still beats.

And damn it, I won't let these two assholes harm Ben in any way.

"We're waiting, Tessa." Garrett's voice slithers like a snake over my skin.

"Get the fuck out of here." I hold up my phone. "I've got 911 punched in. All I have to do is hit send."

"Do that," Garrett says, "or call anyone else, and Ben Black goes up the river."

Do they think I'm stupid? "Ben Black is a billionaire," I say through gritted teeth. "And the best man I know. Save your idle threats for someone who believes them."

"I think you might need to talk to my brother," David says.

"I don't need to talk to anyone."

"Open the door," Garrett says, "and we'll tell you everything we know."

"You'll tell me lies, and I'm not interested. Now get the hell out of here." I reach to hit send on the 911 call, but something holds me back.

Why won't they leave? Why do they think I won't call the cops?

They've both done something horrible to me, and now that I remember what David did, I can have him arrested too. I think I can, anyway. I'm not sure about the statute of limitations.

"I'm not going to prison for a little cunt like you," Garrett seethes.

"Uh...yeah. You are."

"Let's put it this way," he says. "Open the fucking door, Tessa. Because if I go to prison, your boyfriend goes too."

"You're full of it. Now get out of here."

Garrett shakes his head. "We tried to warn you. Have it your way."

They walk down the hallway and out of view of my peephole.

I shiver as I slide down the wall into a sitting position, my phone still ready to call 911.

Rita rushes to me, but I can't bring myself to pet her.

I'm numb. Frozen. My heart has gone mad. And my skin feels like ice.

Do they truly have something on Ben?

They can't. It's not possible.

Still...

I can't call their bluff. I can't risk it. I delete the one, the one, and the nine.

Then I wrap my arms around my knees and stay there.

CHAPTER FORTY-EIGHT

Ben

After my ten o'clock meeting, I grab Braden's arm while he's returning to his office.

"We need to talk."

"I've got a lunch meeting in half an hour."

"Cancel it."

Braden raises an eyebrow. "Excuse me?"

He doesn't mean to be rude. He's reacting because I take this business as seriously as he does, sometimes even more so. He's confused as to why I'd tell him to cancel a meeting.

"I have to talk to you, Braden, and it can't wait."

He cocks his head, raises the eyebrow again, and then rubs his stubbled jawline. "All right. My office."

We're silent as we walk together.

"Cancel my lunch meeting," Braden says to his assistant Claire when we turn the corner of the hallway.

I follow him to his corner office on the opposite side of the top floor as mine. They're both the same size, but his is decorated in his classic downtown-style flair with large picture windows looking out at Boston.

"What is it?" he asks once his door is closed.

"You'd better sit down."

"Thanks, but I'll stand."

I sigh. "Have it your way." I run my hands over my head, trying to ease the ache erupting in my brain. "Then *I'm* going to sit."

That way I'll have to actually get up if I change my mind about this.

But no.

No more changing my mind.

I'm laying my fucking cards on the table, and I'm calling. My hand is shitty, but I have no other choice at this point.

If I don't, Dirk Conrad will never go away.

I plunk my ass down in a chair across from Braden's large desk.

Here goes nothing.

"Something has come back to bite me in the ass," I say, "and it's not pretty, brother."

"We'll make it go away, then."

"It's not that simple."

"Benji, we've got billions at our disposal. Whatever is going on, I promise we can fix it."

It doesn't escape my notice that Braden used my childhood nickname. Brady and Benji. He hasn't used it in at least a decade. He must sense this is bad.

I shake my head. "God, if only…"

Braden takes a seat next to me. Next to me, not behind his desk. Guess he decided to sit after all.

"I'm your brother. Spill it, and I'll take care of it."

"Braden, if that were the case, I could have taken care of it myself."

I could have, and I thought about it. I could have hired someone to off Dirk Conrad. But that makes me guiltier.

I didn't kill anyone all those years ago, but if I have Dirk offed? Then I may as well have plunged a knife into a chest same as he did.

"Bray, do you remember back in the day, during my senior year of high school, when I didn't show up to work one day after school?"

He wrinkles his brow. "No."

"You read me the fucking riot act. How can you not remember?"

"I read you the fucking riot act a lot back then, Ben. How am I supposed to remember each specific time?"

He's not wrong. "All right. Here's what happened. Fuck." I sink my head into my hands. "I can't believe I have to tell you this after all these years."

"Tell me, and we'll fix it."

"God, I wish you could."

"I can. But not if you don't tell me."

I look down at my lap, clasp my hands together. Then I look up, meeting my brother's blue gaze. There's care in his eyes. He thinks he can fix this.

He's wrong.

"I got in with some bad guys at school. Only one time, but I was sick and tired of working all the time. Never having a minute to myself or a penny to spend on myself. So I met these guys after school one day, and they wanted to rob the convenience store."

"For God's sake, Ben. You robbed a convenience store?"

I shake my head. "I wish."

"Fuck. What happened?"

"They wanted to rob a store that's open twenty-four-seven

and only holds about a grand in cash. It was a stupid idea."

"True that. Good for you."

"Not so good for me." I draw in a breath, determined to just spill everything quickly. "Remember that small warehouse Dad used to do business with? The one we had a hunch was dealing in stolen goods?"

"Yeah…" Braden says slowly.

"I was on an errand for Dad one day, and I found a stash of about fifty grand hidden there. I left it, of course. To this day, I don't know who it belonged to. The owner, one of the workers, I have no fucking clue. Anyway, I knew the code—"

"How the fuck did you know the code?"

"Ansel was closing one day when I left with supplies, and I saw him punch it in."

"And you memorized it?"

"I couldn't help it. You know I have one of those memories. I swear it's a curse."

And it is. I remember every detail of that night. Every excruciating detail of the following several weeks when the search was on for that convict who escaped, whose photo I recognized. Whose fate I knew.

I spill it all to my brother.

The break in. The theft. The murder. Everything.

"You pulled out the guy's teeth?" Braden says, his eyes wide.

"Hell, no! I didn't. Jerry Thompson did." A chill runs down my spine. "He knew exactly what to do. It was psychotic."

"So you didn't do anything."

"Not exactly true. It was my tarp we wrapped the body in, my truck we used to transport it to the bay."

"And no one saw you?"

"Jerry again. He knew exactly where to go," I say.

"Fuck." Braden rubs his jawline. "No wonder he's doing time."

"I know. Anyway, the next day the news came on and showed that dude's mug shot, and I recognized him."

"How'd he get in the warehouse?"

"I have no clue. My gut tells me he got in during the day and hid. Whether he was going to use it as a hiding place or he was going to rob it, I have no idea. He could have known about it on the inside if he was dealing in stolen goods."

Braden nods. Keeps nodding.

I wait.

I wait for him to blow.

Then I realize he won't. Not Braden Black. Not the master of control.

Minutes tick by. Minutes that seem like hours. Until—

"This was fifteen years ago, Benji. Why are you telling me now?"

I press my lips together. "Because Dirk Conrad got in touch with me three months ago. Asked for cash. I told him to fuck off, and he did. Or so I thought. Now he's back."

"And he wants more cash?"

"Ten million," I say, "and he seems willing to go down with me if I don't pay."

"So we pay him," Braden says.

I drop my mouth open. "Who are you and what have you done with my brother?"

"Don't for a minute think I'm happy about this," he says. "But it's pennies to us, and—"

"And he'll come back for more. He'll want fifty next time. Then a hundred. It won't stop, Bray. If we give him an inch, he'll take a mile." I shake my head vehemently. "No. That's not how I want to handle this."

"If the guy's got a tooth—" Braden holds up the tooth on the chain I gave him.

"He doesn't have it. We have it. And it means nothing if there's no DNA on file to match it."

"But the guy was a con. His DNA is on file somewhere."

I sigh. "I know."

"If we don't pay him off and this gets to the media—"

"I know. So here's what I want to do." I run my fingers through my hair. "I've gone over and over this in my head, and there's only one way to deal with it, especially now that Tessa's involved."

"Wait, wait, wait… How is Tessa involved?"

"Dirk's brother David is a few years younger. He was a bartender in Jamaica."

"The one with the light brown hair? Light brown eyes?"

"Yeah. I had him fired because he said some nasty things about her. Anyway, he wants Tessa, and Dirk somehow found out about Garrett Ramirez as well. So now that's part of the deal. Not only do I have to pay up, but I'm supposed to get Tessa to drop all the charges against Garrett."

"Oh, hell, no."

"Exactly."

Braden shakes his head. "Fuck."

"I know. So I'm…" I draw in a breath. "I'm going to the DA, Bray. I'm going to confess, tell the whole truth. I'm no killer. That's on Dirk. But I was there, and I helped hide the body. That's on me."

"Unless they find the body…"

"I know, and it's long gone by now. No body, no charges. But we can get Dirk on blackmail. The problem is the news, Bray. It's going to fuck us up."

"Jesus fuck, Benji."

"So as of now, I'm—"

Braden's phone rings. "It's Claire. She wouldn't interrupt unless it was important."

I'm not sure what could be more important right now, but I nod to my brother.

"Yes?" he says into the phone.

Pause.

"Really? And you haven't heard anything?"

Pause.

"I'm on it. Thank you, Claire."

"What's that about?" I ask.

Braden rubs his forehead. "Tessa didn't come in to work this morning."

My heart drops. "What?"

"She didn't report to work, and she didn't call in."

"I've got security on her. I ordered it yesterday."

"Good thinking, but I bet they haven't deployed anyone yet."

"Fuck." I stand. "I'm going over to her place."

"I'm right behind you," he says, "and I'm calling the cops."

CHAPTER FORTY-NINE

Tessa

'm not sure how long I sit, huddled with Rita. I almost called Ben five different times, but what if Garrett wasn't bluffing? I'm about to finally hit send when someone knocks again.

Rita scurries out of my arms, barking, as she runs toward the door.

My heart feels like a herd of wildebeests is stampeding over my chest. I gulp as I rise, walk to the door, and look through the peephole.

I heave a sigh of relief. It's my neighbor, Laura Templeton, holding a bouquet of flowers.

"Hi, Laura," I say through the door, hoping my voice doesn't shake. "I'm not decent. What's up?"

"I'm sorry to bother you, Tessa, but I heard about your father. I just wanted to drop these flowers by. I'll just leave them here in the hallway."

"That's kind of you. Thank you."

"My pleasure. If there's anything you need, please don't hesitate to call me. I can pick up groceries for you. Anything at all."

"I appreciate that." I pause a moment. "Actually, Laura, is anyone else out there in the hallway or the stairwell? Two men?"

Laura looks side to side as I watch through the peephole. "Not that I saw. Were you expecting someone?"

"Yeah," I lie. "Thanks, Laura. I really appreciate the thought."

I watch out the peephole until Laura is out of my view. She lives one floor down, which means she took the stairs.

Thank God. That means they're gone.

I have to get to work. It's only my third full day, and I'm already late. But first I have to warn Ben.

I doubt Garrett and that horrid altar boy could truly have anything that could threaten Ben, but I can't take the chance. Once I talk to him and he assures me they're bluffing, I can call the police and have those two psychos arrested.

Rita scurries around my legs. She probably has to go out. I grab her leash and fasten it to her collar.

My heart thuds as I unlock my deadbolt. I look up and down the hallway.

They aren't still here, are they? Laura would have seen them in the stairwell. I probably should have called 911, but I couldn't take that chance. I'll protect Ben at all costs.

I walk toward the stairwell—

And Rita begins yapping like a rabid dog.

"We knew you'd have to come out sooner or later," Garrett snarls, grabbing me.

Where did they come from? Rita lunges at Garrett and sinks her tiny teeth into his leg.

"Fucking dog!" Garrett yells, kicking at her.

I let go of her leash. "Run, Rita! Go!"

But she doesn't leave me. She takes a shot at David next,

but one woman and one scruffy dog are no match for two men. Garrett punches me in the face.

Pain explodes through my head as blood spurts from my nose. The coppery liquid crawls down my throat, and I swallow it down along with the nausea.

"I hope you like prison!" I shout at him. I grab for my phone, but it slips through my fingers.

"I hope your boyfriend likes it too!" he yells back.

I spit a glob of blood out of my mouth. "You drugged me, you asshole. You laced my alcohol with ketamine, and it caused a reaction with the Echinacea I took for my allergies. I almost fucking died, Garrett!"

He looks me up and down and then rolls his eyes. "You don't look dead to me. Now you're going to drop those charges."

"At least let my puppy go!" I yell at David. "Please!"

"She'll just slow us down," Garrett says. "Let the dog go."

"Fine." David releases a wriggling Rita, and she runs back toward my apartment.

I pray silently that Laura or another neighbor will find her until I can get back to her.

And I *will* get back to her.

I won't let these two degenerates get the best of me.

I tug against Garrett's strength, looking for a weak spot. His groin, if I can get to it. I'm wearing stiletto pumps. I can do some damage with those.

"Let me go!" I yell.

"Not until you drop the charges," Garrett says.

"I can't. It's the DA's call. Not mine."

"Without you as a witness, there's no case."

He's right, of course. Nothing is worth this. Nothing is worth anything happening to Ben. "Fine," I say. "I'll drop it. But you have to swear never to come near me again."

"I'm only too happy to abide by that request, you little bitch."

"You have to let me go first," I say.

"Nope. You're calling the DA right now. Here in the stairwell. Tell him you've changed your mind, and you're withdrawing your complaint."

"My phone is—"

"It's right here." David shoves it in my face. "But you're not calling here, where anyone can walk by. We're going back to your apartment."

"The hell we are." I wipe more blood from my aching nose.

They drag me back into my place, anyway.

Rita scurries inside and into her kennel. Poor baby is scared to death.

Garrett's face is red with anger as David shoves my phone into my hands.

I look down at the screen and start to tap in the number for the DA's office. Then I pause, my finger hovering above the keypad.

I look back at Garrett.

He leers at me. "You going to do it, or do I have to chop your fingers off and put the number in myself?"

"Yes, sorry." I blink several times and look toward the ceiling. "Just can't remember the number offhand. And I don't have it saved in my contacts."

"Look in your recent calls. You've called them before, haven't you?"

I nod my head slowly.

He raises a fist. "Then *move it*, bitch."

I recoil at his fist. Where is the justice here? How can I allow this man, this rapist, to roam the streets free? He won't be able to slake his thirst with my body alone. Don't I owe it to his future female victims to take a stand here?

"I swear to God, if you don't call that motherfucker right *now...*"

I put up a hand in defense. "I'm going."

But I don't type anything into the phone. I tap the screen a few times, then put the phone to my ear.

I've called this number several times. It's an automated line. First they ask for my extension, and then I'm connected directly to Trish.

I wait a few seconds and then pretend to type a few more numbers. "I'm putting in her extension," I explain.

Garrett doesn't respond.

I wait a few more seconds. Then I start speaking.

"Hi, Trish. This is Tessa. Tessa Logan."

I pause for what I hope is a believable amount of time.

"Yes, I'm calling about my complaint regarding Mr. Garrett Ramirez."

Another pause.

"Yes, I would like to withdraw—"

But I'm cut off by my phone's ringtone. I look in horror to see that my mother is calling me. Probably checking up on me after the funeral, making sure I'm doing all right.

God, she has no idea how much she just fucked me over.

Garrett reacts immediately and pounces. He tackles me to the ground, his hands wrapped tightly around my wrists. My phone clatters to the floor.

"Do you think I'm a fucking *moron*?" he asks through gritted teeth.

My whole body trembles underneath him. "No...of course not..."

"You think you're clever, you little slut?"

I shake my head. "My phone...it's..."

He chuckles. "What are you going to say? It's broken? It has some weird defect where incoming calls interrupt ongoing calls? Do you think I'm that fucking dumb?"

I don't answer.

He slaps me across the face, hard. Then he lets go of my wrists and clamors for my phone.

Shit, that stings. I bring my hand to my face and rub it.

He shoves the phone back in my face. "Fucking call the DA. And this time, you'll be putting it on speaker."

David squats down next to me. "I'd do what he says, gorgeous. Don't want that pretty little face of yours to get fucked up, do you?"

I stifle a sob as I get to my feet. I look around my apartment. Poor, sweet Rita is still shaking in her kennel.

I'm out of ideas.

I take my phone, tap in the number of my contact at the DA's office while Garrett glares at me and David locks the deadbolt on my door. I press the speaker button so Garrett knows I'm not trying to trick him this time.

"Thank you for calling the Suffolk County DA," the recording says. "If you know your party's extension, enter it now."

I tap in the numbers.

Shit. Goes to voicemail. "This is Trish McCoy with the DA's office. I'm sorry I can't take your call. Please leave me a detailed message and I'll return your call as soon as I can."

"Hi, Trish, it's Tessa Logan. I'm calling because"—I clear my throat—"I've had a change of heart. I'd like to withdraw the charges against Mr. Ramirez. Please give me a call. Thanks."

I throw my phone down. "Satisfied?"

"I will be," he says, "as soon as you take off those clothes."

My jaw drops.

He laughs wickedly. "Not for me, of course. Been there, done that. For my pal David here. Seems he's had his eye on you for fifteen years. Since you fit into those little white panties."

"No." I back away. "Absolutely not."

"You're going to show me that grown-up pussy," David sneers. "Or Ben Black goes down."

I gulp.

Ben didn't *do* anything. He couldn't have. He's a good man. An honest man.

The man who helped me see myself as I truly am—a strong and independent woman who's no one's victim.

The man I *love*.

Rita runs out of her kennel, barking and snarling. She leaps at David, clawing at his leg.

He kicks her away. "Get this fucking mutt off me!"

"Rita, baby. Go to your den."

She snaps at him again.

"Rita, den. Now!"

She cocks her head at me, and for a moment I think she's wondering why I'm not letting her protect me.

"Go, Rita."

She finally walks back into her den and lies down.

"Fine," I say to David. "Do what you want to me, but first, at least tell me what Ben did. Why you think he's going down."

"How about you ask him about Travis McKee?"

I furrow my brow. "Who the hell is that?"

A grin spreads over David's face. "He never told you?"

"Aren't you two *in love*?" Garrett pokes me in the chest. "Can't believe he'd keep secrets from a conniving little cunt like you."

I try not to react from Garret's physical contact. "Ben would never do anything wrong."

David takes a step toward me. "Really? He'd never, say, knock the teeth out of a corpse to keep it from being identified?"

My stomach drops to my feet. "You're lying…"

Garrett shrugs. "To be fair, he did kill the poor fucker before he did that."

I swallow. "Ben would never—"

"He's a fucking murderer," Garrett says. "Like I said, ask him about Travis McKee."

"For Christ's sake, who is Travis McKee?"

"The escaped con that your boyfriend dumped in the Boston Bay fifteen years ago. After he stabbed his poor ass to death while orchestrating a failed robbery." David takes my white panties out of his pocket and holds them to his nose. "Around the same time I was getting these from you," he says with a snakelike grin.

I grimace at David, but then the gravity of what he said hits me like a ton of bricks, and the last thing I'm thinking about is my communion panties.

Ben?

A killer?

No. No way.

"It's not true. Ben wouldn't—"

"Ben *would*," David says. "And he did. My brother has proof. But that proof will never see the light of day, as long as you let me do what I want."

I gulp down the nausea again. My nose has stopped bleeding, and I feel the blood drying and crusting over my chin and neck. I'm sure I look like something out of a horror flick. It no doubt turns this psycho on.

If what they're saying is the truth—and I have a really awful gut feeling that it is—then I have no choice. I don't want Ben to go down for this. All I have to do is let David have his way with me, and the man I love will be free from his past.

"Why you want a full-grown woman when you obviously have a thing for little girls is beyond me."

"Shut up, bitch." David stalks toward me and punches my jaw.

This pain isn't like when Garrett broke my nose. This is dull and throbbing, rather than sharp and shattering.

Damn it. No. Just no. He can take what he wants from me, but he'll have to fight for it.

If he wants my clothes off me, he can rip them off himself. I swallow, cross my arms, and glare at him.

"Oh, she wants to play hard to get, does she?" David runs his spindly fingers down my arm.

I shudder.

He grabs my wrists, forces my body to the ground, and pries them away from my chest. "Lucky for you, I like it when a girl resists. Makes the pursuit all the better."

I dart my gaze over to Garrett.

"Don't mind him," David says. "I agreed to let him watch."

My stomach flips over on itself.

Garrett's gaze burns into me as he starts rubbing his crotch. "I always wanted to know what it looked like to see you get fucked, Tessa. I always felt like an actor who never got to watch himself on stage."

I don't respond, but I wriggle my wrists in an attempt to free myself from David's grasp.

"I might need you to help just a little," David says. "Hold her wrists down so I can unbutton her blouse the rest of the way."

"Be glad to." Garrett gets on his knees behind my head and holds my wrists down. I can see his erection tenting his pants.

I swallow down the gag. Puking all over these two will only make it worse.

David undoes a button. "This is a nice blouse, Tessa. Nice fabric, nice color." He looks into my eyes. "Though I always preferred you in white."

Oh my God. I can't believe this demented piece of shit.

I spit in his face.

He closes his eyes in reaction, and in that split second I twist my body to maneuver my feet into the right position and kick him straight in the balls.

He keels over on his side, yelping.

"Crafty little bitch, aren't you?" Garrett sneers. "But how are you going to take on two of us?"

I look up at him from the floor. From this angle, every feature of his face is overpronounced, bringing out the true ghoulish nature of his soul.

It's weird, but right now I'm feeling that old Tessa spark burning brighter than it has since this asshole took it from me in the first place.

"You might be able to overpower me, but I won't make it easy for either of you."

Garrett releases my wrist and draws his arm back for another punch. But I react quickly, grab my phone, and batter him right on the forehead with it.

It's not much, but he's stunned for long enough for me to get to my feet. I get to the door, fling it open, and run down the hallway—

Thud.

Right into the hard chest of a police officer.

My heart skips. "Help me. Please!"

Another officer arrives out of the stairwell. "Ms. Logan?"

"Yes, that's me. Help me! There are two men in my apartment—"

"Tessa!"

Ben's voice. Thank God!

"Ben!" I yell. "Help me!"

A moment later, the door is open, the two uniformed officers enter my apartment, guns drawn.

Ben and I stand in the doorway. I shiver in his arms.

"You two," one officer says to Garrett and David. "Hands behind your head. Now!"

Relief swirls through me as Garrett and David are placed under arrest.

I melt against Ben. I had gotten away on my own, but knowing he's here eases my burden. "You came for me."

He pushes me away slightly, looks into my eyes. "We need to get you to a hospital, baby. Your nose, your jaw. Are you okay? Are you hurting?"

The pain explodes in me. I wasn't feeling it much before, but now? With my adrenaline draining?

God, it fucking hurts.

Ben's jaw is rigid and clenched. "Did they…?"

I shake my head. "No. Just my nose and face."

"Your blouse is unbuttoned."

"But they didn't. I swear it, Ben."

He pulls me against him. "Thank God."

Braden—who I'm only now realizing is here as well—turns to us. "Get her to the ER," he says to Ben. "I'll take care of this for now. But the cops are going to want a statement from you, Tessa."

"I've got a fucking statement to make too," David blurts out. "And you know what it is, Black." He sneers at Ben.

"What's he talking about?" I ask, hoping Ben will deny it.

He wraps his arm around me and leads me out of the apartment. "Nothing for you to worry about. Come on."

CHAPTER FIFTY

Ben

Tessa is admitted to the hospital for observation after being treated for her broken nose and bruised jaw.

"This is ridiculous," she says. "I'm fine."

"You do what the doctor says," I tell her. "You've been through so much, Tessa. Just when you were healing, you got the added trauma of your father's death, and now those two—" I crush my hands into fists. "Neither of them will ever see the outside of a prison cell, if I have anything to say about it."

"Ben, please..."

"I know. Assault and attempted rape doesn't carry a lifetime sentence. How do you know David Conrad, anyway?"

"He was the bartender in Jamaica."

"I know. I didn't know who he was at the time. Only that you had a bad reaction to him, and that he made some comments about you that I didn't appreciate. So I got rid of him."

"He's..." She clears her throat. "He was an altar boy at my first communion fifteen years ago. He..."

My insides churn as anger pulsates through me. "He *what*?"

I grit out.

"I didn't remember for a long time, but it was after my first communion that I started to pull away from the church. Now I know why. He… He *touched* me that day. Took my panties."

I draw in a breath. Tessa doesn't need me going all rogue on her. Not right now, anyway.

Besides…she and I can't continue. I realized the truth of that when I was talking to Braden earlier. But I can't tell her that. Not yet.

I want to know the details, yet I don't. I don't want to hear about such a heinous act, but I need to know exactly what he did to her because I'll make sure the same damned thing happens to him in prison.

"Please…" she says.

"Please what?"

"Let it go, Ben. Whatever it is that has you so wound up. Please. Let it go. For me."

"I can't."

"You can. It's not easy. I know that." She reaches her arm out and touches my face. "But you helped me. You helped me see how much good there still was in my life. Please."

I don't reply.

"Ben, I—"

I place my fingers over her lips. "Don't. Please."

"I love—"

"Please, Tessa."

"Damn it, Ben. Why don't you want me to say it? Didn't you mean it when you said it to me?"

"With all my heart, Tessa."

"Then why?"

I lean down and kiss her lips. "You need to rest. We'll talk later. I'll tell the cops you can't make a statement until tomorrow."

"I'm fine to make a statement." Then a giant yawn splits her face. "Ow! That hurts."

"Get some sleep, Tessa. I'll be here when you wake up."

. . .

I spend the rest of the day talking to the Suffolk County DA, Marjorie Akins. With Braden at my side, I tell my story.

"It's up to you," I say to her. "Charge me if you can. I'll gladly pay the price. I can't go on keeping this secret any longer."

"Mr. Black," she says.

"Ben, please."

"All right. Ben, this is a fifteen-year-old crime."

"With no statute of limitations."

"On the murder part, yes. On the theft, my hands are tied. But the theft doesn't concern me. It sounds like that warehouse was dealing in black market goods. I can't be sure, of course, but around that time we had a rash of that stuff going on in South Boston. As for the murder, you didn't do it, Ben."

"No. But I was there. I transported the body."

"And no body was found then, so it won't be found now." She clears her throat. "I'm not condoning what you did all those years ago, Ben, but you weren't even eighteen yet. You were a stupid kid."

"I won't disagree with you there," I say.

Braden says nothing.

"I can't charge you for anything. I can't charge the others at this point, either, but I'll remand your case against Dirk Conrad to federal court for prosecution under the federal extortion laws."

I nod.

"Can we keep this out of the media?" Braden asks.

"They won't hear it from me," she says, "but the Conrad brothers will probably sell their story to the sleazy rag that offers them the most money."

"What if *I* offer them the most money?" Braden asks.

"No," I say. "If that were the answer, I'd have paid Dirk off in the first place. Don't you see? He knows our pockets are bottomless. He'll keep coming back."

"Your brother's right, Mr. Black," Marjorie says.

"So the only answer is to drop all charges against both Conrads and Garrett Ramirez," Braden says.

"That's not our call on David Conrad and Garrett Ramirez," I say. "It's Tessa's."

"She'd probably do it for you," Braden says.

"No." I shake my head. "I don't want her to do it for me. She needs to see justice served."

He narrows his gaze at me. "Ben…"

"No, Braden. Absolutely not."

"I agree with you," my brother says. "Tessa is more important than any stain on our reputations."

"If that's all, gentlemen"—Marjorie nods—"I'll thank you for bringing this to my attention, but frankly I have no choice but to consider the matter closed."

I rub my temples. "I feel like I should be punished."

Braden turns to me and raises his eyebrow. "Why? You heard Marjorie. You're free to go. This is all going to blow over."

I get to my feet, my heartbeat rising. "I don't *want* it to blow over. Because if it does…"

"Then what?" Braden grabs my arm and yanks me back into my seat. "You won't be good enough for Tessa anyway?"

I blink. That's *exactly* why.

I bury my face in my hands. "She deserves someone so much better."

Braden lays his hand on my shoulder. "She deserves someone who loves her. And it's clear that she's found that in you, brother."

I shake my head. "She'll change her tune when the news breaks about all of this. You can bet your ass that Ramirez and Conrad are going to sell this story to the first shitty tabloid that comes calling."

"You don't know that," Braden says. "Tessa has been through a lot, and you've been the one who got her through it. And I'm not just talking about all the shit that went down at her apartment. I mean her father's death, getting through her initial trauma with that asshole…"

I don't respond.

Marjorie clears her throat. "If I may," she says, "there might not be any legal recourse for you to deal with, Ben, but perhaps there is something you can do to alleviate these feelings of guilt."

I nearly pounce onto the desk. "What is it?"

She shuffles through some paperwork. "It would seem that Mr. McKee, the victim in question, had a daughter."

I raise an eyebrow. "He did? I thought he had no family, that's why we got away—"

She raises her hand to quiet me. "I would advise you not to say anything you wouldn't want held against you in a court of law."

I clamp my mouth shut.

"Since he was a detainee of the Commonwealth of Massachusetts, we have every scrap of information about him at our disposal. It would seem that shortly before he went to prison, a former girlfriend of his claimed he was the father of her daughter." She pushes a document to my side of the desk.

I pick it up. On it is a picture of a young girl, no more than four or five years old. "Tascha McKee?" I read.

Marjorie nods. "The mother insisted that the child have his last name, even though she never proved that they were actually related."

"She didn't insist on a DNA test?" Braden asks.

"He wouldn't consent to one," Marjorie says. "She could have filed a motion to get a court to force him to take one, but by the time that would have gone through, he was already in prison. He wouldn't have been able to pay child support anyway."

I swallow. "What happened to the daughter?"

"Look at her date of birth."

I scan the document. "She's about to turn eighteen."

Marjorie nods. "I bet she would be beside herself if a certain billionaire covered her college tuition."

I widen my eyes. "Is she going to college?"

Marjorie shrugs. "How should I know that? But she's the age. You could reach out to the family, perhaps under the guise of trying to serve underprivileged kids. You could start a whole foundation in your name, and she could be your first beneficiary."

I stare at the picture. Tascha is—or was, at least—a cute kid. Chubby cheeks, dark curly hair, and eyes that look just like—

Christ.

They look just like her father's. You never forget the eyes of a man you watched die.

I put the picture down. "Is the mother still around?"

"As far as I know." Marjorie slides another document my way. "Her contact information is on here."

I grab it. "Thanks, Marjorie."

She looks me dead in the eye. "Don't thank me for anything. You did *not* get that information from me, you understand? The paper fell off my desk, and you snagged the information while I wasn't looking."

I nod. "Got it."

Marjorie rises. "I can't say it's been a pleasure, but I know you'll do right by this, Ben."

We rise as well.

I hold out my hand to her, but she declines to shake it. Can't say as I blame her.

"Thank you," I say.

Once Braden and I are outside the building, he turns to me. "Are you going to help out that girl?"

I pause for a moment and then nod. "Yeah. She's half an orphan because of me."

"Ben, the father wasn't even in the picture. Her life isn't any different for her father being dead."

I shake my head. "You don't know that. Maybe he was after that fifty grand to give her a better life."

Braden rolls his eyes. "Yeah. I'm sure it was that and not to get his hands on a shit-ton of heroin."

I hold my hand up. "There's no way of knowing either way. And hell, if I can put a little good out into the universe to counteract the errors of my past, I'm going to do it."

Braden wrinkles his forehead at me but then smiles. "You're a good man, Benji."

"Thanks, Brady." I give him a quick hug. "You too."

He breaks the embrace, and his smile fades. "I guess we wait for the rags to report on this."

"I guess so."

"You sure you don't want me to pay off Conrad?"

"It won't do any good. Ramirez and David Conrad are already going down, and they'll sing like canaries just to get the focus off them."

He nods.

"So I'm prepared to make an official statement," I say, "along with my resignation from the company."

"No. We're not going down that road. You're as big a part of Black Inc. as I am. I couldn't do this without you. We'll just conveniently announce your new foundation for underprivileged youth before any story breaks. That'll soften the blow. And God knows I've done some stupid shit in my life. You know about most of it."

"Most?" I ask.

"Brother, some things I'm taking to my grave." He slaps me on the shoulder.

I silently thank God for my brother.

And then I ask for the strength I need.

The strength to reach out to the daughter of a man who's dead because of me.

And the strength to let Tessa go.

CHAPTER FIFTY-ONE

Tessa

After another week off work to deal with the fallout from Garrett and David's visit to me—three grueling sessions with my therapist and an awkward conversation with my mother about my first communion, after which she threatened to leave the church but I talked her out of it—I'm back at work again.

But I'm good.

I didn't go back to the dark place. I've learned a lot about myself, and I know now that my strength was inside me the whole time.

Ben helped me see that.

He's been busy with his new charitable foundation, and I haven't seen much of him. Just as well, as it's taken that long for me to thoroughly work through the memories of my first communion and the attack by Garrett and David. Plus, my face is finally starting to look normal again.

Ben's charity endeavors have me wanting to reach out as well. I've been thinking a lot about what I can do to help others who have been through sexual assault. I smile as I remember Nana's story of Saint Rita, about how she was willing to go through pain so others could be saved.

I can't say I was willing to go through the pain in the first place. I didn't have a choice in that. But I could do some good with it. Figure out a way to help others in similar situations.

I hum in my kitchen. I invited Ben over tonight, and I'm making him dinner. He hasn't called me back to confirm, but I know he'll be here.

This time I'm making simple tacos with homemade guacamole. No margaritas as I can't drink alcohol until I finish my pain meds.

I turn the TV on to keep me company while I cook. Right now it's a commercial for dog food. A different brand from the stuff I buy Rita. I know the jingle by heart, though. I sing along to it as I mash some avocadoes.

Then the commercial cuts short and the musical intro to the evening news plays.

I ignore it and add a couple tablespoons of olive oil to my guac.

I'm chopping up some cilantro when I hear a familiar name on the TV.

"Benjamin Black, the younger brother of the famous blue-collar billionaire Braden Black…"

Ben's in the news?

But he's a pretty famous guy, especially in Boston. His name is probably in the news all the time. This is just the first time it's happened since we met.

I return to my preparations.

"Allegations made by Garrett Ramirez…"

I nearly drop my chef's knife.

What about that asshole?

I thought he was out of my life.

I walk into the living room and take a seat.

"*Mr. Ramirez, who is currently awaiting trial for assault and battery of Ms. Tessa Logan, who is currently dating Mr. Black, claims to have evidence that Mr. Black is responsible for the death of Mr. Travis McKee, who escaped from the Massachusetts Correctional Institution fifteen years ago...*"

The words slow down, are drawn out, as if seeping out like blood oozing from a wound.

My breath catches in my throat, but I close my eyes, force it out slowly. My stomach knots, and a mix of nausea and disbelief make my legs cramp, my arms turn to jelly. This can't be happening. My thoughts race as I try to process what I'm hearing through the garbled words on television.

Garrett and David *weren't* making it up.

Or if they were, they've gone public with it anyway. If they have enough evidence for the evening news to take this seriously, then...

I have to call Ben. I swallow, force my body to work.

I grab my phone and—

Ben: *I'm sorry. I can't make it tonight.*

Of course he can't. He's probably on the phone with his lawyers right now.

Or the authorities.

My stomach twists further into knots.

If I want to talk to him, I'll have to go to his house. He may not be there, but I'll wait. He'll have to show up eventually.

I breathe in, shaking out my arms. I needed Ben's strength. Now he needs mine.

I hastily pack up the dinner, give Rita a quick kiss goodbye, and hail a cab.

Thirty minutes later, I'm knocking on Ben's door, a bag of food in one hand and the pearl inside the small silk bag in the other.

"Ben, it's me!" I yell. "Open up!"

He doesn't answer.

Oh, God. Has he been arrested already?

I pound on the door. *"Ben!"*

Still no answer.

Fuck it, I'll break in if I have to. This is the man I love. And damn it, this time he'll listen when I say those three words.

I check some of the windows by the front door. All locked. I walk around his massive yard to the back of the house. I eye the security cameras as I walk through.

If they alert him to my presence, all the better.

I make it to Ben's back door and try it. It opens, thank God.

I run inside. "Ben, are you here?"

Silence.

I run upstairs. One door is closed.

I knock. "Ben?"

No answer.

I try the door. It's locked.

He must be in here. The door doesn't lock from the outside.

And he wouldn't have left his back door open if he wasn't home.

"Ben!"

Silence.

Fuck it. He can afford to fix the door.

I throw my entire body against the hard wood. Once, twice, three times.

I rub the ache springing up in my shoulder as I lift my right foot in the air, ready to try to kick the door down, but—

It opens instead.

There stands Ben, looking luscious in jeans, a white T-shirt, and nothing else. Even his feet are bare. But something is definitely wrong. His dark eyes are sunken and…tormented.

"Tessa, what are you doing?"

I collapse into his chest. "I thought they'd gotten you!"

Ben rubs his eyes. "Who?"

I sob. "The cops."

"Why would the cops…" His face darkens. "Oh."

We stand there in silence for a moment. Then he grabs me by the shoulders. "Tessa, we need to talk."

I lift my head from his chest. "I brought the dinner I made. We can talk after we eat."

"No, we can't."

"Ben, we've been through too much together to—"

He quiets me with two fingers to my lips. I pucker and kiss the tips.

"Fuck, Tessa."

"Fine." I whip my hands to my hips. "Tell me what happened with that escaped con. Tell me if you're going to go to prison. Tell me if you want to end things between us."

"I love you," he says.

"And I love—"

His hand goes over my mouth again, and I bite his finger.

"Hey!"

"I love you, Ben! Why on earth don't you want to hear that?"

"Because…" He rakes his fingers through his hair. "Because it just makes this harder."

"What?" I cup his cheek.

His eyes are glassy, almost as if he's hiding unshed tears.

I look into the room. It's littered with empty liquor bottles, and his bed is covered with dirty dishes and food crumbs.

My God. He's in bad shape.

He's known this was coming for a while.

"Ben...what is it?"

"Oh, Tessa. Damn it all. I wanted to help you. You were so lost, and I wanted..."

"You *did* help me, Ben." I lay a hand on his chest. "You showed me what's truly important. That my life is far from over. That even though I can't change what happened to me, I can change my attitude about it. I can choose happiness."

"I'm so glad you found happiness, Tessa."

"I found it with *you*."

He shakes his head. "You don't understand. I've done terrible things. And now the whole world knows about it."

"I think you've made mistakes. Like all of us have. You're flawed. But you're the flawed man I love. I never even understood love before you. I mistook physical feelings, infatuation, for love. But with you—"

"Stop!" he roars. "Just stop it! I can't take it."

My lips tremble. "Ben, I won't let you do whatever you think you're going to do here. I'm not going to—"

"Don't you see? You don't have a choice."

I smile weakly. "But I do. *You* taught me that, Ben. You showed me that. I have a choice...and so do you."

"Tessa, listen to me. The story about me is out. We can't put the toothpaste back into the tube. Before long, there will be news cameras at my doorstep, a media circus. I just can't..." He puts his head into his hands.

"You can't what?"

"It's not going to be pretty, Tessa. And I don't want you to have to deal with it. I did something terrible, and I've kept it a secret all this time. It's been eating at me for years. But in truth? I'm glad it's coming out. Part of me is so damned relieved. And the funny thing is? Without you, I'd never have had the strength to do what I've done. Tell my story. Cop to my part in it."

"Tell me the whole story, Ben. I only heard a little from those two jerks, and I was only listening to the news for a few minutes before I came over. What's your side?"

He leads me to his living room and onto his couch. "Sit down."

But he doesn't sit next to me.

He's creating distance between us.

I don't like it.

Words pour out of him, then.

Jumbled words, but I get the gist.

Seventeen and stupid.

Tired of working so hard.

Got in with a bad crowd.

Robbed a warehouse.

David's brother, Dirk, stabbed and killed an escaped convict who walked in on them.

Teeth.

Tarp.

Dumped in the bay.

No body recovered.

No charges.

My skin freezes.

Ben. My Ben.

How could he?

I was sure Garrett and David were spouting lies. Or at least embellishing.

But every gritty detail was true, except that Ben didn't do

the killing.

Ben is devastated. This is eating at him. Has been eating at him for so long.

Ben Black. Jovial Ben Black. All this time hiding a terrible secret that's been gnawing his insides out. Those demons he talked about when we first met? The demons I doubted he could ever have? They were real. So real.

"So you see?" he finally says. "I have to let you go, Tessa. You deserve so much more than someone broken like me."

I rise, pace around his living room a few times.

"Go," he says. "I know you want to."

Really? That's what he thinks? I absolutely do *not* want to leave, and I won't.

I turn, face him, and I hope he can see the fire inside me. "I don't want to go, Ben."

"This story is going to be in every rag in the country by the end of tomorrow. All over the internet. I'm going to be swamped with reporters following me around. Lies will be told, Tessa. And the truth is bad enough."

I sit down on his knee, cup his cheek. "I'm not going anywhere."

"You have to. I won't put you through this."

"I'll go willingly."

"No." He rises, setting me on my feet. "I won't let you. This isn't your problem. You've been through enough, with Garrett, that asshole David Conrad—"

"I didn't even remember David Conrad until recently," I say. "Even after Garrett, I didn't remember."

"Only when you met me." He rubs his forehead. "Look what I've done to you."

"Don't be ridiculous. Maybe I had to remember him once I

met you. Maybe I had to be whole, whether that's good or bad, to be with you. To be with the love of my life."

He grabs me then, crushes our mouths together in a raw and passionate kiss.

But he breaks it just as quickly. "You are everything to me, Tessa. You're the reason why I was able to face this. To tell my story. And that's the reason I have to let you go."

I grab his face. I have to stop myself from shaking him. "No, you don't."

"I do. I can't ask you to take this on. It's not fair."

I grip his shoulders, force him to meet my gaze. "I'll tell you what's not fair, Ben. It's *this*. You thinking you have to do something noble and let me go. I won't allow it."

He digs gaze eyes into me sadly. "God, I love you. I never even imagined loving someone the way I love you."

"And I love you!"

"You don't *know* me. You didn't know me when you fell in love with me."

"But I did." I squeeze my fingers harder into his shoulders. "Do you think this changes who you truly are? What kind of man you are? It was different with you from the beginning. You were gentle with me, but you didn't coddle me. You helped me find my strength again. Now let me help you find yours."

He shakes his head. "I can't give you what you deserve."

"I deserve to be with the man I love."

Ben sighs. "He doesn't exist, Tessa."

"You're wrong. He *does* exist. He's gentle when he needs to be, but his strength is unequaled. He's kind and giving and the smartest man I know."

"A smart man wouldn't—"

"Do something stupid when he was a kid?" I draw in a

breath. "Damn it, Ben, we've all done stupid shit. I went back to Garrett Ramirez when I knew better. I could have saved myself a lot of headache and heartache if I hadn't. I wish I could take this all away for you. I wish I could go back in time and knock some sense into your head that day. But I can't. It is what it is, and you have to live with it. You've been living with it all this time. It will never go away, but the burden *will* lessen."

A tear slides down his stubbled cheek. "It's unreal how much I fucking love you, Tessa."

I slap his shoulder. "Then fight for us, damn it! Take what the world is going to throw at you, and I swear to God, I'll be right by your side. Just like you've been beside me to help me fight my demons, I'll stand by you as you take on yours." I place my hand on his chest. "Your heart still beats, Ben Black. Your heart still beats. And so does mine."

I kiss him. Hard and raw and passionately.

He stands, lifting me in his arms, and he carries me out of his living room and into another bedroom that isn't cluttered with garbage.

He lays me gently on the bed, hovers over me, gazes into my eyes. "Just when I thought I couldn't love you more…"

I push his hair over his forehead. "And I love you just as much. Always, Ben. Always."

EPILOGUE

Tessa

"Do you, Skye Margaret Manning, take Braden Robert Black to be your husband? In sickness and in health, for richer or poorer, until death do you part?"

"I do."

Skye turns to me, and I hand her the thick gold band. The glint of my own engagement ring catches the light of the candle.

Braden spared absolutely no expense on the wedding to the love of his life. We're at a sprawling estate with manicured gardens and a breathtaking view of the Atlantic Ocean.

The wedding party is standing under towering arches of fresh flowers, painstakingly arranged in hues of ivory, blush, and sprayed gold. A red carpet, lined with crystal-studded pillars, led all of us to the marble altar. A canopy of white silk billows over us, held in place by crystal chandeliers that reflect the golden candlelight. The chairs for the guests are draped in satin and adorned with custom-made gold cushions monogrammed with the initials BB or SM, depending on which side they're on.

A string quartet is poised to play the recession music the

second the officiant declares them husband and wife. They're off to the side on a small platform embellished with gilded accents and surrounded by towering floral sculptures. The whole thing feels like a fairy tale.

Skye slips the ring on Braden's left ring finger.

"Now, by the power invested in me by the State of Massachusetts, I pronounce you husband and wife."

Thunderous applause echoes throughout the church as Skye and Braden turn to face their guests.

"It gives me great honor to present to you, for the very first time, Mr. and Mrs. Braden Black!"

The organ and string quartet leap into the "Trumpet Voluntary," and Skye and Braden make their way down the aisle.

Ben holds out his tuxedo-clad arm, and I take it, smiling up at him.

"Wasn't it beautiful?" I say. "All those gorgeous flowers, and the music of the string quartet. I had to force myself not to cry."

"Not nearly half as beautiful as ours will be, baby." He kisses my left hand.

As he lifts my hand, my engagement ring catches the light from the chandeliers. It's a beauty. A dazzling round-cut diamond serves as its centerpiece, and it's set in a lustrous platinum band. The diamond is gorgeous, but my favorite part is the customized setting that Ben added.

Above the diamond, dwarfed in size but not in significance, is the tiny iridescent black pearl. The one the shucker gave me when Ben and I got oysters together when we first met. The night I found him at his place, he asked if he could hold onto it for me, said it gave him strength to face what was to come. I had no idea what he ultimately had in mind.

I was already crying when Ben proposed after I stood next to him at his first press conference, but a fresh wave of tears came when I saw the pearl.

I look forward at Skye and Braden as Ben and I follow them up the aisle. They have eyes only for each other.

"They make a fantastic couple," I say. "I'm so happy for them."

He squeezes my hand. "You'll be the next Mrs. Black, and I'm never letting you go."

ACKNOWLEDGMENTS

I shed more than a few tears over this one. *My Heart Still Beats* is one of my only standalone novels, and I poured my own heart and soul into it. I hope you love Tessa and Ben as much as I do! For those of you who haven't read Skye and Braden's story, it's a rollercoaster of a ride that begins with *Follow Me Darkly*.

Huge thanks to my brilliant editorial team, Liz Pelletier, Lydia Sharp, and copy editor Jessica Meigs. You all helped *My Heart Still Beats* shine. Thanks also to my proofreaders, Greta Gunselman and Briana Cohen, for your excellent catches. And of course Bree Archer and Elizabeth Turner Stokes, who design the most beautiful covers. Thanks to everyone else at Entangled whose tireless efforts always amaze me—Jessica, Meredith, Curtis, Heather, Katie, Ashley, Lizzy, and so many more.

Thanks also to the women and men of my reader group, Hardt & Soul. Your endless and unwavering support keeps me going.

To my family and friends, thank you for your encouragement. Special shout out to Dean—aka Mr. Hardt—and to our amazing sons, Eric and Grant. Special thanks to Eric for helping with this book before I turned it in to Entangled.

Thank you most of all to my readers. Without you, none of this would be possible. I am grateful every day that I'm able to do what I love—write stories for you!

*Don't miss the exciting new books
Entangled has to offer.*

Follow us!

@EntangledPublishing

@Entangled_Publishing

@EntangledPub

AMARA

an imprint of Entangled Publishing LLC